M000031679

VINNY

Alvarez Security Series

By

Maryann Jordan

Vinny (Alvarez Security Series)
Copyright © 2015 Maryann Jordan
Print Edition

All rights reserved. No part of this book may be reproduced or transmitted in any form or by any means, electronic or mechanical, including photocopying, recording, or by any information storage and retrieval system without the written permission of the author, except where permitted by law.

If you are reading this book and did not purchase it, then you are reading an illegal pirated copy. If you would be concerned about working for no pay, then please respect the author's work! Make sure that you are only reading a copy that has been officially released by the author.

This book is a work of fiction. Names, characters, places, and incidents either are products of the author's imagination or are used fictitiously. Any resemblance to actual persons, living or dead, events, or locales is entirely coincidental.

Cover Design by: Becky McGraw
Editor: Shannon Brandee Eversoll

ISBN: 978-0-9864004-7-6

Acknowledgements

First and foremost, I have to thank my husband, Michael. Always believing in me and wanting me to pursue my dreams, this book would not be possible without his support. To my daughters, MaryBeth and Nicole, I taught you to follow your dreams and now it is time for me to take my own advice. You two are my inspiration.

My best friend, Tammie, who for twenty years has been with me through thick and thin. You've filled the role of confidant, supporter, and sister.

My dear friend, Myckel Anne, who keeps me on track, keeps me grounded, and most of all – keeps my secrets. Thank you for not only being my proofreader, but my friend. Our friendship has grown and changed and you mean more to me than you can imagine.

Shannon Brandee Eversoll has been my editor for the past five books and what she brings to my writing has been amazing. She and Myckel Anne Phillips as my proofreader gave their time and talents to making Gabe as well written as it can be.

Thanks go to my beta readers who devote their time to make sure my books will have readers who love them!

My street team, Jordan Jewels, you are amazing! You volunteer your time to promote my books and I cannot thank you enough! I hope you will stay with me, because I have lots more stories inside, just waiting to be written!

My Personal Assistant, Barbara Martoncik, is the woman that keeps me going when I feel overwhelmed and I am so grateful for not only her assistance, but her friendship.

Most importantly, thank you readers. You allow me into your home for a few hours as you disappear into my characters and you support me as I follow my indie author dreams.

If you read my books and enjoy them, please leave a review. It does not have to be long or detailed...just that you enjoyed the book. Reviews are essential to indie authors!

Dedication

My mother made sure that my brother and I learned how to play the piano and other instruments. She had never had that training, but it was essential to her that we knew how to play classical music. My piano teacher, Mrs. George, was a believer in learning classical music. She used to say, "If you can play the classics, you can play anything." My elementary school music teacher, Miss Ruth, also spent years dedicating her life to helping children understand the importance of music in our lives.

My brother went on to become a trumpet performer and I played the flute in my younger years. My daughters also learned the piano, flute, clarinet, and took voice lessons. While those days are long gone, the appreciation for music has continued through the years.

So I dedicate this to Mrs. George and Miss Ruth, for their tireless efforts in teaching young people. I also dedicate this my mother, the first person in my life to show me that music can uplift, speak to our souls, bring us joy and heal our sorrows.

CHAPTER 1

THE MISSION HAD the squad of Special Forces men crouched behind a rock, watching the village below. Like other Nuristan villages, where many of the men had been killed, they could see a preponderance of women. The sun was setting behind the mountains casting shadows on the scene in front of them.

The twelve men of the squad were tired, angry—some with minor injuries. The mission was partially successful, but it was not without cost. They accomplished the first part of the job, but it turned deadly when the man they had been sent to rescue decided at the last minute to try to assault one of his sleeping captors, making their presence known. Trained to do whatever it took to make the mission successful, the twelve men worked as a complete team to get their target out of captivity, but now were traveling through a threatening area to their safe rendezvous, with the enemy behind.

Moving off of the beaten path, they came across a group of women in a rocky field. In this country, where women were afforded little rights, they often turned to agriculture to feed their families.

How they eked a living from the craggy mountainsides, Vinny Malloy could not imagine as he shifted ever so slightly to keep an eye on the villagers below. He did not need to shift his gaze to know exactly where the rest of the squad was. Several years of training to be the best the Army had to offer, this squad was more in tune with each other than any he had served with.

His twin brother, Gabe, was about ten yards to his right. Gabe and he were both Medics, but Vinny was also the Weapons Sergeant and undeniably the best marksman and long-range shooter. Captain Tony Alvarez, the leader of the squad, was about fifteen feet to the left and Vinny knew that Tony's eagle-eyes were trained on the activity in the village.

Chief Warrant Officer Bryant and the Engineer Sergeant moved behind several outcroppings of rocks to check their location. Jobe, another Weapons Sergeant, watched their rescue mission settle among the rough terrain and fall asleep.

Just a few more minutes, Vinny thought and they could continue toward the rendezvous. Trained not to feel fatigue, he nonetheless felt the slight drain of energy after the adrenaline of the fight. Suddenly, the sound of music reached his ears, jerking his gaze back to the women entering the village. The soft, lilting sound of the Afghan song rang through the night, sounding as foreign as the land around him. *Women rarely sing, at least not in public.* A few of the women were playing jaw harps, the unusual twang adding a layer of harmony to the song. Then the sound of a crude lyre sounded in the night.

As different as the music was to his ears trained to heavy metal bands, he found it soothing. Comforting. As though in the middle of a war zone, something could be as normal as a woman singing. Her tune was unfamiliar, but the universality of music calmed his soul. Taking a deep breath, he listened as the sound carried across the evening sky.

Glancing to the side at Gabe, he noticed that his twin was listening too. They shared the same love of music. To his Special Forces squad and to his friends back home in Virginia, he was a hard rock lover. But their mother had sung Irish lullabies to them as children. As they had gotten older they sometimes complained about her singing all of the time.

"Bocht an fear bhíos gan cheol," she used to say, quoting an old Celtic phrase. *Poor is the man that's without music.* He suddenly realized that as soon as this mission was over, he needed to call home. His mom deserved that from both of her sons.

CWO Bryant quickly signaled Tony. With a few short words, he alerted their Captain that the enemy soldiers that had been following them were coming from the road, straight for the village below them. The women singing as they came from the fields were in danger and had no idea. All eyes jerked quickly to Tony, who gave an imperceptible shake of his head.

They were to stay hidden, keeping the mission safe.

All of them followed orders. Never wavering. Never questioning. The sounds of music were abruptly halted, giving way to tortured wailing before the Afghanistan men could be seen continuing down the road.

Tony jerked his head forward in silent communication. Vinny and Jobe headed down toward the village, stealthily moving until they were just outside the largest building. With Jobe standing guard, Vinny leaned around the corner. The crying women surrounded another woman lying on the ground. She was covered in blood and he could see the lyre lying next to her on the ground. The harp was broken…and bloody.

Slipping back into the night, they reported what they had found to Tony whose jaw was tight with anger. The Communications Sergeant signaled that their transport was near so they began to move back through the rough terrain to the rendezvous. Jobe rousted the sleeping mission, hustling him on his way.

The silence of the night was punctuated only by the slight noise their booted footsteps made. Vinny focused on the task at hand—nothing else. Nothing else mattered but securing the mission. They met at the rendezvous and quickly helicoptered back to their base.

After the normal post-mission debriefing, the group headed to the showers. Vinny hung back after the others, not able to celebrate the success as easily as he normally would have. Gabe came back into the room, clad in only briefs, as he walked over to his locker. Pulling out clean sweats and a gray t-shirt, he looked over at his twin.

"You okay, bro?" Gabe asked.

Vinny sat silent for a moment, knowing that Gabe would wait patiently until he was ready to talk. Finally shaking his head, not able to get the vision out of his mind, he said, "Fuckin' music."

Gabe said nothing, waiting.

"I listen to music all the time. I like it loud, hard, fast, and rockin'." Rubbing his hand over his face, he added ruefully, "Kind of like how I like to fuck."

Gabe chuckled, settling his large frame on the bed across from Vinny. "Nothing wrong with that."

"Yeah, I know. I just realized that most of what I listen to I like because it's hard and fast. Don't really feel anything other than getting pumped up." He lifted his gaze to Gabe's. "Remember mom singing?"

Nodding slowly, Gabe said, "Sure. Every night, those Irish songs sent us to sleep. First as little kids and then, hell...she would sing them in the other room when we got older. Used to drive us nuts." Another silent moment passed before Gabe inquired, "What's got you thinking about mom and her singing?"

"When Jobe and I went down to the village to check on things, I could see the woman who'd been singing. After the men came through, they made quick work of killing her."

"I'm sorry, bro," Gabe said gently, with heartfelt sympathy.

Vinny sat with his forearms on his tree-trunk legs,

head hanging down. "And that fuckin' harp. Not only was she killed but that harp thing she was playing was busted. Like they had to completely silence the music."

Gabe stood, placing his hand on his twin's shoulder. "You gonna be okay?"

Heaving a huge sigh, Vinny nodded. "Yeah. I just don't think I'll ever feel about music the same way. Something about that sound was haunting and made me think of mom when she would sing to us. It hit a little too close to home, you know?" Looking up at Gabe he said, "I think I'll try to get a call off to mom later. You in?"

"Absolutely. Just let me know when."

Nodding, he watched as Gabe walked out of the room. Sitting alone, he finally stood and opened his locker to grab clean clothes to take to the showers. The bottom of the locker contained some of his personal effects that included a few CDs. He bent to look at the titles—mostly heavy metal which he put back into his locker. The few that were lighter music were tossed into the trash. *From now on music's gotta be for getting pumped—for forgetting. Never for feeling.*

He tried to remind himself of that at night when the memory of the village woman's simple song haunted his dreams and the sight of the broken, bloody lyre filled his nightmares.

CHAPTER 2

FIVE YEARS LATER

THE PLANE TOOK off from the Richland International Airport an hour late, causing Vincent Malloy to continually check his watch. Having turned off his cell phone, he anxiously wondered if he was going to make his connecting flight to Los Angeles. Rubbing a hand over his face, he settled back into his first-class seat, knowing there was nothing he could do about it now.

Sitting in the window seat, he glanced at his row partner, a businessman having to be reminded for the third time to turn off his phone and shut down his computer. *Jesus, man, I know you fuckin' fly all the time. Turn your shit off.*

The man barely glanced at him before looking around the cabin and calling over the flight attendant to ask if he could move to another empty seat. Her eyes darted over to Vinny, but what flashed through her expression was lust. Vinny smirked, knowing he looked a little rough. Six feet four inches tall and over two hundred twenty pounds of muscle, with tats showing on his arms, he knew he was intimidating to other men. And interesting to women.

The attendant helped the other man settle into a different seat, giving Vinny the opportunity to stretch his legs out the way he wanted. He watched her as she winked while moving back toward the front. A moment later she came by with his coffee, bending low to place it on his armrest holder. While her uniform was not overly revealing, he noticed that she had unbuttoned the next two buttons on her tight blouse, allowing a tantalizing view of her breasts.

"Sir, if you need anything at all on this flight, please don't hesitate to call for me. Or if you happen to be near the attendant's station," she said, nodding toward the front where the bathrooms were, "just ask for me. I'll be happy to see to your every need."

Vinny just nodded, wondering for a second if he would take her up on her blatant invitation. *Maybe if I hadn't just partied like hell last night.* Even though he was only going to be gone for two nights, his buddies had given him a send-off. *Or maybe I gave myself a send-off. Whatever, it was fun and I wouldn't mind finding that blonde again for a repeat performance.* As he leaned his head against the headrest, his mind went back to the previous evening's fun.

He and some friends had gone to a bar and the sound of loud, hard rock music with a deafening beat pulsated through him, firing his blood. It did not take long for several women to begin circling the group of tall, muscled, tatted men. Rubbing his hand over his face, he realized his interest was waning for the same old, same old. He had spared a glance at Gabe, who had no problem fending off the ladies, letting them know he was definitely off the market. His brother's wife was a dynamite little lady...beautiful and a real sweetheart as well. Glad for his twin, he sure as hell had not found anyone like that. Where had that come from? I've got no interest in being tied to one woman now. Startled at where his musings had taken him, he reached for the tall, stacked blonde who had been trying to get his attention for the past thirty minutes.

Taking her down to the dance floor, he pulled her into his body feeling her ass grind into his crotch. As tall as she was, her ass hit just the right spot. Oh yeah, it's time to quit this joint. She turned to face him, pressing her enormous breasts into his chest.

"You want to go back to your place, sweetie?" she cooed.

"Nope. Not my place. You in the mood, we go to yours. I'm a one-night, one-stop kind of guy."

Her heavily made-up eyes lit with desire. "I'm totally good with that," she agreed, pulling him off the dance floor.

Several hours later, he moved from her bed knowing he needed to go back to his place to get ready for the trip. Looking down, he stared at her body sprawled out naked on the bed. She was pretty, he had to admit. Long legs that had wrapped around his hips. A full ass that gave him something to grab when taking her from behind. And those breasts. He knew they were real because of the feel of them, but the size? Fuck. Enormous handfuls, with large dark nipples, that swayed back and forth with each pounding. She leaned up in the bed, her face slack with a hangover and makeup smeared around her eyes.

"You goin', sugar?" she asked, rubbing her hand over her chest. "You don't want more?"

"Gotta go, but thanks. Maybe I'll see you around sometime," he said, noncommittally. Standard line. Always meant the same thing. Once I've tasted, I don't come back.

A flash of irritation flew through her eyes, but he walked out nonetheless. He had to get ready for work.

"WILL YOU BE in Los Angeles for long?" she purred once again.

Startled, Vinny jerked his eyes open seeing the flight attendant leaning over him again. Shaking his head, he replied, "No. Just for the night. I'll be flying back tomorrow."

"Then you'll definitely have to try to get in as much as you can as quickly as you can," she smiled.

Chuckling at her invitation, he shook his head saying, "The coffee'll do me for now."

Watching her walk back to the attendant station, it was hard to keep his eyes off of her ass. The rear view of her was almost as good as the front.

Once in the air, he leaned his head back again. He felt like he should be reading up on his security escort case, but Tony had purposefully kept him in the dark. Tony Alvarez, his former Captain, had opened up his own Security Agency once out of the Army. Several of their squad were being discharged at the same time and gladly joined him in his growing business, filling it with his brothers-in-arms who had left the Special Forces as well. Men from their squad. Men they trusted. Men whose skills were unparalleled. Tony's agency now handled not only installing state-of-the-art security systems, providing security to any number of dignitaries or functions in the area, but also helped the Richland Police Department on a number of cases where their budget constraints did not allow for the equipment that he had.

Closing his eyes once again, he thought back to the conversation between them a few weeks ago.

Gabe and I were in the main Alvarez area working on a new security system when BJ walked by, calling out to me.

"Boss wants to see you. He's in his office."

I immediately headed to Tony's office, finding him at his desk with files spread in front of him. "You called for me, sir?"

Tony looked up at me, staring for a moment before saying, "Business has been steady and we've got a good reputation in Richland and now in Virginia. But I've got a new request for someone who travels in and out of the state. That kind of recognition has come from hard work and dedication and I'd like you to take it. This could take our company to a whole new level."

My interest piqued, I waited to hear more about it.

"Got a request for a security detail to escort someone from Los Angeles to Richland." My face must have shown interest...and concern. Gabe had gotten tangled up with a diva actress on an assignment before meeting his fiancé, Jennifer, and it had turned out to be a cocked-up situation.

"Nope, not an actress. A musician," Tony clarified.

"Just an escort detail?" I asked, willing to take any mission assigned, but curiosity getting the better of me.

"Yes, they'll have a concert in LA where you will meet them. You'll escort them on their flight to Richland."

"Concert?" I was definitely interested at the idea of spending a couple of days with a female musician, preferably a beautiful rock star. "Who is it?"

Tony sat quietly for a moment, staring at the file in front of him. Rubbing his chin in thought, he finally looked up at me and said succinctly, "Not saying."

"Not...saying? Sir?"

Tony looked deeply at me before continuing. "Vincent, you're one of my best. Ever since the first time I laid eyes on you and your twin, I couldn't have asked for better. One thing about you was that when you were on a mission, you gave me one-hundred percent. Off mission, if you thought with your dick it didn't matter. You still work just as hard for me as when we were in the Special Forces, *but I need your head on this mission and not thinking with your dick."*

I started to protest, but Tony put up his hand. "I want you on this mission, regardless of who it is."

Understanding what was at stake, I agreed. Male, female, old, young...it did not matter to the mission. Standing, I nodded to the leader I trusted with my life. "When do I leave?"

"I'll have the details by the end of the week and you need to be ready to fly to California next week."

LOOKING AT HIS WATCH as they landed in Chicago, he knew he missed the connecting flight. Hurrying to the ticket counter, he waited impatiently as they managed to get him on the next flight to LA. Nodding his thanks, he made his way to the gate.

There was no need to pull out the assignment instructions again. He had them memorized. He was originally going to check into the hotel and have time to change before taking a taxi to the concert hall. Given backstage access, he would be there for the concert. He would meet the manager, the agent, and then after the concert...the artist. Escort them back to the hotel, where they would be staying, and then to the airport the next day for their flight back.

Tony had been specifically obtuse about the identification of the musician. The realization that his boss and friend was unsure of his professionalism with a hot rocker had Vinny grimacing. Vinny decided against checking concerts in the LA area, wanting to maintain complete control over the mission regardless of who he was escorting. It did not matter to him if she was a big name or not—he was taking this mission as seriously as all his other missions. He knew there was no danger involved or Tony would have briefed him completely. This was purely an official escort mission. *What's the worst that can happen? I have to scare a few paparazzi?*

Hearing his flight being called, he made his way on board for the last leg of the trip. Settling down, he checked his watch one more time. *I'll have just enough time to get to the hotel and change before heading to the concert hall.*

An hour later, he was seething as the plane was just taking off. Mechanical difficulties, the pilot had said. Re-running his schedule through his mind, he knew he would have to take his luggage with him and catch a taxi directly to where he was meeting the musician. Glancing down at his attire, he was traveling for comfort. His jeans, while clean, were slightly worn. His black t-shirt stretched tightly across his chest, only partially hiding the Malloy tattoo on his arm. His hair was trimmed neatly, but still long enough that it was standing on end from all of the times he had run his hand through it in frustration.

Sucking in a deep breath and letting it out slowly, he settled back. *It'll be fine for a musician. In fact, I'll probably fit right in with the crew.*

Several hours later, he jogged to the line of taxis outside of the LA airport. Rattling off the name of the concert hall, he hopped into the back. The concert had already started, but that would be all right. He was there on a job, not to listen to some chick sing. *That was just going to be a bonus!*

The taxi driver pulled up to the Walt Disney Concert Hall, then looked at Vinny in the rear-view mirror. "You say you needed to go to the backstage door?"

Vinny replied in the affirmative, but leaned over looking at the large hall with the sign **Los Angeles Philharmonic**. "Are you sure this is the right place?"

The driver nodded, saying, "Oh yeah, man. LA's finest orchestra."

Vinny chuckled at Tony letting him think he was escorting some young, female rocker. *You got me, Captain,* he thought. Knowing that he would be working with an older lady, he knew he would have to charm her a bit to get past his outer appearance. *No worries. I got this.*

Paying the taxi driver, he pulled his bag out of the back and jogged up to the door, passing security once he showed his identification. The hall's security guard showed him where he could stow his bag and then pointed him in the direction of the backstage area. Moving through the people milling around, he heard the sounds of the orchestra growing louder as he approached. The guard had radioed ahead and he saw a man coming toward him, dressed in a tuxedo. Looking at his own casual attire…*Shit.*

He walked over to shake the man's hand.

"Mr. Malloy?"

"Yes, sir. Vinny," he replied.

The man nodded, then added, "Good to have you on board. I'm her agent, Gordon Fisher. If you'll follow me, you'll be able to watch the last part of the concert from the wings and then we'll head back to Ms. O'Brian's room afterward."

Vinny followed the young man and as they moved into the wings, he could see the large orchestra on the stage. The women all in long, black dresses and the men in tuxedos. Glancing out toward the audience, he saw that the house was full.

The orchestra was playing and Vinny shifted uncomfortably in his stance. It had been a long time since he had listened to anything without a strong heavy beat and the harmonious sounds reminded him of times better left forgotten. The orchestra built to a climax and then fell silent as the soloist continued to play. The harp. The melodious chords filtered through the concert hall and resonated deep within Vinny's chest. His eyes sought out the woman in the center of the stage with the harp gently resting on her shoulder. His breath caught in his throat as his gaze took her in.

Long, thick, dark hair that curled down her back. A porcelain, heart-shaped face, eyes closed as though in prayer as her fingers nimbly moved quickly across the strings. Her slim body encased in a sky blue evening gown, setting her apart from the others dressed in all black.

The tones moved through him as no other music had in years—not forcing him to remember a time of sand and death, but taking him to a place of respite and peace. Entranced, he watched her face in quiet repose as her fingers connected to his soul. The last time he allowed his being to be carried away by the enchantment of the music...*Nope, not going there.* Shaking himself out of his reverie, he tore his eyes away from the beautiful harpist and gazed across the rest of the orchestra wondering who he would be escorting back to Richland.

Gordon touched his arm and Vinny followed the man to a hall backstage. Multiple doors opened into the hall, but they headed to one near the far end. "They're on the last song. After they take their bows, the orchestra will release and I will have Ms. O'Brian's manager bring her straight back here."

The agent left the room, leaving Vinny in the small space looking around. A small settee was against one wall, with a chair facing the mirror on the other. A garment bag hung on a hook on the wall and a cosmetic travel bag sat on the floor nearby. Hearing voices coming down the hall, he straightened, awaiting to meet his mission.

ANNALISSA O'BRIAN WAS being pushed along with the crowd as usual. She hated being bounced around and wished for the umpteenth time that she were taller…or bigger. *Then I'd push back*, she thought. Todd Levine, her manager, on one side and Gordon Fisher, her agent, on the other. Both talking to her at the same time, trying to move her through the crowd toward her room.

Finally bursting through the door, she was propelled forward.

"You were fabulous, darling," Todd was saying. "I told you this concert would take you places."

"Todd, I don't care about going pla—" she tried to interject.

"Of course you do," Gordon interrupted. "Todd, we need to talk tomorrow to see what we can get set up next."

"I'm thinking a trip to Chicago, then possibly Dallas. See what you can get worked up."

"Annalissa, what a show. Honey, you look marvelous and your playing? Oh my God, I absolutely cried," came the voice of her hair stylist, Parker, behind her.

Sharon barged into the room, grabbing the cosmetic bag. "I knew your makeup would hold up under those hot lights. I'm telling you, I know my shit."

"Gordon, I want you to check on the Hall in New York. See what they have next year," Todd's voice cut over the cacophony of others.

"Sirs, are you ready to allow any of the VIPs to have

entrance to Ms. O'Brian?"

The room grew small and Annalissa could feel the noose tightening around her neck. Closing her eyes, she tried to block out the sounds, but could feel her breath coming in spurts. Everyone was speaking at once and she could feel the panic rising. *Please, not now. Don't let me fall apart now.* She had suffered from panic attacks for years, but only in unfamiliar crowds—never on the stage. Her father considered it a sign of weakness and she had tried to hide them for years.

Numerous hands came forward, all connected to voices clawing for her attention. Until one clear voice in the crowd spoke out.

"Quiet!" came the bark from…her eyes widened as she looked to see who had managed to shut everyone up. Her gaze landed on him. She had no idea who he was, but he looked like a god. Tall, muscular, with the bottom of a Celtic tattoo showing below the arm of his t-shirt. The only man in the room not dressed for a symphony concert and yet the only man in the room that appeared to be completely at ease with himself.

Blinking back the tears as they threatened to fall, she watched as the crowd parted instantly for him as he stalked over. Stopping directly in front of her, she leaned her head way back to hold his gaze. He bent down to whisper, "Breathe, darlin'."

Gasping in air, she realized that she had indeed been holding her breath. He took her hand in his much larger one, bringing it to his lips. A barely there kiss was placed on the back of her fingers and then he said, "Ms. O'Brian? It's my honor to meet you. I'm Vincent. Vinny Malloy. And I'll be your security escort back to Richland."

The room had grown strangely quiet, but before chaos could once again ensue, Vinny's voice carried out. "I've just met Ms. O'Brian, but it's obvious to me that she's exhausted. As of this moment, she's under my care and my protection. I and I alone will determine who may be let in to see her and when we will leave."

Annalissa's eyes darted around quickly, awaiting the uproar that was sure to follow. Todd's mouth hung open while Gordon's face grew red and his eyes narrowed. But she noticed he did not argue with the large man still holding her hand. *Still holding my hand?* Pulling her fingers out of his soft grip, she immediately felt regret at the loss of his touch.

Suddenly remembering the reason her father wanted to hire a security escort, she glanced around quickly, "Where's Easnadh?"

Todd immediately answered, "The stage crew is bringing it here."

Visible relaxing, she turned her eyes once more to the man still standing a few inches away from her, a questioning look in his eyes.

VINNY HAD WATCHED with curiosity as the group

pushed through the door, all talking at once. Then stunned, he stared at the exquisite woman they were crowded around. The harpist. The Celtic beauty whose playing had him entranced just thirty minutes earlier.

Well played, Tony. No wonder you kept this one a secret, he thought, his eyes never leaving the woman. Expecting a diva personality, he was again stunned when she appeared to be completely overrun by the noise and confusion of her entourage. He watched her eyes, once again tightly closed, but this time as though trying to push out the uproar around her, then saw the tell-tale signs of her chin slightly wiggling, as she fought to keep from crying.

Before he knew what he was doing, he barked out, "Quiet!" and walked over to her. Her eyes flew open as they found his and they were…green. They drew him in as he reached to kiss her fingers. The same delicate fingers that played the most amazing music.

After almost falling apart, he watched as she suddenly came to life and with the only forcefulness he had seen from her, she questioned the whereabouts of someone named Easnadh. Hearing the response, he assumed that was the name of her harp.

She had pulled her hand away from his and he immediately missed her touch. *Of course, the last thing she probably wants is someone holding her fingers in a grip that could crush them.*

He had no idea why her father had requested an escort from Alvarez Agency and while he would have

21

fulfilled his mission to the letter, from the moment she looked up at him with trust in her eyes, he knew he would do anything and everything to ease her trip back. And if that included keeping her own entourage at bay, then he had no problem doing just that.

The noise in the room stayed subdued for just a moment and then people began to talk again. Vinny noticed that Todd and Gordon moved closer to each other and began to speak in low tones. The man who had raved about Annalissa's hair smiled at him and then gently pulled her over to the chair in front of the mirror.

Vinny could hear the young man talking to her in low, soothing tones as he carefully took all the pins out of her hair and began brushing it.

"Ms. O'Brian," Vinny addressed her, watching as her gaze darted up to his in the mirror. "Do you want to meet anyone tonight?"

"I…um…," she faltered as she looked over to Todd and Gordon. "I'm not sure what they've agreed to."

Already taking a dislike to her agent and manager, he turned to them. "Gentleman, does Ms. O'Brian have a contractual obligation after the concert?"

Todd stiffened at the tone. "No, not in her contract. But it's considered—"

"Then I suggest we allow Ms. O'Brian to get her things and then I'll escort her to the hotel."

Just then a noise sounded from the door and a man, wearing a stage crew identifying t-shirt, walked in carrying a harp case.

"Here you go, safe and sound," he said.

The harp case was not as large as Vinny had expected, then realized that when she was on stage she was not dwarfed by a large harp.

"It's a Celtic harp," came her soft voice from beside him. He glanced down at her, seeing her smile as she walked over and placed her hands on the case. As she was getting ready to open it, another man pushed his way into the room. An older gentleman, tall and reedthin, he made his way directly toward Annalissa.

"Mr. Feinstein," she cried, rushing to the man's outstretched arms. "I wasn't sure you'd be able to get back here."

"Oh my dear, I wouldn't have missed this for the world. You were superb."

Annalissa felt a presence come up behind her. Glancing upwards, she saw the tight look on Vinny's face. Rushing to explain, she said, "This is my teacher, Mr. Maurice Feinstein."

Vinny shook the older man's hand and then moved back allowing them to visit.

Annalissa opened up the harp case and she and Mr. Feinstein looked over the harp carefully, checking to make sure it was well protected. Todd moved over next to Vinny and said, "We haven't been formally introduced. I'm Todd Levine, her manager. I knew her father was hiring someone to escort her back to Richland, but you should know that his priority is Easnadh.

The harp. It's an antique Celtic harp and worth quite a bit of money."

Vinny's gaze cut sharply to the man next to him. Todd exuded an air of importance that rubbed Vinny the wrong way. Short, with dark hair neatly trimmed, wearing an expensive suit, he managed to look down his nose at everyone in the room despite his height.

"You're telling me that her father wants the harp escorted more than his daughter?" Vinny bit out.

Gordon walked over, hearing the end of their conversation. "No, no, you mustn't misunderstand Todd. Her father does want her protected, but the harp is well…very valuable."

The more the two men talked, the more Vinny disliked them. Turning back to Annalissa, he spoke again to the assembly. "I'm calling it a night for Ms. O'Brian." Turning to Todd, he asked, "Does she have transportation?"

"Oh yes, we have two limousines to take us to the hotel. We'll all go together and then Easnadh will be transported over by a hired company."

"Fine," Vinny growled. "Ms. O'Brian goes with me in one limousine and the rest of you go in the other."

The group erupted in complaints, but were silenced quickly by the look on Vinny's face. *Hell, you people are sucking the patience out of me and I've only been around you for an hour.* Sparing a look over at Annalissa, he saw her wide green eyes taking in the scene in front of her. But what he especially noticed…she did not seem upset in the least with him being in charge.

The group quickly dissembled and he gently took her by the arm as they left the room. The others trailed, carrying their various parcels. Parker had the garment bag, Sharon had the cosmetic case, and Todd and Gordon were following with a crew member carrying the harp case.

Maurice kissed her goodbye and told her that he would see her in Richland. He planned on staying in Los Angeles for a couple of days visiting old friends.

Outside, there was a small crowd waiting and she offered a genuine smile to them as Vinny assisted her into the limousine.

CHAPTER 3

ONCE INSIDE THE LIMOUSINE, Annalissa eyed Vinny warily. Used to people taking over her life, making demands, she wondered what made his different. So far, while he appeared at ease pushing others around, she noticed that he was not forceful with her.

Peering at him from across the seats, she nervously fiddled with the beading on her long skirt. "I um…want to thank you…for back there…when you…got…um…everyone quiet," she said haltingly.

"Ms. O'Brian, you don't have to thank me," he said genuinely.

Smiling, she nodded. *Of course. I'm a paid job for him.* Sucking in a deep breath, she said, "Well, if we are going to be together for a day or so, you really should call me Annalissa."

He smiled, watching her face carefully for signs of fear or fatigue. He saw none of the former but plenty of the latter. "I'm sure you don't need me telling you how beautifully you played tonight. It was…" he faltered uncharacteristically. Every word his mind came up with seemed lacking. Looking directly into her green eyes, he said honestly, "Soul changing."

Her eyes widened at his words and he cursed himself for sounding like a fool. He started to apologize for his lack of eloquent phrases when she leaned across the space and placed her hand on his arm.

With tears in her eyes, she whispered, "That's beautiful. Thank you so much."

Chuckling, he said, "Well, I'm sure there were more appropriate musical descriptions I should have used."

"No, no. Please understand. What you said about my performance…soul changing…that's all I've ever wanted to do with my music. Truly, thank you."

Annalissa felt the power of his arm under her fingertips. Suddenly heat filled the limousine as the air crackled around them. Licking her lips nervously, she leaned back in her seat removing her hand, once again missing the energy from his touch.

Vinny watched her sit back, avoiding his gaze as though nervous about what seemed to happen when they touched. Admittedly, he had no idea what was happening either. *She looks young. Probably at least five or six years younger than me.* His eyes could not help but roam down her body, showcased perfectly in the blue dress that set off her dark hair and green eyes. The bodice was tight, covered in sequins. The gentle swell of her breasts, while not large and heavy as he usually preferred, seemed perfect. The layers of silk in the long skirt had swayed gently as he had ushered her before him into the limousine.

Giving himself a mental shake, he thought, *Not for me. Not even my type. And that's good. She's a mission. And one I will see through to my utmost just like any other mission.*

They arrived at the large, exquisite hotel and he alighted from the limo first and then, after quickly scanning the area, turned to assist her from the vehicle. With his bag in one hand and her hand tucked into his other, they entered the tall glass doors and walked to the reception desk.

Before she could speak, he nodded to the manager and said, "This is Ms. O'Brian. You will have a reservation for her. I am Vincent Malloy. We have a reservation for adjoining rooms, regardless of where her original placement was to be. Her harp case, when it arrives, it to be brought to her room."

The hotel manager looked askance for a moment, then turned to Annalissa and said, "Mr. Levine booked you in a suite of rooms with several others from your group. We have Mr. Malloy on the floor below."

The manager seemed to want her to make a decision, but she felt unsure. Todd always made the arrangements and he could be such a bear when he did not get his way. Glancing up at Vinny, her eyes implored him to see her dilemma.

Leaning down, Vinny saw the confusion in her eyes. He whispered, "You look very tired. I thought that you would like to be away from the others, have some dinner sent up to your room and relax with your harp. And," he added. "I can't do my job if you're a floor away."

Hearing the noise of the rest of her entourage coming through the door made up her mind. Looking at the hotel manager she smiled as she pulled herself up and said, "Yes, please. I would like to have you follow Mr. Malloy's instructions. Immediately, if you please."

Giving her arm a squeeze, Vinny grinned and turned his attention back to the manager who was handing him their room keys.

"Annalissa dear," Todd called out. "I'll take care of all of this and you can go on up with Sharon and Parker."

"I'm not staying in the suite," she announced. She winced when her announcement was met with the outcry that greeted her.

Vinny had been proud of her statement, realizing that she often felt overwhelmed by the strong personalities in her life, but his protectiveness grew as soon as he saw her wince.

"She has her room adjacent to mine. It's the only way I can be assured of her safety," he declared.

"It's not her safety that needs to be assured, you overgrown guard. It's the harp that her father wants to be protected," Gordon bit out.

Annalissa reared back as though slapped. She wondered why her father had hired a security agency to escort her back to Richland. *I should have known it was Easnadh.* As much as she loved the harp herself and recognized its value, it still hurt to realize that was where her own father's concern lay.

"You ass," Todd said, turning on Gordon. "What the hell's wrong with you? I have a good mind to have her find a new agent for all you're worth."

"Me? You wouldn't be anywhere if it weren't for me," Gordon argued.

Vinny watched the players begin to squabble like children, but felt Annalissa press into his side as though escaping the unpleasant scene in front of her. Before he could drag her away, Parker came up to him. Tall, dark-skinned, with a handsome smile he said, "Security dude. I really like you. 'Bout time this girl had someone looking out just for her."

Vinny acknowledged the compliment and turned with her tucked into his side. He caught the eye of the hotel manager and jerked his head toward the harp case.

"Yes, sir. It'll be sent straight up."

With that he, Annalissa, Parker and Sharon made their way into the elevator.

THAT NIGHT, AFTER PARKER AND SHARON helped Annalissa out of her clothes and makeup, they said their goodbyes and she fell into bed. Laying there, unable to sleep, she almost got up and played her harp. That was what she did at home when she could not sleep. Deciding she did not want to take a chance on waking Vinny next door, she stayed where she was. In bed. Alone as always. But this time, her mind full of the man in the connecting room.

Turning over, she punched her pillow and tried to force herself to sleep. But she could not get his take-charge attitude off of her mind. *I'm surrounded by people trying to take over my life, why did he seem so different?* Then it came to her. *All the others try to control me to get me to do what they want me to do. What's good for them. My manager, agent, teacher, father. But Vinny? When he took control, it was for me. What was good for me.*

Never having been around a man like him, she felt overwhelmed. He was larger than life, like a hero from one of her romance novels. Tall, handsome, powerfully built. A face that would make women swoon. A panty-melting smile. Sighing, she wondered how many women had swooned at his feet or had their panties melted right off of their hips before he…*Stop! Geez, I'm so lame. He's just a man and he's certainly not interested in me. I'm just a job. Well, Easnadh is his job actually. I'm just a by-product.*

Finally giving up on sleep, she rose from the bed and settled in the chair with her harp on her lap. Stroking the strings she began to play softly, slow lullabies from her childhood filling the air.

IN THE ROOM a few yards from hers, Vinny found sleep lacking as well. He heard her moving around earlier and now that it was silent, assumed she was in bed. His mind rolled back over the events of the day.

The first late plane from Richland followed by the next one delayed out of Chicago. The rush to the concert hall only to be blown away by his assignment. Her music had stilled him. Filled him. Moved him in ways he had not been moved in years. Familiar sounds from her harp took him back to a time when his mother sang to him and Gabe every night. Haunting sounds from the last time he allowed music to fill his soul only to be ripped from him in violence.

He had been stunned when the creator of that music was none other than his mission. First shocked. Then bowled over by her beauty up close. Dark, silky hair hanging in waves down her back with small jewels woven throughout. The sky-blue evening gown swirled around her slender form, giving her a princess look. *And when I barked at everyone to be quiet, she gave me a look…like I was the prince in her fairytale.*

Fuck, I'm no prince, he thought ruefully. But for the first time ever, the idea that he could be someone's prince appealed to him.

Listening carefully and not hearing any sounds coming from the connecting room, he called Tony. "Yeah," came the sleepy response.

Oh yeah, Virginia was three hours ahead so it must be about three in the morning there. "Wake up, Captain.

Just thought I'd report in."

"Okay, okay," Tony said. "Let me get up so we can talk."

Vinny heard Tony murmuring to his wife, Sherrie. He knew Tony would not want to disturb her rest and was probably going to another room.

"Okay," Tony answered, "So I guess you know by now why I didn't give you the name of the mission."

"What the hell, man? He contacts you to protect his daughter's harp, which just happens to have a name. And who the hell knew that musicians named their harps? But what I want to know is did you know who played that harp?"

Chuckling, Tony said, "Here's the full story, Vinny. I was contacted by Mr. O'Brian saying his daughter was flying with a group of people to Los Angeles for a concert but he wanted her and her harp back the next day and not to wait for anyone else. He kept talking about some Asnev, or however the hell it's pronounced. I had no idea he was talking about a harp's name until the actual contract came in. By then, I'd seen the daughter and even saw a YouTube of her playing her harp."

"You could have told me," Vinny said.

"No, I really needed your head in the game. This girl's got talent, but seems to be surrounded by people that push her one way and another. I wanted you there, without any predisposed ideas about the players. Yes, I need you to escort her and the harp back tomorrow, but more than that...I thought you'd be the right man for making sure that both the harp and *the harpist* were safe."

Vinny nodded, smiling to himself. Tony had always been the best leader he had ever served under. He knew his missions. He knew his men. And Tony never had a problem matching up the two.

"You anticipate any problems?" Tony queried.

"Not at all, boss. I'll be with Annalissa and her harp until we have it checked at baggage. Everything will go like clockwork, Tony. No worries on this end."

"I knew you were the man for the job," Tony added. "Safe travels and I'll see you when you get in."

Vinny's mind went to the beautiful woman lying in a bed not twenty feet from his. He tried not to think of her. *She's a mission. An intriguing, talented, musical, beautiful, totally charming in the most innocent way mission.*

Shifting over in his bed, he wanted to ignore the call of the wild as his dick pressed against his boxers. *Down boy. She's not even my type. I like 'em blonde, tall with long legs, curvy hips, and big tits. Loud and brassy for me. Not petite, dark-haired, green-eyed, women who looked like they would run away if someone said 'Boo' one minute and the next minute protecting a named harp.* His mind went back to the change in her when she realized that she did not know where Easnadh was. Suddenly the mouse could roar.

And what would it feel like to take that untapped pas-

sion and teach it, tame it, turn it toward him? Groaning, he knew that if he kept this up he would need a cold shower. Sighing once again, he thought of the mission. *It doesn't matter how much I'm noticing her as a woman, I've got to tamp that down.* Ruefully he realized, even if she was not a mission, her purity was not for him. He would protect. Care for. See safely home. But nothing more.

Then he heard the soft music drifting from her room. The tinkling sound of the harp drifted over him, calming his mind. But stirring his heart. Running his hand over his face, he tried to block out the memories. *There's nothing the same between this music and the unfamiliar sounds of a woman singing in the middle of a goddamn war. So why the hell does it make me crazy? That Army psychologist told me that I now associated it with the loss of control. Fuck that. No way I'm not in control now.*

The music finally stopped and the quiet of the night once again penetrated his mind. He laid in bed a few more minutes, running through the needs of tomorrow trying to take his mind off of the woman in the connecting room. He had already checked on the limo service that would take him and Annalissa to the airport, as well as ordered breakfast from room service to be delivered to them. It would be a tight fit, but since her harp was a smaller Celtic harp, it would be able to travel in the limo with them. Then it would be checked for the flight. And they had a non-stop flight to Dulles International Airport in the D.C. area. Then another limo ride to Richland.

Perfectly planned. All those years of Special Forces training taught them to plan extensively for every mission...and then be prepared when things go wrong. But what could possibly go wrong?

CHAPTER 4

ANNALISSA WOKE TO the sound of knocking on her door. Sitting up on the bed, she pushed her sleep-tousled hair from her face as she tried to remember where she was and who would be knocking. Suddenly, the connecting door to her room opened and in stalked Vinny. He winked at her as he walked to her main door and opened it to the tantalizing smells of breakfast.

After tipping the server, he set the tray on her table and nodded at the food. "I ordered some breakfast for you. It may be a while before we get to the airport and their food is sometimes less than desirable." Giving her another wink, he walked back through the connecting door and closed it.

Stunned, she ate quickly before heading into the shower. Thirty minutes later as she emerged from the bathroom, hair washed and a touch of makeup applied, she walked over to the door and knocked. Her hand shook as her nerves gave out on her. Turning, she started to walk away when the door opened and Vinny filled the doorframe.

"You need something, Annalissa?" he asked, the deep timbre of his voice sliding over her.

She looked down, seeing his cowboy boots first. Legs, encased in well-fitting jeans, were long and muscular. As her eyes traveled upwards in curiosity, his waist was narrow but his chest and arms were just as powerfully built as his legs. The square jaw with the tiny chin dimple had her suck in her breath. Then her eyes reached his. They were twinkling with mirth as she had been caught ogling the man in front of her.

Suddenly unsure of herself, she realized her hand was still lifted in a knocking position. "Uh, I was just…it was…breakfast. You really shouldn't…um…"

"Annalissa," he said softly. "You don't have to be afraid of me."

Her gaze shot back up to his and he noticed that with a tiny lift of her chin, she drew herself up, defiance in her eyes.

"I'm not afraid. I was just wondering…" she began to falter again. *Dammit, it shouldn't be so hard to just say what I'm thinking.* Trying again, she said, "I wanted to thank you for breakfast, but it was…um…kind of…presumptuous. But nice. Um…I didn't know this door was…open…or rather…unlocked."

Sighing, she looked back down. *God, I'm such a wimp. He must think I'm a stupid child who can't even speak.*

Vinny watched in fascination the woman standing in front of him, struggling to ask him why he barged into her room. *She has everyone taking over her life and I just fell right in with the rest of them.*

He reached out and lifted her chin with his fingers, hoping she would not be afraid. "Annalissa," he said softly. "You're right. It was very presumptuous of me and I apologize."

Her eyes widened, sending shock waves through him. Looking into her large, green eyes, he felt a punch to his gut. *Stop looking at her as though she were a woman. She's the mission.* The internal struggle was in full swing and he knew it was still early in the day. He had to get through the entire day, keeping his hands to himself.

"Oh, Vinny," she exclaimed. "You shouldn't apologize. The breakfast was lovely." Looking down at her feet, she could not help but notice his large boots standing in front of her tiny, pink-tipped toes. Sucking in a huge breath, she lifted her gaze back to his smiling one. "How did you know I liked scrambled eggs and bacon?"

Laughing, he confessed, "Of everyone around you yesterday, Parker seemed to be the one most in tune with you, so I asked him."

Her mouth dropped opened at his simple act of kindness. Giggling, she said, "Todd usually orders what he likes and then fusses when I don't eat." Leaning forward as though sharing a secret, she added, "I hate poached eggs."

"Duly noted," he smiled. "I'm glad Parker got it right."

Smiling shyly, she backed up and turned to move

over to her suitcase. He watched her every movement. Delicate, and yet with purpose. He realized she was painfully shy, but not standoffish. *And obviously tired of everyone around her taking over.* They only had today together, but he found himself wishing for more. *I wonder if I could see her when we get back to Richland? Friends, maybe?* Looking at the talented musician who would soon be traveling the world, he scoffed to himself. *Yeah, right. What would she need a friend with a womanizing reputation like mine for?* Filled with a strange sense of recrimination, he wished he had more to offer her, but felt lacking.

Watching as she walked over lovingly caressing her harp case, he pulled himself up to his full height, determined to offer them both his protection as long as they needed it.

"We'll head to the limo in about fifteen minutes," he said, as she turned and graced him with a full smile. It rocketed straight to his heart.

FINALLY SETTLING INTO the first class seats on the straight flight from Los Angeles to Dulles, Vinny and Annalissa both heaved a sigh of relief at the same time. Looking at each other, smiling, they acknowledged hating the crowds and security lines.

"I always dread that, don't you?" she asked. "Just trying to push through the crowds."

"With my size, I usually just glare and people move away," he admitted.

She looked over at the man filling his seat and the long legs stretched in front of him. "Come to think of it, you did manage to get us through the crowds without me getting squished. I don't think that's ever happened before," she grinned.

"Then maybe you should keep me around as your crowd mover," he joked.

Her smile reached her eyes, as she admitted, "I'd like that. I've never had that before. Usually Todd and Gordon are either meanly pushing people away or they walk ahead talking which leaves me to find my own way."

He forced his smile to stay on his face, but what he wanted to do was get up, go back to the hotel, and punch those two.

She sat in the window seat, nervously wiping her hands on her jeans. She had worn her nice jeans, slip on shoes to make it easy to get through security and a lightweight sweater, not knowing if she would be chilly on the plane. She should have known that being a few inches away from Vinny would have her warm. Way beyond warm.

"Nervous?" he asked.

"Not too much. Just take off and landing," she said, looking over at him. Looking down, she saw that he had turned his hand over, palm up, and gave her a questioning look. He was offering his hand. Not grabbing hers. Letting it be her choice.

Reaching out hesitantly, she placed her left hand on top of his upturned right one. He closed his fingers around hers gently. Not squeezing. Smiling, she looked back out of the window as the plane taxied to the runway.

"Don't worry," he assured. "Nothing's going to happen. I'm sure this flight will be as uneventful as all my other flights."

He felt the slight pressure of her fingers as her grip increased during takeoff. Aware of her delicacy, he was also aware of the strength in those fingers. *Of course. She uses her fingers every day as she plays the harp.* Like her. Delicate and yet with strength underneath.

Hearing a deep sigh as they were airborne, he turned to see her smiling at him again. Releasing her hand regretfully, he asked, "Why Easnadh? Do all harpist name their instruments?"

Immediately her eyes sparkled as she spoke, "The Celtic name for music or musical sound is Easnadh. It's pronounced *As na.*" Giving a little shrug, she added, "Not all harpist name their instruments, but I suppose I'm sentimental. She's a beautiful instrument and when I play her, it's as though I'm a part of her sound. Her music." Looking back up at him, she blushed. "I'm sure that sounds silly to you, doesn't it?"

He wanted to tell her that some soldiers name their weapons, but assumed her world would never understand that piece of information when all she brings is joy from her instrument. Instead he just said, "I think the name and the harp are beautiful, but not nearly as much as the player that brings out the music."

Annalissa was used to compliments. About her talent. Her music. Even the way she looked when all made up for a concert. But it had been a really long time since a man told her she was beautiful as though he really meant it just for her. Blushing, she looked back out of the window, unable to keep the smile off of her face.

A female voice from the side broke the moment. "Mr. Malloy, how nice to see you again. Is there anything I can get for you? Anything at all?"

The seductive purr had Annalissa's head swinging around quickly. The flight attendant was bending over Vinny's seat, her breasts straining at the navy blouse that was unbuttoned a couple of buttons below what was surely regulation. The woman's face held a sensual expression, her mouth opened slightly as her tongue slipped out to moisten her already glossy lips. Annalissa's gaze flew to Vinny's face and she could not help but notice his eyes drop to the woman's chest before lifting back to the attendant's face.

The attendant leaned closer, whispering to Vinny but in a voice loud enough for Annalissa to hear. "I don't know if you remember, but we met the last time you took a flight out to California. We had a very good time the night you were there."

Annalissa thought, *Of course. That would be exactly*

what a man like him would want. Worldly. Sophisticated. Ready to jump into bed at his panty-melting smile. She started to turn her head back to the window, refusing to see the interest flare in his eyes, when his hand came to rest on her arm.

He leaned over to her and asked, "Do you want anything to drink? It's going to be a long flight, do you want some coffee or juice?"

Her gaze shifted back to his, seeing him looking directly at her and not the attendant, who still had a smile on her face that now did not reach her eyes. "Some juice would be nice," she answered. "If it's not too much trouble."

Turning back to the attendant, whose body language had stiffened, he gave their order before giving Annalissa's hand a gentle squeeze. He felt her pull her hand away from his and place it in her lap. *Shit, I would have to run into someone I've fucked before.*

Leaning back he closed his eyes, his mind whirling. *What is it about Annalissa?* The attendant was exactly what he had been going for ever since getting out of the Army. Stacked. Exuding confident sex. Easy. *Easy? Yeah,* he admitted to himself. *Always easy. Nothing I had to work for. No one to have to explain things to, make excuses to.* Relationships took too much work and when he had been in the Army and since working for Tony…that was all the work he wanted to concentrate on. *No one to impress other than my prowess in bed. Get 'em off, get me off, and get outta there.*

Opening his eyes as their drinks were served, he noticed a different attendant now. *Good. One less thing from my past right in my face.* Looking sideways at the woman next to him sipping her juice, he was overwhelmed with the desire to know her. Really know her. He snorted. *But what the hell would she want with me? At least we have several hours together.*

"Tell me how you got started with the harp?" he asked, hoping she was still talking to him. Her shy smile was the response he craved.

"My mother was a violinist. She was amazing," she said with conviction. "Not just with her musical talent, but as a person."

"Was?" he asked, curious, then instantly hating the sadness that flashed through her eyes.

"She died about five years ago. I had just finished the music conservatory when she lost her battle to cancer." Lifting her gaze back to his, she added, "But she did get to hear my senior recital. They wheeled her in from the hospital just so she could be there."

"That must have meant a lot to her. And to you," he said simply.

Nodding, her gaze was unfocused, years away in her mind. "Yes," she agreed softly. "She said…" her voice broke and she swallowed several times to battle back the emotions that threatened to overwhelm her.

He sat perfectly still not wanting to interrupt, but watching her carefully. He saw her battle back the tears and lift her chin a little higher. *She does that,* he realized. *When she's steeling herself for strength, she lifts her chin.*

"She told me," Annalissa said, her voice stronger, "That listening to me play the harp was like listening to the angels welcoming her into heaven." Neither of them spoke for a moment and then she added, "The next day, mama died peacefully."

He looked down at their clasped hands, not even remembering when he reached over to take hers. Her tiny, yet strong fingers, were intertwined with his. *When was the last time I held hands with a woman?* He could not remember, but this felt right.

Rubbing her palm, he began to feel the tingles of electricity jolting between them. Her gaze shot up to his and he knew she felt it too. Jerking his hand away, he cursed himself. *Keep your mind on the job. But damn, I didn't even give her time to finish telling me about her music.* Glancing back over, he saw her turn to the window effectively blocking him out.

Disappointment flooded her as she felt him his hand move away. Turning she looked out of the window again, the clouds below them, and wishing once more that her mom was still around for her to talk to.

VINNY SAW THAT ANNALISSA had finally fallen asleep and leaned his head back as well. Movement to his left caught his attention as the older man in the seat across the aisle loosened his tie, grimacing. His complexion was pasty and Vinny was instantly on his feet, his Army medic training kicking in.

"Sir, do you have chest pain?"

The man nodded as Vinny assisted him in removing his tie and unbuttoning his shirt. The man's wife began to panic, trying to grab her husband while Vinny spoke to calm the woman. The flight attendant moved over quickly and said, "I'll alert the captain," before moving away. Another attendant came to assist and Vinny barked, "Get your AED."

Annalissa was instantly alert, watching the activity across the aisle from her, wishing there was something she could do. Seeing the wife getting in the way, she maneuvered past Vinny in the aisle and moved to the empty seat behind the woman. "Ma'am, please come back here so your husband can lay down."

In her panic, the woman appeared unable to understand, crying and grasping at her husband. Annalissa stood and placed her hands on the woman's arms, pulling them away. Speaking sharply, she continued to talk and pull the woman back. The wife finally turned and looked at Annalissa, fear in her eyes.

"I'll help you, but you must move to let them help your husband," she said, more gently. As the woman finally understood, she allowed Annalissa to assist her over the back of the seat. It was rather undignified, but with the help of a gentleman in another row, they managed to get the wife settled where she could see but not be in the way.

Vinny glanced at Annalissa as he laid the man down across the double seats, shooting her a look of gratitude. By then the attendant returned with the AED. "The captain needs to know if you have done this before."

"Army Special Forces Medic," Vinny answered, gaining a nod of approval from the attendant. With Vinny attending to the man, Annalissa sat with her arms around the now crying woman, soothing her as best as she could.

The Captain announced that they would be making an emergency medical landing in Kansas City and shortly they began their descent. Vinny and a nurse from the back of the plane had the man as stabilized as they could, but he was hoping they would land soon. He did not like the coloring of the man's face, nor the erratic heartbeat.

Suddenly, the plane lurched slightly and Vinny was immediately aware that the plane was at a slight angle at it came in. *What the hell?* He jerked his eyes over the seat to Annalissa knowing she hated landings. "Hold on," he shouted to her as the plane landed hard, veering to the right. The shuddering of the aircraft told him that they had landed too hard on one of the wheels, but the pilot managed to right it so that they were able to come to a stop.

The hard landing caused the oxygen masks to fall

from the overheads and the screams of several passengers could be heard.

Goddammit, he cursed looking at the dismay on Annalissa's face as she sought his eyes for reassurance. "We're okay, babe," he said, reaching back to grab her hand.

She gave him a curt nod, keeping one arm around the woman. The captain explained that they were safe, but that an ambulance would be out to remove the ill passenger and then the aircraft maintenance would need to see about the plane. All passengers would have to disembark and be moved to the terminal for the duration.

This was, of course followed by apologies from the Captain and grumblings from the fellow passengers. The ambulance arrived shortly and Vinny stepped back to allow them access as they removed the ill man and his wife.

He looked down at Annalissa seeing the affects of stress etched on her face, and without thinking pulled her into his arms. Tucking her in tightly, he cupped the back of her head against his chest, her face resting against his heart. The other hand encircled her small waist, pressing her into his warmth.

She went willingly, enveloped in his protection. Comfort. Care. After a moment, she was aware of the sensations of being held so close by such a virile man. She felt the strength of his arms as hers gripped his biceps. She was aware of her breasts pressed against his stomach. And against her stomach…she could feel the bulge of his arousal.

Vinny's awareness was also heightened. Her breasts, which had seemed much smaller than he was used to when holding a woman, pressed firmly against him and he could swear her nipples were actually poking his abdomen. Her cheek against his chest had his heart beating loudly, sure that others could hear as well. And his dick…it had a mind of its own and right now was telling him that this woman in his arms was all woman. And very desirable.

Pulling back regretfully, he kissed the top of her head saying, "Let's go, babe. We need to get off with everyone else."

Sorry for the loss of his heartbeat against her face, she knew that he was just comforting her. Nothing else. *Even if he called me 'babe'. I've never been anyone's 'babe'. But I know him…he probably calls everyone that.* Determining to be brave, she pushed away, nodding.

"I thought you said this flight would be uneventful?" she joked.

Shaking his head, he smiled at the beauty in front of him. "Guess I was wrong about that. But surely we've had our share of excitement for one trip. Hopefully, it'll be smooth sailing the rest of the way."

CHAPTER 5

HOURS LATER, THE HOTEL near the Kansas City airport was filled with the passengers from the flight. The airline determined that their flight would be canceled and they were shifting the passengers to other flights. Wanting one more day with her, Vinny agreed to take a flight the next day and she readily acquiesced. Once again, they had connecting rooms in the nearby hotel. Easnadh had been unloaded along with their luggage and they were comfortably settled.

Vinny called Tony to give him an update before calling Gabe. Assuring them both of their safety and comforts, he hung up listening to Annalissa talking to her father.

"I'm fine. We just had an emergency landing and are having to spend the night in a hotel in Kansas City. Yes, Easnadh is with me. Yes, right here in the room. No, I haven't checked her but the landing wasn't that hard. Yes, dad, I'll take her out tonight and make sure. Mr. Malloy is in the room next to mine. Dad, I'm not leaving Easnadh with him. The harp is perfectly fine in my room."

Vinny listened, his anger growing. *The man hardly*

asked about his daughter, only caring about the instrument. He heard her hang up and moved away from their connecting door. Waiting a few minutes before knocking, he entered. She sat on the bed, a faraway look on her face. Startled, she jumped when she saw him standing there.

"You were lost in thought," he said, slowly walking toward her.

"Yes, I was…um…just…well, I had to call my father," she stammered.

Vinny noted her demeanor. *Back to being shy. Cowed. Now I understand why. She not only has Todd and Gordon bullying her, it appears that her father is the worst bully of all. And the last thing she needs is another dominant man in her life. And that's what I am.*

Looking at her tired face, he thought, *she needs someone soft. Someone who will let her…* He realized that he wanted to be what she needed but had no idea if he could or not. Shaking his head, forcing the battle of thoughts from his mind, he stuck out his elbow and quipped, "May I have the honor of taking you to dinner, Ms. O'Brian?"

She giggled, the first laugh she had had all day. Standing and taking his arm, she agreed. "Why yes, Mr. Malloy. It would be my pleasure."

ONCE AGAIN VINNY laid in bed, his thoughts a tangled mess. *What the hell happened to the man who had all the*

answers? His mind wandered back to the dinner he had shared with Annalissa.

She asked about being a medic in the Special Forces, really listening as he described what he did. Well, the gentle version. He did not think that she could handle the realistic version. *But then, she's stronger than she seems. Stronger than she thinks.* Her gaze focused on his eyes as he spoke. Not looking around to see if there was someone else who would be a better catch for the evening. He had always taken pride that most hook-ups considered him to be the prize but now realized that it was due to what they thought he could do for them in the sack...but not him as a person. This was different. She smiled when he talked about being a twin and laughed at his jokes. And all it took was one look at her guileless face to know that she was as sincere as she appeared.

When was the last time I had that? Have I ever had that? He told her tales of his brothers-in-arms, now coworkers for Alvarez Security. He talked about his friends and the women they had all fallen in love with and saved.

Realizing that he only opened up to friends he wondered, *Is this friendship? Is that what's happening here?* If it was, he liked the feeling. A lot. Enjoyable, comforting, relaxing.

And then? *Oh, Jesus, what a fuck-up.* She had excused herself to go to the ladies' room when two women approached him.

"We've been waiting forever for that little mouse to leave," one of them had said, immediately drawing his ire.

Standing, he pushed his chair back, saying, "Not interested, ladies. Now if you'll excuse me."

He turned to signal their waiter so that he could pay, when the other woman grabbed his arm, saying, "That child could not possibly keep a man like you interested. What'd you say to a threesome, big boy?" She pressed against his arm, her low shirt showing her impressive breasts.

Looking down at her smirk, he knew she thought he was a sure thing. An easy man for an easy fuck. But for the first time, his dick did not even respond. Nothing about the woman was appealing. But the thought of a petite, dark-haired, green-eyed harpist stirred him like no other.

A slight gasp sounded to his right. Turning his head, he saw the look of surprise on the face of the woman that was filling his thoughts, just before she turned and walked away. Disentangling himself from the two interlopers, he told the passing waiter to put the meal on his room tab and jogged after Annalissa.

The elevator doors were just closing as he rounded the corner in the lobby. *Fuck.* He took the stairs to the third floor, arriving about the same time the elevator doors opened. He caught her wide-eyed expression, knowing that she had hoped to be in her room by the time he arrived.

She quickly schooled her expression, but he could still see the embarrassment. She tried to move past him, but he took her arm escorting her to her door. "Annalissa," he said softly.

"Thank you for a lovely dinner, Vinny. I'll just be turning in and you can…uh…enjoy your…um…evening." She graced him with what she hoped was a bright smile.

No way, baby, am I letting it go like this. Not used to having to explain himself, he rushed in. "I was enjoying my evening…with you. What you saw? They came up and I was trying politely to move them along. I have no interest in being with anyone else."

Her eyes peered into his, searching deeply. Cocking her head to the side, she asked, "Do you usually find women from bars to…um…be with?"

Dropping his head, he wanted to scream "No" but found he could not lie to her. "Yeah." He sighed, shrugging his shoulders. "Yeah."

"Please, Vinny," she said. "I know I'm a job, but I'm here in my room safe and sound. You can come in and check to make sure my harp is here. But then you may go do…um…whatever you want to do."

He stepped closer, his hand on her face, and could see her fighting to keep from leaning into his embrace. "I only want to be here. I have no desire to be with anyone else." *Please believe me.*

He watched as she lifted her chin slightly, away from his hand and he missed her touch. "Goodnight,

Vinny," she said, turning and entering her room.

Her door shut firmly with a click and he heard the bolt latch.

And now, he was laying on his bed listening for any sound from next door. *What did I think was going to happen? That she'd have a change of heart and come knocking on my door?*

He had heard the shower and movement for a little while after they parted and now nothing. *She must be asleep.*

MILES AWAY, A MAN placed a call, anxiety coursing through his veins.

"Talk," was the only response when the call was answered.

"It ain't here. I searched everywhere. Even went back to all the planes. Looked through everything. I'm telling you, it ain't here."

"Goddamnit! You must have missed it."

The line was deathly silent for a moment while he swallowed loudly a few times.

"Or else you decided to take it for yourself."

"No, no, I swear it. I ain't lying. It ain't here. I looked everywhere," he said, sweat trickling down his face.

"Well, find it. Search the apartment in case it was picked up and taken there." Rattling off the address, they said, "And do not fail to locate where it is if you want to keep your job. And your life!"

The line went permanently dead at that point, leaving him to wipe his brow once again.

What have I gotten myself into, he wondered as he looked down at the address he had written. Heading toward his car, he hoped the trip would be successful, trying to push the consequences of failure from his mind.

ANNALISSA WAS SITTING up in bed. Sleep was not coming and no matter how much she tried to tell herself that it did not matter what the women in the bar said, it still hurt. *Mouse. I'm not a mouse. Maybe I'm not an in-your-face kind of person, but that doesn't make me a mouse.* Glancing down at her slim body, she thought of their tight shirts with tons of cleavage showing. Taking her hands and pressing her breasts together, she giggled. *There. If I did this all the time, then I could have men ogle my boobs too.* Letting her hands drop, she sighed. *I know that's what he likes. That's what he's used to having.* Heaving another sigh, she shook her head. *It doesn't matter. I'm who I am and what I am. I never had a shot at a man like him anyway.*

She padded over to her harp case, realizing that with all the events of the day she had not taken Easnadh out. Laying the case on its side, she unsnapped it and lifted the lid. The sliver of moonlight coming in through the curtains cast a shiny shadow across her beloved instrument. As was her habit, she lovingly gazed over the entire harp, noting with pride the exquisite restoration work. Everything looked perfect...until her gaze fell upon the pedestal. Flipping on the light next to her, she peered down into the case to see what caught her eye. *What is that?*

The base of Easnadh's pedestal was slightly crooked. It would not be noticed by anyone other than someone intimately acquainted with every inch of the beautiful instrument. *How did that happen?* She carefully lifted her harp from its case and walked over to her bed, laying it down for further inspection. Running her fingers carefully over the wood, she noted that the harp was completely as it should be, except the base.

Bending over her task, she saw that the screws that held the base onto the pedestal were almost perfect—except for one. And it was not screwed in all the way flush with the wood. *How did the screw become loose?* Not wanting to leave anything to chance, she moved over to her cosmetic case, looking for a nail file to use as a screwdriver.

Lifting the harp, she turned it upside down and heard a noise from inside the hollow pedestal. Turning it back down in the correct position, she heard the noise again as something slide back down. Her brow knitted as she moved the harp several times, each time greeted with the same noise.

What's in there? And how did something get there?

Instead of screwing the errant screw back in tighter, she removed all of the screws carefully and slowly removed the wooden base. With the harp still on the bed, she leaned over to peer inside.

Seeing several plastic bags, she reached her fingers toward the foreign objects. Stopping at the last minute, her hands hovered over the bags...*someone's put something in here.* Her heart began to pound in her chest as realization slid over her. Too many nights watching TV when she could not sleep and her fingers ached from harp practice had her assuming what the bags were. Something white was in them. *Oh, Jesus, someone's put drugs in Easnadh's case.*

Whirling, she ran for the connecting door. "Vinny!" she screeched.

Hearing her cry, Vinny blew through the door, belatedly realizing he almost hit her as he rushed to her aid, his weapon drawn.

"What? What's wrong?" he bit out as she rushed into his arms. His gaze flew around the room ascertaining that no one else was there. Seeing the harp case opened, his heart dropped. *Oh, shit. Is something wrong with her harp?*

"Something's there," she muttered, pointing to the harp.

His brow creased as he struggled to understand. Pushing her gently away from him, he said softly, "Sit down. Let me see."

He moved over to the instrument lying on the bed

and instantly knew what he was looking at. He looked over at her pale, shaking form. Stalking to her, he knelt in front of her.

"Tell me what happened," he said. Her eyes found his but appeared dilated with shock. "Annalissa," he said a little louder and noticed her eyes re-focused. *That's it, baby. Stay with me.* "I need you to tell me what happened."

Nodding, she described that she had forgotten to check on Easnadh, so she went over, opened the case and explained why she began looking.

"Oh Vinny, what'll we do? Do we call the police?"

"No, not the local police." His mind raced with possibilities. Hearing a choked sob, he turned his attention back to her.

"Who would have done this? Someone from the airport?" she asked, tears glistening on the tips of her lashes.

"Possibly. Someone could have stashed it in the airport in LA and then had someone else get it out in D.C. before it went to the claims section." While that was the easiest explanation, he knew that it would have taken an organized effort to hide them inside of the harp. He knew instantly that the mission just became a lot more complicated.

Looking around the room, he said, "Babe, I need you to get dressed and pack your things. We're going to a different hotel."

She looked at him with big eyes, a confused expression on her face. "But why?"

"If someone in the Dulles airport was supposed to get it then they know by now that you didn't land. And if someone wants this," he glanced over at the still open case, "and they will want it, then I don't want us in a room under our names."

She licked her lips nervously, nodding her understanding. Quickly standing, she moved around the room gathering her belongings and throwing them in her suitcase.

He watched in admiration as she moved to the task, no tears and no hysteria. And he had to admit that seeing her again in the old fashioned, cotton nightgown from another era was breathtaking. She hurried into the bathroom, emerging a few minutes later, dressed and ready to go.

Smiling, Vinny thought, *Stronger than she thinks she is.* He closed up the harp case and grabbed it and her bag, ushering her into his room.

It only took a couple more minutes for him to secure his belongings as well. A quick trip in a taxi took them to a nearby hotel where he went in and paid by cash. For just one room. As he carried her suitcase and Easnadh to the room, she carried his much lighter travel bag. Opening the door, he entered quickly checking out the space.

"Where's my room?" she asked, following him in.

"This is it," he answered. Seeing her eyes widen in surprise, he quickly explained, "I need to keep an eye on you and I sure as hell can't let over a quarter of a million dollars worth of cocaine out of my sight."

Her mouth opened into an "O" and he found himself wanting to lean in and kiss the surprise right off of her delectable face.

Before she could find an objection, he added, "And I've got to get the Agency on this. I need everyone here together so I can do my job and watch you too."

She pulled her lips in, hiding the hurt. *His job. I'm his job. And now it just got a lot harder.* Nodding her agreement, she went into the bathroom.

IT WAS ONE A.M. in Kansas City and three a.m. in Richland, but Tony had immediately called his team together with one phone call from Vinny. Rendezvousing at the agency they gathered around the large conference table with the live feed from Vinny's secure computer up on the screen. Gabe and Jobe immediately showed up. Lily, one of their computer software experts, along with BJ, another computer expert and security agent in training, rounded out the crew. Lily's husband, Matt, was a detective for the Richland Police and good friend, but he was not there. Vinny had requested that Matt and his partner, Shane, go to Annalissa's apartment and check it out.

Gabe was the first to speak, worry for his twin utmost in his mind. "Bro, you okay?"

Vinny nodded and answered in the affirmative. "Just letting you all know that I've got Annalissa here with me. We changed hotels so that there was no trail to where we were."

He explained everything that had happened since meeting up with her the day before. Succinctly going through everyone they had been in contact with and all the times when the harp case had been out of their sight. "Annalissa checked it before we left for the airport and we saw it sent to claims ourselves. We picked it up in claims once everything was taken off the plane in Kansas City. So it could have happened when we were at dinner, but my guess is that it was part of a drug run from LA to DC."

"Do you think it's personal?" Tony asked. "It could be that an airport worker at LA just picked whatever case was convenient on a non-stop flight to DC and then would have plenty of time to let their partner know which case to look in when it landed."

"No," Gabe growled, "it was someone who knew how to get into the base of the harp. It was someone who knew her and knew her schedule."

Vinny was about to answer when there appeared to be some movement on his laptop screen as he could see people at the table shifting around. Matt and Shane came into focus.

"Vinny, is Ms. O'Brian there with you?" Matt asked.

Vinny turned around, looking at her sitting in a

chair in the corner of the room. Her knees were drawn up with her arms around them, as though to ward off any more unpleasantness.

"Annalissa, come over here, honey," he called gently, not thinking about the others listening. As he was looking at her, he missed the glances shared by the ones back in Virginia when they heard his endearment.

Tony's crew watched the screen as a slim, dark-haired woman came into sight. Her face was pinched with worry, and Vinny placed his arm around her protectively. He pointed to the laptop screen and introduced them all. "Annalissa, these are my friends and co-workers. Everyone, this is Annalissa O'Brian."

Lily moved the camera around so that it focused on Matt and Shane. "Ms. O'Brian, we're from the Richland Police Department and while we have no jurisdiction where you are now, Vinny asked us to go check out your apartment."

She nodded her understanding, although she felt as though she were in a fast paced movie and was one step behind on the plot.

Matt continued, "Ms. O'Brian, I hate to inform you, but your apartment was broken into. And from the looks of what we saw, it was trashed."

Gasping, her hand flew to her mouth. "But why? I have nothing of value," she cried. Vinny's arm tightened around her shoulders, his mouth set in a tight line.

"Our assumption at this point is that whoever was

expecting those drugs at the airport, may have not realized that the flight was canceled and just thought they missed you. That could be why they headed to your apartment to look for them."

"Oh my God," she said, slumping back into Vinny. "What do we do?" she asked, fear written on her face.

Tony spoke up, "Ms. O'Brian, let us handle things. Our job is to make sure you're safe and Mr. Malloy is just the man to do that. We're going to talk to him for a while and figure out our next step. Just make sure that you listen to whatever he tells you to do. Have you told anyone about what has happened? A call or text?"

"No, no one. I need to call my father in case he wonders, but honestly he wouldn't even miss me until tomorrow. Or today. Or...oh I don't even know what day it is!"

"Don't worry about it. But for now, if you do talk to anyone, and that includes your father, just tell them about the plane delay but say nothing about the drugs at all. It is imperative that you keep that information completely quiet. We don't want to tip off anyone that it has been found."

Nodding her understanding, Vinny noticed her chin lift slightly. *That's my girl.* Standing with his arm still around her shoulders, he walked her over to the bed. "Babe, go ahead and get ready for bed and see if you can relax. I've got to finish the briefing so we'll have a plan."

Moving back to the small table where his laptop

was set up, he worked with the group on different scenarios. Tony had walked away for a few minutes and then came back into view.

"Vinny, I was just in contact with Jack Bryant." Jacques "Jack" Bryant had been their Special Forces squad's Chief Warrant Officer, and he now ran a different type of Security Business. More clandestine. Government contracts. And definitely flew under the radar. He had pulled together a team of former SEALs, Special Forces, DEA, FBI, ATF, and others.

"His former DEA agent is going to fly out there tomorrow…rather later today…and meet you. You'll be able to hand off the harp to him and he'll bring it back here safely. He has a two seater so he'll only bring the harp now. He'll work with his former DEA contacts. Lily's making alternate flight arrangements for the two of you. You can fly in after meeting with the agent."

Vinny finished his briefing, closed his laptop and leaned back, running his hand over his face. Sighing deeply, he realized he had not slept much in two days. *Damn, in the Army I was trained to go without sleep.* Shaking his head, he looked up as he felt a small touch on his arm.

Annalissa was standing in front of him, with the same nightgown on. A soft, long sleeved, old-fashioned gown that looked like something from several centuries before. Nothing like the wisps of fabric that most of the women he met wore. Thongs and bits of material they called nighties. And yet...*I've never seen anything so fuckin' sexy.*

She saw the weariness in his eyes, then something different flickered in them. Giving his arm a pull, she said, "Come on. Come to bed."

He eyed the single bed in the room and said, "No, I'll sleep in the chair."

She let go of his arm, cocked her hip and began tapping her foot. He looked up at her face. *Yep, there goes that chin lift.*

"Vinny, we're both dead on our feet and need some sleep. I trust you." She held out her hand toward him.

Chuckling, he allowed himself to be pulled up. Several minutes later, he was in the bed, her on one side and he on the other. She yawned loudly, exhaustion overpowering her almost instantly.

He could tell when her breathing evened out and sleep had laid its claim on her. Looking down at her dark hair spilling across the pillow, her cherubic face relaxed in slumber, her thick eyelashes forming a crescent on her cheeks. And her lips. Perfect. Plump. Kissable. She sighed, rolling over onto her side facing him, unconsciously moving closer to his warmth. He could not remember the last time he had slept with a woman that he had not fucked. Ever. In fact, he could not remember being in bed with a woman that he was not banging and then leaving. Ever.

And then he was filled with the realization...that he had never wanted to until now. *This woman.* And he felt a jolt to his heart. Smiling, he let sleep overtake him as well.

"IT'S NOT THERE either. I looked real good. I looked everywhere. Don't think she's been there yet." He hoped his explanation would appease who he was reporting to.

"I want to know what the hell happened. Where the goddamn plane went to and why the case wasn't there. Do you understand me? I want to know where it is!"

"I'm just a handler. I ain't got no special knowledge," he protested.

"You find out what you can. I'll look on this end. But listen and listen well—you had better get me some facts and damn quick."

Protesting again, he said, "I didn't sign up for this shit. I was just supposed to get it when it landed. That's all I've ever done. That's all I was told I'd be doing."

"Well, the job description just changed. And you'd better accept the change and get me the information I need or we're all dead!"

As usual, the line went silent leaving him to wonder how they were ever going to get out of this mess alive.

On the other end, the cell phone was tossed with an expletive. *Think, think. Where the hell is she and where is that harp? What was the name of the goon she was with?*

Oh, yeah. Vincent Malloy from Alvarez Security. Not willing to wait on the plebe from Dulles airport, they pulled up their laptop, clicking through a variety of screens. Finding the news from the airport, they learned of the plane's detour. *Work the problem. Where would they be?*

Smiling at their cleverness, they continued to search...and plan.

CHAPTER 6

T HE SUN WAS peeking through the slit in the hotel's room-darkening curtains when Vinny opened his eyes. The evening's events flashed through his mind as he looked down at the woman sprawled across him. Her leg was across his and her arm was slung over his chest. Her head rested on his shoulder and just as he had not been able to remember sleeping with a woman, he knew he had never woken up with one. But as she stretched her lithe body over his, he realized what his brother had been talking about. When Gabe first met Jennifer, Vinny had been glad for him but not envious. Never envious.

But now? I could wake this way every morning with this woman and be happy. The knowledge that he felt this way about a woman that he had not had sex with made him chuckle.

Annalissa felt the deep rumble underneath her cheek and she opened her eyes to the most handsome man she had ever seen. And he was staring right at her. Her eyes flew wide open as she realized she was laying half across his body.

Jerking back, she rolled to the other side.

"Morning," he said, his sexy, raspy voice growled, as he smiled at her.

"Good morning. I…um…seem to have…moved a bit…in the night," she stammered, blushing furiously.

"No complaints here, babe," he said, hoping she would not discover just how much he liked waking up to her. His morning wood was tenting his boxers and he would bet she had never experienced anything like morning sex. And since he never stayed with a woman overnight, he was used to taking care of it himself in the shower. *Ugh, stop thinking about sex with her.* Forcing his mind to other things, he nodded for her to head to the bathroom first.

While she was getting ready, he checked the harp case once again, making sure nothing had changed with the package. Thirty minutes later, a taxi was driving them back toward the airport to meet with Jack's DEA contact. Since he would be flying in on a small, private plane to another airport, Vinny was going to rent a car just to meet the contact. Then when their business was finished, they would make their way back to the airport for a flight straight to Richland.

Feeling Annalissa stiffen against him, he jerked his head over to her side of the taxi. The hotel where they had stayed last night was in their view. Police cars and police dogs were moving around the area. She started to ask him if they were there for them, but his quick head shake kept her quiet.

Her gaze landed on the taxi driver and she realized

her almost blunder.

The taxi driver noticed their gazes focused out of the window. "Heard someone broke into one of the hotel's rooms and the manager saw 'em. Called the cops and caused a ruckus. The man that was there is missing and I reckon they're looking for him."

It did not take long to circle by the airport, heading to the rental center.

Shit, Vinny thought, knowing that they were being sought after. He glanced to the side seeing Annalissa's green eyes, huge with fright. He tried to offer her a smile, but the look on her face told him she was not buying it.

As the taxi pulled up to the rental car agency, Vinny prayed that whoever was looking for them would be watching the airport, assuming they would be joining the other displaced passengers from the previous day. The rental facility had no police around, so Vinny left Annalissa in the taxi as he went in to get a car. Using cash and one of his fake IDs, he was soon pulling around to the side in a small SUV. Paying the taxi driver in cash also, he quickly moved their items to the rental and took off.

Several minutes later he pulled into a nondescript shopping center and parked. Calling Tony on one of the secure cell phones he carried, he relayed their change in plans. "Get the message to Jack's contact. We've got to come up with an alternate meeting location. They're definitely after her."

Listening to Vinny discuss the events calmly did not help the pounding of her heart. *After me? For the drugs I didn't even know about? Were they planted there on purpose or was Easnadh just the random case they picked?*

The sound of him disconnecting the call jerked her out of her frantic musings. He turned to her, seeing the fear in her expression.

"We're going to start driving. I'm going to take care of you, but we've got to hit the road and get out of here. Tony is setting up a new location for us to get the harp case to DEA, but for now…you and I are going to hit the road."

Watching her lick her lips nervously, he wanted to lean over and lick them himself. Part them and take the kiss deeper then…*nope. Not now.* Sucking in a huge breath and letting it out slowly, he pulled out of the parking lot and headed on the highway towards HWY 70 E towards Missouri.

"Where are we going to meet the person?" she asked, trying to still her nerves.

"We're going to get to the east side of Kansas City and Tony is arranging a meeting place not too far into Missouri."

Watching the skyline of Kansas City come into view, she stayed quiet as they moved through the city quickly. She had never been traveling through the country by a car before. *If I wasn't scared out of my mind, I might actually like this.* But she was scared.

Glancing over at Vinny, he seemed calm. In charge. In control. But there was a slight tick as he gritted his teeth and just looking at his face she could tell that his mind was racing. Planning. *How can I know that about him in only two days?*

He was doing exactly what she thought he was. His mind raced through the possibilities. It could still be that her harp case was randomly chosen to transport drugs from someone at the airport and when the case did not arrive, the D.C. receiver got nervous. But that would have taken coordination. That person would have had to make quick contact with the person at Kansas City, found out who the harp case belonged to, found out their address, and made a visit to trash the place.

Possible. But not very plausible. He had to accept the very real scenario that she was targeted before getting to the airport yesterday morning. Someone planting the drugs or planning on having the drugs planted...specifically in her harp case.

As his mind continued to roll over the possibilities, he was aware of her glancing at him. He knew she was nervous. While wanting to assure her that everything was fine, he was glad she was concerned. *Heightened awareness means more prepared.* And right now, he wanted them prepared for anything.

SEVERAL MILES DOWN HWY 70 once in Missouri, Vinny drove the SUV into a strip-mall shopping center parking lot and pulled up to the third light post in front of a Chinese restaurant. Eyes alert, he checked his watch before looking over at Annalissa. Her pale face stood out in stark contrast to her dark hair. Her hands were clasped in her lap, the knuckles white with tightness.

He reached over and placed his large hand over hers, saying, "We're going to be fine. I promise."

She smiled, but it did not reach her eyes. "You'll tell me, won't you? I know you think I'm weak, but I'm really not. I just need to know."

Lifting his eyebrow in question, he asked, "What is it that you want to know?"

"Everything. What you're doing. What you're thinking. I…I don't want to be in the dark." Her large green eyes implored him as her fingers unconsciously squeezed his.

Nodding, he agreed. "Okay. I'll keep you in the loop…and keep you safe."

"Well," she said, licking her lips. "Isn't this kind of public for a meeting?"

"This shopping center is not very crowded as you see and they only have security cameras facing the front of the stores. We're out of any camera range."

This time her tremulous smile was genuine. His gaze jumped from her face to outside the window behind her and she jerked her head around. A black

SUV with dark-tinted windows pulled directly next to their vehicle.

Giving her fingers a warning squeeze, he let go of her hand and said, "Annalissa, stay in the car. Don't get out, you understand?" Seeing her nod her head, he moved out of the rental and walked around, meeting the man who emerged from the other vehicle.

Vinny instantly assessed the man, knowing that he was being looked over as well. The other man took off his aviator glasses and stuck out his hand. "Taggart," he said, introducing himself while lifting his hand forward.

"Malloy," Vinny answered back, shaking the man's hand. He liked what he saw. The man oozed confidence, but not arrogance.

"Bryant talked to Tony and says you have a package for me to deliver."

Nodding, Vinny walked to the back of the SUV and lifted the hatch. The harp case lay on its side in the back. Before he could stop her, Annalissa jumped from the passenger seat and came to the back, her fingers fluttering.

He started to growl, but she lifted her chin. "I can't stay in there. Not when you're talking about Easnadh."

"Who?" Taggart asked, his gaze quickly scanning for someone else.

"Easnadh," she said softly, her hand reaching out to touch the case. "My harp."

"Harpists will sometimes name their instruments," Vinny explained, then offered his fiercest glare to her indicating that he wanted her back inside the vehicle.

Ignoring him, she turned to Taggart, begging, "You'll take care of her won't you?"

Before Vinny could say anything, Taggart took her hand as he introduced himself to her. "Ms. O'Brian, I'll take the best care of your harp."

A brilliant smile beamed at Taggart and Vinny found himself uncharacteristically jealous. *Jealous? I never get fuckin' jealous!* But he could not deny that the sight of her hand in Taggart's made him see red.

"You gonna hold hands all day or take this off of ours so we can hit the road?"

Chuckling, Taggart dropped her hand and leaned in to open the case. Seeing the packages of white powder inside next to the instrument silenced his mirth.

"Someone went to a lot of trouble with a half-million dollars of cocaine," Taggart said. Closing the lid and securing the latches, he lifted the harp carefully and put it in the back of his SUV. Turning to Annalissa, he looked her in the eye and said, "Ma'am, it'll be completely safe in my hands. Malloy here knows how we operate and I promise you'll get your harp back."

She wanted to ask more. *Where are you taking Easnadh? What will you do when you get to where you are going? How will you get her there?* But she knew this man would not answer and Vinny already looked angry enough that she had gotten out of the car. *And that Taggart had held her hand. Was he jealous? No way, not over me.*

Taggart drove away as Vinny took her gently by the arm leading her over to the passenger side. Assisting her up, he leaned over to buckle her in, putting his face right in hers. Their lips almost touching.

"Next time I tell you what to do and you don't do it…you're gonna find out just what kind of punishment I can hand out." With that, he slammed the door before walking around and hopping up in the driver's side. As he got in, he noticed her head slightly down. *I don't want to scare her but she's got to listen to me if I'm going to keep her safe.*

As he started the vehicle, she spoke. "I just had to explain about Easnadh. He had to understand," she said, her eyes imploring Vinny to synpathize.

Sighing, he reached over and clasped her hand again. "I should have realized that parting with your harp was going to be difficult and I'm sorry. But, babe, I can't keep you safe if I don't know where you are or what you're doing. So you gotta listen and obey. Can you do that?"

He saw her chin lift slightly as she answered him, "Yeah. I can do that." With a final squeeze of her fingers, he pulled back out onto the highway, heading east.

"I GAVE YOU the information about the plane and the hotel, I can't help it if they weren't there." The person who had been threatening the airport handler was now in the dubious situation of reporting to their contact. And not liking the feeling at all.

"What went wrong?" came the cold voice on the other end of the phone.

"I sent the handler to her apartment and he looked carefully and then said they weren't there. Then I found out about the plane being delayed in Kansas City."

"I know that, you imbecile. That's what you told me last night."

"You must have sent someone in, but they got caught. Police were there and now the girl and that guy she's with have disappeared."

The silence on the phone was ear-piercing. "I pay you to get my stash across the country, not fuck up and get the police involved."

Whining, the person objected. "That's not my fault. I did my part."

"Where are they now?"

"I'm telling you, I don't know. They didn't get on the plane in Kansas City."

"Then they must be traveling by car. Did you check the rental agencies?"

"Yeah, of course. But no one with their names got a car. I checked all of them."

The man in California closed his eyes in frustration. Not used to incompetence, he growled, "Go back you fucking moron and give them a description. Find that couple and the fucking harp. When you do, let me know and I'll send someone to take care of them."

"I'll try," came the fearful response.

"Just fucking do it!" he ordered before disconnecting. Sitting in his office he wondered how such a brilliant plan had gone all to hell. Rubbing his hand over his face, he knew that failure would not be acceptable. Not to Don Juarez. Don had not risen to be one of the largest drug lords in California by surrounding himself with incompetents. Sucking in a huge breath before letting it out slowly, he picked his phone back up, making his next call.

THE NEXT HOUR passed in silence, the highway rolling before them. Annalissa was quiet, her face turned toward the window. Her mind was churning once again, the events of the last two days so far out of her realm of experience that she had no idea what to think. Heaving a sigh, she closed her eyes wondering if sleep would come. *Or would it be fueled by nightmares?*

"Annalissa?" Vinny interrupted her thoughts. "Where are you?"

Giving a small smile as she turned toward his smooth voice, she said, "Right here."

"Oh no, darlin'," he replied. "You were a million miles away."

"I just have no…idea what to think about…all of

this," she said hesitantly, her hands fluttering as she shrugged in frustration.

"I know. I know you're tired and I know you're scared. We'll figure it out and keep you safe, I promise."

He saw her look down as her hands clasped together once again. *She does that when she is nervous.* "What are you thinking? You got questions? Go ahead and ask. I'll answer if I can," he assured.

"Well, I know we don't know who put the drugs in the case or if they were targeting me. But…well…I was…kind of…" her voice trailed off. *I hate being introverted.* Sucking in a deep breath, she lifted her chin, determined to sound more confident, and said, "Why did we not call the police right away?"

Seeing her resolve, he nodded, "Good question, and I'll tell you what I know." He glanced sideways, noticing her twist in her seat so that she could focus on him. "If we'd called the local police, they would have confiscated the harp and its case. They would have taken us in for questioning. They would have immediately begun investigating you and me, both. All the while, the ones who put it in your case and the ones expecting it would have had more time to cover their tracks. By me calling Tony, we have our agency plus the services of another…uh…security business that we are working with. Friends who have a variety of backgrounds and contacts themselves."

He saw her nod slowly, digesting this information.

Hesitating for a moment, he continued, "And we have to face the possibility that with the police and dogs at the hotel this morning, someone could have been trying to frame you." Her sudden intake of breath had him looking over.

Her green eyes were wide with fright, her mouth opening and closing like a fish. *Her delectable, kissable mouth.*

"But who'd want to frame me? I'm...I'm...not...," faltering, she snapped her mouth shut in anger.

"I don't know who'd do that or why, other than to take suspicion off of themselves. But right now, your har...I mean, Eashadh is heading with a former DEA agent who will meet with a group of other DEA and FBI agents to analyze the situation and let Tony know how to plan for your safety."

Silence filled the car once again as she mulled over his answers to her question. Deciding to pull her out of her musings, he said, "You never finished telling me about your mother and how you became a harp player."

She turned back to him, a little smile once again on her face. "That's right. Well, I told you that my mother was a violinist, but she also taught music. My father was an orchestra conductor. He's...not a patient man, but mom had all the patience in the world. She loved playing, but I think she loved teaching more."

"So did she teach you?"

"At first, yes. I had my first violin when I was four years old," she admitted.

His eyes jerked over to hers, a look of confusion on his face. "Four? How the hell did you even hold it?"

Laughing, she answered, "They make them sized for children. Mine was tiny."

He loved hearing her laugh. *Hell, I love hearing her speak. I can't remember the last conversation I had with a woman that didn't involve 'flip over' or 'are you coming yet'.* Suddenly feeling like a world-class prick, he ground his teeth together. He glanced back over at her, now facing the front window, watching the scenery pass by, her profile a study in perfection. Long, thick, dark hair pulled back with a clip away from her face, a few strands loose and framing her face. Even her neck was delicate. He saw her pulse beating and wanted to pull the SUV over long enough to just taste her neck. Feel the life of her beat under his lips. *And maybe give her a little bite…just enough to taste…and mark her as mine.*

He had not given a woman a love bite since high school and yet the desire to do so now, with this woman, was almost overwhelming. Shifting slightly to ease his erection, he said gruffly, "Continue."

"I'm sorry. You must think me a terrible story teller," she giggled. "I suppose I always get this way when talking about mom. Anyway, she taught me the violin when I was very young. I also learned the viola and cello. But my love was the harp. When I was only ten and at one of their symphonies, a beautiful harpist was the soloist for the evening. She floated out in a gown...I thought she was a princess."

Vinny thought about seeing Annalissa at the concert the other evening and could understand the comparison. *I sure as hell thought she looked like a princess.*

"My mom bought me a Celtic harp and that began my love affair with harps. My father wanted me to learn. He liked the idea that his daughter was not just going to be in the orchestra but would often be front and center. He...likes the...showmanship of the instrument as much as the sound."

He heard the faltering words when she talked about her father and continued to dislike the man even before meeting him. And he would be meeting him.

His eyes stayed on the rear-view mirror for several miles while listening to her. He wished he could focus just on her, but he had noticed the same vehicle behind them for a while. She did not seem to notice, for which he was glad. He wanted her to focus on happy times and princess dresses...not on the probability that she was in danger.

"Celtic harp?" he queried.

"It's a mid-sized harp, although you can get them small enough to sit on your lap. They're much smaller than the large standing pedal harps. I can play any of them, but my favorite is the Celtic."

"Is that what Easnadh is?" he asked, wanting to keep her talking but also finding that he wanted to learn everything about her.

"Yes, although her story is very interesting. An old woman died in New York without close relatives and when the city sent some people in, they found that her house was filled to the brim with…stuff. The old lady had gone dumpster diving for years and her three-story brownstone was filled with a lot of junk and some antiques. The auction company contacted my teacher, Mr. Feinstein, when a few old musical instruments were found because he is also an expert on antique instruments. Most were old but not antique. But then they brought him an old, beat-up harp, strings broken and in horrible shape. But he recognized its value and bought it from them and then spent almost a year meticulously restoring it. He had it analyzed and, believe it or not, it was a true antique. Over one hundred and thirty years old! Can you even begin to imagine all of the people that have played her? And to think that I'm one of them!"

Vinny glanced over once more and his breath caught in his throat. Her green eyes sparkled with excitement and her smile lit up his world. A foreign feeling swept over him, one of passion born of…*what? Protectiveness? Concern? Friendship? Is this what I feel? After only three days?* All he knew was that at that moment, the idea of waking up to that face, those eyes, that smile every day was all he wanted. He moved one hand from the steering wheel to rub his chest, a strange ache in his heart. *What would I give to have that passion aimed toward me?*

CHAPTER 7

"SO WHAT HAPPENED to the harp?" he asked, finding himself truly interested in her story.

"After Mr. Feinstein restored it, he gave it to me."

"Gave it to you?" he asked incredulously.

"I know, right?" she said, nodding vigorously. "But he said that I was his best student and that I should have the honor of playing on it always."

Her voice became soft once again and he looked over to see the wistfulness in her expression. "My father loved the publicity," she added. "The New York Times ran a huge article on the restored harp and the conductor's daughter who plays it."

"I take it you didn't like the publicity?"

"I'm just...not that into...the spotlight. I play because I love it." Laughing, she added, "But I do get to dress up like a princess. I named the harp Easndah because it is the muse for my music."

Several more miles passed on the long straight highway, the scenery flying by. Vinny had lost sight of the car he thought may have been following, but he was not letting down his guard. Traffic was not heavy, but he knew they could have just backed off.

"Anyway," she sobered, "mom died and I had my degree in music performance but stayed an extra year to obtain my teaching degree as well."

"Teaching?" he asked.

"That's my first love, besides playing Easndah. I'd love to teach, but my father was furious when I stayed that extra year. He refused to pay, so I worked in small clubs and taught on the side to make the money I needed."

As much as Vinny wanted her to tell him all about herself, he was getting more and more angry at her father. *Sounds like an asshole.*

Watching the flat land all around, Annalissa was fascinated with the scenery. She relaxed back into her seat, feeling peaceful. *When was the last time I talked about my mom? Or talked about my father without getting so nervous.* She realized how easy it was to talk to Vinny. Sliding her gaze sideways, she watched his profile. *God, he's gorgeous. He seemed genuinely interested in me, but then he probably has lots of women that want to talk to him.* Remembering the actions of the flight attendant, a frown crossed her face. *I'm such a dork. What would he ever want with me?*

"You getting hungry?" he asked, his rich voice pulling her out of her thoughts. The growl coming from her stomach was his answer. Chuckling, he said, "I'll take that as a 'yes'. There's a stop up ahead where I can get some gas and we can grab some food."

"That's perfect. To be honest, I could use a bathroom break as well. Too much coffee this morning," she said with a blush.

Fuckin' adorable, he thought, but wished she had said something earlier. "Babe, if you need to stop for any reason, you let me know. I don't want you uncomfortable."

She nodded, the blush still visible from the tops of her breasts to her hairline. They pulled into a large truck stop convenience center and parked close to where he could keep an eye on the vehicle from inside.

By the time she was unbuckled, he had appeared at her door, offering his hand to assist. Walking toward the building, he wrapped his arm around her shoulder as they went in. Looking up at him, she wondered about the act of intimacy. At least it was intimate to her. *To him? I'm sure he's had his arm around tons of women.* Wishing this assumption did not bother her as much as it did, she lifted her chin slightly as they entered the building.

He nodded toward the back where the restrooms were and she quickly took care of her business. Exiting the room, she saw him standing against the wall across from her, one leg crossed in front of the other, his muscular arms crossed over his chest. His face relaxed into a sexy smile as soon as she saw him.

"Are you waiting for me?" she asked, looking around.

He pushed off of the wall toward her, swinging his arm around her shoulders once again as he propelled them toward the food court. Curiosity filled her as she wondered why he seemed to stay so close but she had to admit, it felt wonderful. *I can pretend, can't I? That he's into me, just for this little while.*

Vinny saw the appreciative looks that came their way. He did not care about the ones aimed at him from the ladies and for the first time realized that he had no interest in them at all. But his blood pressure rose from the ones coming from the men, openly ogling Annalissa. Looking down at her, he saw that she was oblivious. *She's got no idea that she's a walking wet-dream.* While he appreciated her innocence, he cursed her niavete. *Awareness could keep her safer.* Giving the men a glare that had them looking away, he marched her up to the counter.

She quickly ordered a hamburger and french fries, with a chocolate shake, before he ordered the same, only doubled.

They found a table where he could keep his eye on their vehicle and dug into the food. She moaned in appreciation as she ate heartily.

"Gotta say I like to see a woman eat like she enjoys food instead of picking at everything," he commented.

She grinned while shoving in a french fry loaded with ketchup. "I love food. It's a wonder I'm not as big as a horse." She saw his eyes roam over her figure, appreciation flaring there. It was a heady feeling to think that a man as virile as Vinny could find her attractive. Blushing, she looked back down to concentrate on her lunch.

As they finished, she headed back to the restroom one more time and when she came out, found Vinny standing like before, right outside. He had a bag in his hand and once again threw his arm around her as they walked to the car.

"Take the bag, please," he gently ordered, handing it to her. She did, remembering his request that she follow his directions even if they did not make sense to her. Seeing his gun holster under his jacket, she realized that with his left arm around her and his right hand now free, he would be able to reach his gun. Suddenly nervous, she began to look around as well.

He felt the tenseness enter her body and rubbed his fingers along her shoulders before sliding them underneath her hair and around her neck. "I got this, babe," he said.

Babe. He sometimes calls me babe. She loved the sound of it as it came from deep inside of him, resonating through her. *He probably calls every woman 'babe'.* But somehow it made her feel special. *If he just called me Ms. O'Brian, I would only be a job to him. But 'babe'? Even if I'm one of a million women he calls 'babe'.*…grinning to herself, *I like it.*

He jumped into the driver's seat quickly as soon as he had her buckled in. She had relaxed as they walked the rest of the way to the car but he knew she was picking up on his tenseness. He eyed the car that matched what had been following them earlier, but was unable to identify the occupants.

The problem with HWY 70 was that it was long and flat and was the main road between Kansas City and St. Louis. Filled with travelers, vacationing families, and truckers. Anyone following could be innocently traveling the road. Or watching them.

Pulling quickly onto the highway again, he kept an eye on the car that was slowly circling the parking lot. Breathing a sigh of relief when he did not see them following, he glanced sideways as he heard a soft voice asking, "Are we okay?"

Reaching over to link his fingers with hers, he smiled, saying, "Yeah. We're good." Giving them a little squeeze he added, "Thanks for listening and following my directions without questioning,"

She smiled at the compliment as she leaned back to get comfortable. "What was in the bag anyway?"

"Snacks."

"We just ate," she exclaimed.

"You never know when we might get hungry," he answered, grinning.

They settled into a companionable silence for a while as the miles of Missouri slid by. Annalissa finally giggled, causing Vinny to look over quickly.

She turned to him with an adorable smile on her face. "This sounds silly, but have you noticed that there are long stretches of cornfields only broken up by the billboards for girlie shows at these places along the road?"

She began to blush as he quirked an eyebrow at her. "I…um…well, I just thought…that the only thing here was corn and porn."

Just then they passed another building in the middle of nowhere with a large sign above, advertising the 'topless dancers', with truckers in the parking light. She could not hold back the embarrassed giggles.

Vinny found himself chuckling, both at her goofy description and the sound of her laughter. He could not remember the last time he shared an innocent laugh with a woman. *Or a laugh with an innocent woman.*

"We'll stop again for a break once we get past St. Louis," he said, when they were close to the city. The traffic was heavier, but he still kept an eye out for anyone who appeared to be following. He called Tony to let him know of their progress.

"Ask him about Easnadh," she whispered loudly.

Nodding, he checked with Tony and then talked to Gabe when the phone was handed off. He could hear the tension in his twin's voice, but assured him they were fine.

"Got a bad feeling, bro," Gabe said, "Just like with some missions."

"Yep," he answered cryptically, not wanting to alarm Annalissa.

"The pretty harp player listening?" Gabe asked, understanding his brother's short answer.

"Yep," came the response.

"She really pretty?" Gabe prodded.

"Uh huh."

"She gettin' to you, considering all you've been hanging out with is bar bimbos?" Gabe continued, knowing he was pushing his brother's buttons.

"What do you think?" Vinny growled.

Gabe laughed, "Thought so, bro. 'Bout time something nice came your way. Listen, you take care and bring the mission home."

"Will do," Vinny responded, knowing his brother was concerned.

Hanging up, he turned toward Annalissa, seeing her head cocked to the side.

"So?" she asked impatiently.

He hoped she had not somehow been able to hear the conversation with this brother, so he tried to adopt an innocent look.

"Vinny? What did you find out about Easnadh?"

"Oh yeah, she arrived safely and is now with the DEA contact."

Sucking in a huge breath, she pursued her lips as her brow wrinkled. "Do you think she'll be okay?"

"You worried about your dad?"

"No, I'm not. I just want to make sure my harp is fine."

"That's my girl," he said chuckling, liking her backbone.

She watched with interest as they passed by the Arch in St. Louis and drove over the Mississippi River.

She grinned with excitement, saying, "We never took vacations when I was little even though we traveled with the different symphonies." Sighing, she added, "I know this sounds weird because of the reason we have to drive, but I'm really having a good time on this trip."

Vinny reached over and put his hand on hers again. "I gotta say it's the best mission I've ever been on."

As soon as the words were out of his mouth he instantly knew they came out wrong. The smile on her face dropped as she slid her hand out from under his, crossing her arms around her.

"Oh, Annalissa, that's not what I meant," he quickly said, wanting desperately to bring the smile back to her face.

Looking out of the window, she said, "It's fine...really. I was just...um—"

Jerking the car into the right lane he pulled off at an exit, driving until he found a small gas station. Pulling to the side, he cut the engine and twisted his large frame to face her. Giving her arm a little tug, he said, "Look at me. Please."

She turned her face to him, trying unsuccessfully to hide the hurt.

How do I make this right? he thought. Realizing he had never felt this way, he wanted to make it better. Running his hand over his face in frustration, he looked into her green eyes staring at his in curiosity.

"Annalissa, you're not...this is no longer...what I'm trying to say is...ah hell," he growled.

A laugh erupted from her lips as she lifted her hand to cover her mouth. "You sound like me," she said with a small smile.

He leaned his head back for a second, trying to still the pounding of his heart. Her soft voice broke through his gathering thoughts.

"Vinny, it's really okay. I know you were hired to take me...and Easnadh back to Richland. I get it, I really do," she said as she laid her hand on his arm. She felt the corded muscles underneath her fingertips and wished that they were surrounding her, even as her words told him what she knew. "I know I'm a job. But that doesn't mean that I'm not having a good time."

He leaned forward, staring into her eyes as he slid his hand under her hair and to the back of her neck. "You became so much more than a mission to me miles ago, Annalissa." He watched as her eyes widened in...*shock? Lust? Approval? What are you thinking, baby? Can you give a man like me a chance even if I don't deserve a girl like you?*

He watched as she licked her plump lips and his cock pressed into his zipper at the thought of kissing her. *Come on, baby, give me a sign. Anything.*

"I...I've never...I...oh damn," she cursed, blinking back tears. "I hate not being very articulate when I don't know what to say," she confessed.

"Just tell me what you're thinking," he prompted, pulling her lips a little bit closer to his.

"You're everything...a woman could want, Vinny.

You have to know that. I know I'm the dorky harpist...the one that someone like you would never see."

"I see you," he said softly. Rubbing her cheek with his rough thumb, he moved in a little closer, his lips now a whisper away from hers.

Her eyes grew large and he watched them drop to his lips. He refused to move closer knowing that if they were going to share a first kiss, she needed to be the one to want it. He already knew what he wanted and it was her. And for a lot longer than one night.

"I don't know the games...you know...the ones that men and women play, Vinny. The pick-up lines or the flirting. I've never...done that. I'm too likely to get...hurt," she said all in one breath, afraid of his response.

"What I feel for you has nothing to do with games. You're strong and funny. You're beautiful and sexy, without even trying. You make me feel things that I've never felt. And all I want right now is to kiss you. But you gotta do it. It's gotta come from you," he said, his thumb now running over her lips.

With hope and a prayer, she leaned in the rest of the way and gave her lips to his.

The kiss started gently. The slow exploration of two people who seemed to have all the time in the world to discover each other. He moved his mouth over hers, relishing the feel of her soft lips against his. With a little pressure from his hand on the back of her neck, he angled her head for better access. Licking the seam of her lips, she opened her mouth on a groan which he felt all the way to his dick. Her arms found their way around his neck and he felt himself pulled closer.

He plunged his tongue into her mouth, exploring each crevice and tangling with hers. Sucking on her tongue she groaned again, this time causing his dick to swell uncomfortably, pushing against his zipper. He moved his hands to cup her face, holding her, cherishing her.

Her innocent kiss led him to wonder if she was innocent in other ways. Slowly he pulled back, immediately regretting the loss of her heat, but knowing she deserved better than to be mauled in the front seat of their SUV in the parking lot of an old gas station.

She mewled at the loss of his lips on hers. As he pulled away, she lifted her fingers to her mouth, feeling her swollen lips as they tingled. Her eyes sought his, afraid of what she would see. *Disgust? Regret? Or worse, a cocky look of conquest.*

As her gaze focused on his face and not just his lips, she saw…care. A slow smile. A look of…

"Annalissa," he whispered her name and she loved the way it moved over her. "You deserve more than a kiss where we are now. But know this and take it down deep in your soul…you're not just a job to me. But you are my mission. Keeping you safe. Keeping you happy. Keeping you."

Her eyes widened again as she tried to understand

what he was saying. "Vinny, I'm no good at this. I told you. You have to speak…plainly, so I get it," she said.

"Okay, baby. Here it is. I want you and I want to see where this goes. You stopped being a job to me, but wanting to make you happy and wanting you with me, is my mission now."

A slow smile spread across her face, illuminating the dark corners of his soul. Leaning over to kiss the end of her nose, he nodded toward the old gas pumps. "We're here so I'm gonna fill up the car. It doesn't look great but do you want to take a bathroom break?"

Receiving an enthusiastic nod from her, he pulled to the pumps and she went in to get the key. She walked around to the side of the building to enter the restroom. It was old and she was afraid of some of the bugs she saw under the sink. Quickly finishing, she hurried outside wanting to rejoin Vinny. Smiling to herself, she thought back to their kiss. *He wants me? Me?*

SUDDENLY, A HAND clamped over her mouth while another hand snaked around her waist in a vice grip. Whirled around, she saw another man coming from the corner saying, "Keep her quiet. Get her in."

Panic set in as she realized they intended to kidnap her. The hand on her mouth was too tight…keeping her from screaming…and breathing. Her feet stumbled as the assailant tried to pull her along causing him to shift her upwards in his arms, giving her the opportunity she needed. Biting as hard as she could on the finger that had slipped into her mouth was her only defense.

He yelled as he dropped her on the pavement. "Bitch!" he bit out. His partner raced back around the other side of the car towards her.

"Vinny!" she screamed as loudly as she could, scrambling up to her feet. A blur flew past her and she heard the sound of flesh hitting flesh. Continuing to move away from the car, she managed to get to her feet before turning around. Vinny had raced past her, landing a punch to the first man, breaking his nose from look of the blood that was spurting out, before whirling around and grabbing the second man around the neck. Squeezing tightly as he held the man, he growled, "Who sent you?" and with another jerk, added, "And I'd better like your answer."

"Don't...don't know..." the man choked out.

"Wrong answer, asshole," he bit out, fury pulsating through his veins. He had already been coming to see what was taking her so long when he heard her scream. *Goddammit, I should never have let her out of my sight.*

"Just...got...text...who to...," the man tried to speak. Vinny let up slightly on his hold allowing the man to gasp out, "who to follow and get."

Vinny reached in the man's pocket pulling out his cell phone, quickly looking through the texts. There it was.

Follow blk SUV, lic TX6590319, get girl, text when accmpl

With a growl, he dropped the man to the pavement and pulled out plastic handcuffs, easily dispatching him as well. Stalking over to their car he grabbed the keys and popped the hood.

Annalissa had moved over to the gas station, leaning against the bricks. She watched as Vinny disabled both men and then cut hoses on the inside of their car. As he walked around, he bent low pulling out a knife from his boot, slicing all four tires. His chest heaved with adrenaline. Then he turned and speared her with his gaze, lifting one muscular arm.

That was all the invitation she needed. Flying across the pavement, she jumped into his arms, choking back a sob.

He enveloped her in his embrace, holding her fiercely, willing his rage to dissipate. His body shook as much as hers. This was different. This was no mission gone wrong. This was personal. All because of the beautiful woman crying in his arms.

Pressing her body as close to him as he could with one hand holding her head against his neck and the other arm wrapped around her waist, he cradled her. Making shushing sounds he comforted her, assuring her that they were fine.

"Baby, we gotta go. The gas station owner is an old man, but he'll be coming around to see what's going on soon. I've got their phone and we need to get somewhere so I can let Tony know what's happening."

She nodded against his neck and lifted her face. He set her down carefully, whispering, "Hold on to me like we're lovers who just fuc...um...have been making out back here, in case he's looking." She gave him a curious look but did exactly what he asked. Wrapping her arm around his waist, she smiled brilliantly at him, giggling appropriately as they walked to the SUV.

Within another minute, they were back on the highway. Calling Tony, he looked at the clock. Tony had him on speaker instantly, having assembled their group back at the agency, knowing that at any time Vinny might need them.

Vinny quickly explained what had happened, hearing cursing in the background. The group began to quickly work the problem and plan the next step of the mission.

Giving Lily the phone number of the cell phone he had taken, she and BJ began working on tracing the phone and the calls to and from it.

Jobe said, "There's no way this could be random at this point. A few people at each airport just randomly sending drugs in luggage aren't going to have the resources to do this kind of reconnaissance. Gotta be bigger and it's gotta be aimed at Ms. O'Brian. Someone knows exactly who has the drugs and is now actively searching for you two."

Vinny agreed, asking, "Anything suspicious on that list of people who had access to the harp case before it left LA?"

Gabe answered, "Still working on it brother. By the time we added the stage crew to the ones that were in her inner circle, there were a lot of hands involved. But we're on it, bro."

"How's she holding up?" Tony asked. "I got the feeling that she isn't made of very strong stuff."

Vinny glanced to the passenger side, seeing her pale face with slight bruises forming on her lips from the assailant's hands. Dark circles were under her red-rimmed eyes, but she was still beautiful to him. *And her fuckin' chin was lifted.* "She's shaken, but okay," he answered.

She jerked her head toward him, knowing he was referring to her, a small smile turning up the corners of her mouth.

"She's a lot tougher than she looks," he added.

"You want me to see if I can get a private pilot to meet you at some airstrip and get you here quicker?"

"Nah. It's already getting late today and I want to stop soon to get some food in her and we'll rest for the night. We can get through to Kentucky in several more hours and will stop at Louisville. Find us a place to stay and rent a room. I'll get there and rent one too, but we'll stay in your room as added protection."

"What about tomorrow?" Tony asked.

"Yeah, see what airstrip is close to Louisville and we'll meet someone tomorrow."

As they ended the strategy call, Vinny tossed his cell

into the cup holder between the two front seats and took her hand again.

"You said I was tougher than I look," she said, smiling at the compliment. Watching his handsome profile, she could not take her eyes off of his lips. Strong. Soft. And wanting them back on hers.

"Lots of women would be screaming hysterically. Hell, lots of men would have been pissing in their pants. But you, girl, you bit that man, screamed for help and stayed out of my way to let me do what I had to do." Squeezing her hand, he said, "I couldn't have asked for more."

He looked over at her, seeing her eyes focused on his lips. As angry as he still was about the attack, he felt his blood rush from his head to his dick. *Oh hell no!* "Babe, you staring at my lips like that makes me want to pull over again and take those lips and hell, take anything else as well. But I'm not doing it. Letting my guard down last time got you attacked and almost kidnapped. Not happening again."

"That wasn't your fault, Vinny." Seeing him about to answer, she continued, "No, it wasn't. I know I'm your mission and you never fail. But even you said this goes beyond a mission."

"Never done this, Annalissa. Never mixed work and pleasure." He thought for a moment and amended, "Not just pleasure. But feelings."

Her smile grew, but she turned to look out of the front window at the woods surrounding them. The sun was almost set and she leaned back, closing her eyes. Her mind churned. *Drugs, her crew, unknown assailants, her father, Todd, Gordon, Easnadh. And Vinny.* He had just admitted to having feelings for her. *And I have feelings for him too.* Sleep was not going to come, but to not distract him she continued to sit quietly as the highway lines passed by.

CHAPTER 8

A S THEY CAME to Louisville in the dark, Vinny called Tony and received the name of the hotel they were staying in and the closest car rental facility. "Room's gonna be 113, on the back side. Lily's got you a rental reserved at the local car rental. It's under the name you used last year."

Pulling off the highway, Vinny acknowledged the information. He and several of the others had various identifications, including driver's licenses.

They made a quick stop at the rental facility, the young man behind the desk more interested in the ball game on his TV than he was seeing who was renting the car. He looked over at Annalissa after they had transferred their belongings to the smaller car. They had not stopped for supper, but then there had been little opportunity. There was an all-night pancake house next to the little hotel. *Perfect.* Not about to leave her alone again, they both walked into the lobby as he got a room on the first floor.

Parking near the room they were registered for, they unlocked the door and moved in. Vinny quickly turned down the covers, messing the sheets up as though they had had a quick fuck as soon as they got in. He wished his thoughts had not gone down that road, the idea of a romp with Annalissa immediately making him hard.

Forcing his thoughts back to the mission, he noticed her standing still to the side, watching him carefully. He walked into the bathroom and ran some water into the bathtub, splashing it on the sides, before getting the towels slightly wet as though they had been used. He rolled some toilet paper off the new roll and flushed it.

Walking back over to her, he looked down into her curious expression. "If anyone comes in while we're getting something to eat, it'll look like we've settled in here. We won't be staying, but they won't know that."

Cupping her cheek with his large hand, he leaned down hesitating a breath away from her luscious lips. *Your call, baby.*

Rising on her tiptoes, she wrapped her hand around the back of his neck, pulling him closer. Latching her lips onto his, she relished the feel of them once again. The electricity shocked her right down to her toes, before coming back to her core.

Delving his tongue in once again, he lapped, sucked, and tasted all of her delectable mouth. Her hair fell like silk over his fingers and he pulled her body tightly against his. Her breasts, natural and perfect, crushed against his chest. One hand slid down to her ass, its globes filling his hands. Thoughts of all other women fled from his mind. There was no one. No one for him, but the beautiful woman in his arms.

"We gotta stop," he said, capturing her moan with his mouth. Pulling away regretfully, he smiled at her pout. "I've gotta get some food in you and then we'll get to the other room."

Heaving a sigh she nodded, her stomach growling loudly giving away her hunger. He entwined her fingers with his as they walked to the pancake house.

Sitting in the brightly lit restaurant, Annalissa felt naked. Her eyes darted all around, nervous about being seen. Or approached. Or attacked. She jumped when she felt his hand cross the table, grasping hers.

"Easy, babe. I got you covered." He met her questioning look and leaned forward. "We're in a booth where I not only can see the door to this place, but I can see the front of the hotel where I left the car. Nothing's happening, but remember if I tell you to do something, then—"

"I do it immediately," she laughed as she finished his sentence for him. "I know. I just can't help but think this is all so surreal. Two days ago I was just concerned with making sure my performance was perfect. Now…" her voice trailed off as she searched for the right words. "Now, everything's topsy-turvy."

Vinny had to chuckle at her choice of words, the realization of her innocence slamming into him once again. *Innocent. I wonder if she is…*

Their food arrived and they both ate heartedly.

Even though he ate twice as much as she did, he was pleased to see her dig in. Finally sated, they headed back to the hotel. Opening up the door, he motioned for her to stay back. She waited by the door before he signaled for her to come in. Keeping quiet, she followed him through the room over to the window. He had her wait as he went back to their bags and inspected them carefully before zipping them back up.

Sliding the back window open, he slipped through and then turned to assist her over the window sill as well. Closing the window, they moved silently, making their way over four more rooms and with quick dispatch, he had opened the window of another room.

Once inside he saw her turn toward him for more instructions. *Good girl,* he thought. "We're okay. This is the room that Tony reserved. From here I can see where I parked the rental. If anyone comes, they'll go to the other room. With the all-night bar down the street, they may assume we're there."

She nodded, the tension leaving her body. Suddenly exhausted, she slumped onto the bed. Then her eyes looked around. Bed. *Bed? One bed again?* Her wide-eyed gaze jumped back to his, seeing the amused expression on his face.

"Don't worry. As hard as it will be to keep my distance, we both need our sleep. And…" he said, stalking toward her, caging her in with his long arms on either side of her forcing her to fall back on the mattress. "When we make love…and I hope to God you feel about me the way I'm feeling about you. Then when we make love, it'll not be rushed. Not when we're fighting danger. And not when I can't give you everything you need."

Lying on her back with the most gorgeous man in the world almost on top of her caused her heart to pound. Licking her lips, she wished he would lean down a few more inches and take her mouth. *And then take everything else.*

He did lean down, but just to give her a quick kiss knowing anything else with her lying under him would weaken his resolve to take things slow and at her pace. Standing up, he took her hand and gently pulled her to her feet.

"Take a shower or a long bath and I'll be right out here. Gonna report into Tony while you're in the bathroom."

He heard water running and made his call. Once again on speaker, he knew that the men were pulling an all-nighter. Updating them on the events of the evening, he let them know they were in the alternate room.

"How you doing, bro?" Gabe asked, hearing the uncharacteristic tension in his twin's voice.

"I want this whole mess to be over with," he answered back. "She's doing great, but she's not used to this. Her adrenaline has spiked numerous times over the past two days, she's running on little sleep and goddamn, if she isn't holding up great."

"Sounds like a winner, if you ask me," Tony added.

The silence across the airwaves spoke volumes. Finally Vinny admitted, "Yeah, she is. But shit, she should be sitting in some room playing her harp and not on the run from whoever the fuck is doing this."

"We're working on it, Vinny," BJ promised. "So far, this is what we've got. The father is a tough cuss to deal with and is pissed that she put the harp on a separate plane. We haven't told him that it will not be going through Dulles. But from everything we've seen, he's clean. So are Todd and Gordon. Both assholes in their own ways, but they don't seem to have any nefarious connections that we can see right now. They both have questionable deposits and withdrawals in their bank accounts but could be just from the entertainment business. We're still looking at the others in her inner crew."

Jobe spoke up, "I'm working on the security cameras that we've tapped into from the airports. Jack Bryant's group is working on this with us."

"What's DEA found?" Vinny asked.

"So far, it looks like pure cocaine, the street value of almost half a million. But here's the part that's gonna upset your girl."

Vinny's heart lifted at hearing Annalissa referred to as his girl and then sank at knowing something was going to concern her. Before he could growl, Jobe continued.

"DEA says that it appears that the screws may have been tampered with at an earlier time, so she may have transported drugs when she was traveling before."

The men continued to plan for a few more minutes until he heard the water stop running. After disconnecting he tossed his phone on the nightstand and pulled the covers down. Turning around as the door opened, his breath caught in his throat.

Long, dark, wet hair hung down her back. Her face, devoid of all makeup was fresh. Beautiful. And she was standing in that fuckin' Little House on the Prairie nightgown with her bare toes peeking out from the bottom. *Fuckin' adorable.*

Finding his voice, he motioned toward the bed. "Go on, babe. You need to sleep. I'll clean up and be along shortly."

Ten minutes later he emerged, finding her already sound asleep. Standing over the bed, he watched her gentle breathing as her face was finally at peace for the first time all day. He knew he had never watched a woman sleep before. Always fucked for the physical pleasure, not wanting to stick around…*not for conversation, not for friendship, and sure as hell not for snuggling.*

Shaking his head, he quickly packed their belongings into two backpacks that he always had folded into his larger duffle and checked his weapons. Just in case.

Crawling under the covers, staying to his side of the bed, he resolved to keep his distance. *Yeah, right.* He immediately rolled over to her, wrapping his body around hers and pulling her in tightly. Then he fell asleep. Soundly. The sleep of someone wrapped up with someone they care about.

THE VIBRATIONS WOKE VINNY, instantly alerting him to the presence of someone in their other hotel room. The clock showed that it was almost three a.m. He had set sensors at the door, with a wireless alarm that was connected to his cell phone, courtesy of BJ. A warm body moved closer to him, the scent of her flowery shampoo filling his nostrils as her head lay on his chest. All he wanted was to stay right where he was, with this woman all night. Kissing the top of her head he slipped out from underneath her, walking stealthily to the window by the door. Barely pulling the curtain back he saw movement by the room they had originally rented. *Fuck.* Turning, he hurried to the bed, gently shaking Annalissa.

"Babe, you gotta get up. Throw your clothes on quickly and only grab what you need. We're going to head to the rental car and leave as quickly as possible as soon as I give the all clear."

With only a few blinks of her eyes, she jumped from the bed throwing off her nightgown as she hurried toward the bathroom, grabbing clothes as she went.

Vinny stood rooted to the floor, his mouth hanging open as he stared at the almost naked image of her as she ran into the bathroom. He knew that no matter what happened to them when all of this was over, that image would be burned into his mind forever.

The door closed and she quickly tugged on her jeans, bra, and a lightweight sweater. She ran back out of the bathroom, hopping as she slid her feet into her sneakers. Just then a loud crackle and then an explosion rocked the building. He threw her down on the floor, covering her with his much larger body as the building shook.

Hearing a commotion outside, he ran back to the window by the door, peeking out. Their new rental car had exploded. *Goddamn, son of a bitch!*

"Babe, we gotta get out of this room. We'll go out the back window just like we came in. Grab this backpack. I've filled it with everything of yours that we can take on foot."

"On foot?" she asked, her eyes darting from the window to him.

He walked over; putting his hands on her face he cupped her cheeks. "Stay with me, babe. Whoever the hell is after you just blew up the new rental car."

Gasping, her green eyes widened in shock and her mouth opened but no words came out. Blinking again as he called her name, she focused on his face. The face that had become so familiar in the past two days. The face that she trusted with her life. Sucking in a deep breath, she lifted her chin.

Nodding, he grabbed his larger backpack and did a quick inventory of the room, seeing that the few items that they left behind were not necessary. Grabbing her hand he headed to the window, once again sliding it open and climbing through it. Turning, he assisted her before sliding the window shut. Tony had specifically picked a room on the back, facing the woods. Under the cover of darkness with the sound of sirens in the background, they hurried straight into the thick forest.

VINNY KNEW THEY needed to get as far away as they could before stopping, but also knew there was no way she could keep up with his normal pace. Special Forces training had him easily moving through the woods in the dark, but with her along he needed to move slower and much more carefully.

Annalissa trotted behind him, fueled by adrenaline and determination. She knew they were not going very fast but was not sure that she could go any quicker.

He pushed branches out of the way for her and tried to point out obstacles in their paths. *Thank God for a full moon.* Even though he could have traversed the woods in almost blackout conditions, the moon-light gave her some illumination.

After almost thirty minutes, they stopped by a small creek. She was winded and plopped down on a log quickly. He cursed as he saw her trying to catch her breath. Pulling out his phone, he called Tony knowing that this time he was at home.

Filling him in on the events at the hotel, he said,

"We're hiking through the woods right now. Got a location on my phone we're heading to. Small town, back off the highway. Gonna need some intel and you gotta let Jack's man know that we won't be meeting him at the airstrip later today."

Tony cursed, knowing the mission had now changed for the worse. He not only had a man in the field, but was now responsible for keeping a woman safe who was unused to the dangers they faced.

"Look Tony, I'm gonna see if I can find somewhere safe to bunk down for a few hours until it gets a little more light. Once everyone is in later, we'll coordinate again."

"I'm calling everyone in now," Tony growled.

"No, don't do it, boss. Let everyone get a few more hours sleep in their own beds and then come in fresh."

"Vinny, you're the best I've ever seen in the field but with—"

"I got this, sir. Nothing's gonna happen to her."

Disconnecting the call, he turned to check on Annalissa, still sitting on the log. Even in the moonlight he could see her fatigue, now that the adrenaline rush was over. Walking over, he knelt in front of her, his massive legs on either side of hers and his arms stretched out, caging her in. "Babe, I hate to do this, but we gotta keep going for a little while."

She looked into his eyes, a smile on her face. "I can keep going," she assured him.

"That's my girl," he said, standing while pulling her

up with him, loving the sound of *my girl* on his lips.

She smiled, the heat of his hand warming her almost as much as the words he had spoken.

He reached for her backpack, but she pulled back. "Nope, I got this. At least for now. If it gets too heavy, I'll tell you."

Giving her hand a squeeze, they took off through the woods once again. The terrain was difficult to traverse and he turned often to keep an eye on her. Several times he heard her grunt in exertion or make a slight exclamation when tripping over a tree root.

Her eyes were trained on the ground below trying to find her footing, while following the large man in front of her. Her breath came in pants as she wondered how he managed to make it look so easy. Her legs burned with the exertion and her aching feet sent shards of pain radiating throughout. Just when she thought she would drop from the inhuman pace, Vinny stopped suddenly.

"You're doing great, Annalissa," he said encouraging her on. Her face smiled up at his in the moonlight, but he could see the fatigue in her eyes. Reaching down to take her hand, he added, "We can go a little slower," and as they continued, he did not let go of her hand this time.

After a while Vinny saw a crude hunter's stand that had seen better days. Moving quickly to it, he tested the pieces of wood nailed to the tree trunk, finding them sound. Scrambling up, he tested the floor as well.

Climbing back down, he said, "It's not the Ritz, doll, but it'll keep us off the ground for a few hours while you can rest."

She eyed the wooden slats suspiciously, but before she could object, she was boosted from behind. Grabbing the makeshift ladder, she felt his hands on her ass pushing her upwards. Landing on the floor of the wooden structure, she moved carefully on her knees, peeking over the edge.

Tossing up her backpack and his as well, he climbed up after her. He tried to move carefully, aware of his body size and the smallness of the platform. He settled with his back against the tree trunk and pulled her back with him.

"Vinny?" her quiet voice rang out in the night.

"Yeah?"

"What's happening?" The fear and fatigue warred within, easily heard by him.

"I don't know for sure, but it looks like whoever discovered that the harp did not make it on schedule is now looking for it."

His statement was met with silence. Uncomfortable silence.

He turned her gently so that she was facing him. Concern and confusion filled her expression. Pulling her into his chest, he promised, "Don't worry. We got away and haven't left a trail. I've got Tony and the group on it. Their job is to plan our new mission and my job is to keep you safe until we can get to a rendezvous point to get back home. And Annalissa?" he said, willing his strength into her. "I never fail."

Within a few minutes they settled down, her face on his chest once again as exhaustion took over. He watched as her face relaxed in slumber and wrapped his arms around her tighter, wanting his body warmth to sink into hers.

Looking up into the star-filled sky, his mind ran back over the events of the past couple of days. Heaving a sigh before stilling his body so as not to wake her, he finally closed his eyes. *Whatever's happened brought this amazing woman into my life,* he thought as he drifted off into a fitful sleep.

DON JUAREZ ANSWERED his phone, noting the call coming from one of his most trusted second in command and cousin. He never greeted anyone on the phone—he simply connected and waited to see what the other person had to say.

"Boss, I'm sorry. But we've got a situation," came the preface.

"I don't have situations," he reminded Jawan. "I only have successes. Those under me might have situations and then they fix them. Still leaving me with only successes."

Closing his eyes, Jawan knew this was going to prove to be more difficult than he had hoped for. "I understand, Boss. I'm working on it now. We've lost a shipment but know who has it and where it is. It appears that who I sent bungled it the first time and the police were involved. So I sent in two more to intercept and they've bungled the job as well."

"This is not boding well for your continued placement in my organization, cousin. Your job is to find the shipment, retrieve the shipment, and eliminate the parties involved. All of the parties involved. That includes the incompetents you sent the first time and the witnesses."

"I understand. I won't fail you, Boss."

"I know. Failure is not acceptable, therefore there will be no failure."

The phone disconnected, leaving Jawan to ponder his fate. Refusing to give up, he placed another call. *Time to show Don that I can handle this situation on my own.*

CHAPTER 9

THE SOUNDS OF BIRDS crept through the hazy fog of Annalissa's sleep. The early morning sun's rays were filtering through the leaves above, giving the woods an enchanted feel. Shifting stiffly to the side, she felt Vinny's hard body next to hers. Smiling, she looked up at his face, his eyes on hers.

"I've never slept in a tree before," she said with a smile. Wincing as she moved, she sat up adding, "But then there's something to be said for having a mattress."

"Babe, when we get out of this, I promise you the softest mattress we can find."

Hearing the innuendo in his voice, she smiled, wondering if he planned on sharing that soft mattress with her.

Seeing her shy smile, he grinned back as he rose to a seated position alongside her. "You think there would be any room in that bed for me, darlin'?"

"Yeah," she said softly, her gaze lifting to his. "I hope so."

Leaning down to kiss her gently, he added, "Then that's all the motivation I need, babe."

He assisted her down and discreetly turned his back as she wandered a little way through the trees to take care of her morning business. As she returned, he handed her a protein bar. "I know it's not scrambled eggs but it'll do you good for now."

Nodding her acquiescence, she dutifully ate the whole bar greedily and drank from the canteen.

Soon they were on their way after a quick call to Tony. The group was assembled again and she was beginning to feel as though she knew all of Vinny's friends.

Lily and BJ gave them the coordinates for a small country store off the beaten path, mostly serving the farming community in the area.

The pace was slightly slower this morning and she found that she was better able to keep up. The sleep and power bar definitely helped. Hiking in the daylight was easier for her to see not only where she was stepping, but gave her the opportunity to look around as well.

"The woods are kind of pretty, aren't they?" she said.

He glanced over his shoulder, glad for the smile on her face. "Yeah, I guess they are."

"You guess? Vinny, it's beautiful out here. Like a fairy forest," she exclaimed, looking at the thick copse of trees around, ferns and moss on the forest floor.

Chuckling out loud, Vinny thought, *Out here, running for her life and she sees beauty.* His eyes, used to scanning for Intel and danger, actually began to look around. She was right. The sunlight filtered down through the thick foliage and now that they could see where they were going, the ground was covered in lush green. Once again, he reached back and gave her hand a squeeze as he handed her the canteen.

Walking for about another hour through the woods, they came to a small river. Vinny assessed the shallowest place for them to cross and hoisted his backpack high on his back. "Follow right behind me and stay close, okay?" he ordered.

Annalissa stared into the slow moving waters. Knowing that it was not deep, she was still terrified.

He saw her stop behind him and he looked up in question. "What's wrong, babe?

"I'm…um…well…it looks…"

Walking back over, he put his hands on her shoulders and bent down to peer into her eyes. "Annalissa, look at me." Holding her green-eyed gaze, he continued, "This is just me. What's wrong?"

Lifting her chin, she stood to her full height, her gaze snapping. "Nothing. I can do this. Just walk right in front of me so I'll know where to go."

He hesitated. "Are you sure?" Getting her agreement, he pulled out a thin rope from his pack and tied it around her slender waist. He left his hands on her for a moment, relishing the feel of her underneath his fingertips.

Moving into the river, they stepped carefully. The

current swirled around their legs, terrifying her, but she refused to be a burden. The water was cold and she found her legs freezing as the depth was up to her hips. Suddenly slipping, she floundered before going under the water. Strong arms quickly lifted her out and tried to still her flailing arms. Screaming, she clawed out, trying to grasp, not realizing that he was holding her above the water.

"Babe, stop," he ordered. "I've got you."

The panic continued as he half-carried, half-dragged her to the other side as she tried to climb her way up his body. Once out of the water he set her down on the ground watching in frustration as she gasped for air. Their clothes were soaked as well as the backpacks.

Kneeling down, he growled, "You wanna tell me what the hell that was back there?"

Peering up at him through a layer of wet hair, she said, "Oh Vinny, please don't be mad. I was scared."

"Scared of what, babe? The water barely came to your hips. The only danger of drowning was you having a fit and trying to climb up on top of me."

Huge tears fell, mingling with the water droplets still falling from her hair. "I…I'm…scared…of…I don't know how to…"

Rubbing his hand over his hair and to the back of his neck, he sighed. "Are you telling me you don't know how to swim? And you're afraid of the water?"

A small nod was her only response.

"Don't you think that maybe you coulda told me that before we got in?"

Another small nod.

Reaching over he slid his arms under hers and stood, lifting her with him. Holding her close, he pushed her sopping wet hair from her face. "Don't cry. I've got you."

Her next nod was against his chest and he felt that one go straight to his heart. Lifting her chin with his fingers, he held her gaze. "But babe? As soon as we get out of this mess, I'm teaching you how to swim."

A small smile curved her lips as she pulled back out of his arms. Looking down at their soaking clothes, she exclaimed, "Oh, no. The backpacks got wet. All your stuff is in there."

"It's all good," he said calmly. Kneeling at the packs, he unzipped them showing her that everything was sealed in plastic bags. Looking up at her he winked, saying, "Always keep your gear safe."

His gaze drug down her wet form, her light sweater molded to her perfect breasts. Chilled, her nipples had hardened to points, tantalizing through her bra. Desire flooded him and all he could think about was latching his mouth over those nipples, first while she was still dressed and then as he peeled her wet clothes off.

Willing his dick to behave once again, he closed his eyes and counted to ten. Feeling a small hand on his arm, he looked down at her concerned face.

"Are you okay? Are you still mad at me?" she asked,

unshed tears hanging on her lashes.

"No, I'm not mad. But we've got to get out of these wet clothes," he replied. *And my case of blue balls may kill me,* he thought, not remembering the last time he was hard and could not pound into a willing woman.

A blush rose from the top of her breasts. "Oh," she said softly. Turning, she dug through the plastic bag to see what clothes he had managed to pack. Pulling out a dry pair of panties, yoga pants, and a t-shirt she stood, looking around nervously.

"Where do we change?"

Chuckling, he looked at her clutching her dry clothes in front of her like a shield. "Babe, there's no dressing room here so it looks like we've gotta do what we need to right here," he said yanking his tight t-shirt over his head.

Oh my God. She just stared at his naked muscular chest. *I always thought those pictures in magazines were photo-shopped. Jesus, Lord have mercy.* His arms were huge with a Celtic tattoo around his bicep. His broad shoulders and chest tapered to washboard abs with a smattering of chest hair. That led a trail to his...

"See something you like?" he rumbled, knowing that if she kept staring at him like that, he would not be able to hide the bulge in his jeans.

Her face flamed even redder as she whirled around, presenting her back to him. Her hand shook as she pulled her wet shirt over her head and reached for her dry t-shirt.

Vinny's voice came from right behind her. "Babe, you've got to ditch the bra."

Clutching her t-shirt to her chest, she said, "But I don't have another one to put on."

She heard a sigh before he continued, "Believe me, I know that. And swear to God, no one wants you covered up more than me. But a wet bra is going to chaff and you've got to let it dry before you put it back on."

"Oh," she murmured. She reached behind her and unclasped her bra, letting it slide to the ground as she put on her clean t-shirt. Glancing behind her to make sure he was turned away, she jerked off her wet jeans and panties, replacing them with dry ones.

Looking down, she saw that the shirt hid very little, but there was nothing she could do about it now. Hearing noises behind her, she kept her back to him assuming he was changing his pants. She had seen the impressive bulge in his crotch and in spite of the embarrassing situation, she could not help but smile. *I don't think I've ever had that effect on a man.*

"I don't want you to be uncomfortable, Annalissa. I assure you, I'll be a gentleman," came his deep voice.

She turned around and saw his eyes drop to her nipples, protruding prominently through the t-shirt.

"Fuck," he growled. "I just lied." Stalking over, he pulled her in, lowering his face to hers once again a whisper apart.

Come on, babe. Please let me in.

Lifting on her toes, she pulled him close, touching her lips to his. Tentatively at first, she moved her mouth over his. *His lips are hard. Soft. And everything in between.* Growing bolder, she licked his lips before sliding her tongue into his mouth, swallowing his groan.

That was all it took. Vinny picked her up, crushing her body tightly to his, feeling her breasts touching his chest, knowing his swollen cock was nestled into her. Walking her backward, he pushed her up against a thick tree trunk sliding his knee between her legs.

Claiming and owning her mouth, he took charge of the kiss, tasting and sucking until he thought he would go mad with desire. He felt her rub her core against his jean-clad leg, knowing she was trying to quench the need for friction. Sliding his hands slowly under her shirt he hesitated just under the soft mounds, waiting for permission.

She thrust her breasts up in silent invitation and he took it. With her back pressed against the rough bark, he moved both hands to cup her pert breasts rolling each nipple simultaneously. The groan from the kiss was nothing like the groan she heard when his hands felt her nipples. She just had no idea if the groan came from her…or from him.

Rubbing her core on his leg was not alleviating the need for friction that was building…it only increased her need. She felt his erection pressing against her and sliding her hand down, palmed him through his jeans.

This time the groan that resonated through the woods was definitely from him. The urge to drop her to the forest floor, strip her naked, and pound into her waiting flesh overwhelmed him, almost to the point beyond reason. Almost. Pulling his head away from her, hating the loss of contact, he rasped, "Babe, are you...have you ever...?"

She shook her head as she dropped her eyes. Panting, he pulled back farther, gently ordering, "Eyes on me."

She lifted her gaze to peer into his eyes, seeing anguish, lust, need, and concern. But no anger. She owed him the truth. *He knows I don't have a clue what I'm doing.* Sucking in a deep breath, she admitted, "No, I've...never." Then as an afterthought as he lowered her to the ground with his hands still on her waist, she added, "I'm sorry."

"Sorry? What the hell do you have to be sorry about? I'm the one who was about to take you against a tree."

"I know you're used to...um...a different kind of...woman."

Sighing, he asked, "Easy, you mean?"

Nodding, she glanced down at her feet.

"Yeah...about that...Listen, I'm not going to lie, Annalissa. I've been the kind of man who worked hard and I admit I've played hard. Haven't been too particular about who I fuc...had...um...sex with." He stammered, realizing how pathetic he sounded. Suddenly the joke from his buddies about being a *fuck 'em and leave 'em* guy did not make him very proud. In fact, he felt rather ashamed.

He peered into her face, seeing a look of misery. *Oh Jesus, how do I make this right?*

"It was only ever physical. Just two people acting on a physical need. Never, ever did I feel an emotion with any of them."

"I see," she said, glancing up at his face that was mirroring the uncertainty she knew was on hers. Sliding from his grasp, she pulled her wet shoes back on saying, "We need to get going if we're going to find a place with some food." Shoving her wet clothes into the backpack, she hoisted it on her back before looking at him expectantly...hoping she was fooling him with the expression of ambivalence.

It did not work...he knew she was disappointed...in the situation. And in him.

MOVING TOWARD THE EDGE of the woods two hours later, they came across a farmer's field, freshly plowed. After such a long time in the dark woods, the glare of blue sky and sunlight was blinding. Vinny looked around, assessing the security. Seeing no one around, he turned to the woman trailing behind. He had taken her backpack several miles ago, with no resistance from her. Her hair was pulled up in a messy bun, held together with two twigs. Her shirt was dirty with sweat and her face was red with exhaustion. And she was limping. Looking down at her almost dry, pink sneakers, he could only imagine the blisters the wet material had caused.

Kicking himself for not noticing sooner, he patted a fallen log, saying, "Have a seat and let me look at your feet. Sliding the sneakers off, exposing the blisters, had him furious. "Goddamn it, Annalissa. Why the hell didn't you tell me earlier that your feet were this bad?"

"I didn't know, you big…jerk," she cried, pulling her foot out of his hand. She looked down and the tears fell faster.

Rubbing his hand over his face, he shook his head in frustration. "Babe, please don't cry." Her sobs increased as he lifted her up and sat down on the log with her now in his lap.

She felt his arms around her, rocking her back and forth. She was tired, dirty, hungry, and in pain. "I'm sorry. I've…never been hiking," she hiccupped. "I've…never done any of this. Not hike. Not swim. Not camp out." Hiccupping again, she felt his arms tighten.

"Babe, get ahold of yourself. Honest to God, I'm not mad at you. I'm a goddamn medic for Christ's sake and I shoulda seen what was happening."

Her tears slowed and she felt his lips on the top of her head. Sucking in a halting breath, she nodded, "I'm okay now."

He lifted her chin with his fingers, kissing her lips gently. Moving so that he was once again kneeling in front of her, he worked on her feet. He used most of their filtered water, cleaning the blistered skin that had broken and even carefully broke some of the larger ones. He pulled out some bandages from a plastic bag in his pack. Wrapping her feet carefully, he taped off the ends. Sliding her feet back into the pink sneakers, he re-tied them.

She watched him at work, his strong hands handling her feet in such a gentle manner. She saw his face, a study in concentration, as he bent to the task. Wincing occasionally, she noticed that each time, he gentled his touch even more.

Standing, she admitted that her feet felt so much better. Smiling up at him, she placed her hand on his arm, saying, "Thank you, Vinny. And not just for making my feet feel better." Standing on tiptoe, she added, "But for everything. Taking care of me, as well."

He leaned forward to kiss her lips, this one soft. Easy. A promise. Suddenly, he pulled back, cocking his head to the side. Seeing her questioning look, he said, "I think I hear a tractor, babe. There may be a farmhouse around here close by. BJ indicated that we would run into some farms before we made it to the road."

Not willing to have her feet become more injured, he swung her up into his arms and began walking toward the sound. He saw the farmhouse in the distance. "Let's get to the farmhouse and see if we can get some help," he said.

Protesting, she cried, "You can't carry me and the backpacks too."

He chuckled as he looked down. "Never insult a former Special Forces, woman. You're light as a feather and I've carried around rucksacks, equipment and weapons much heavier."

She had to admit that it felt good to be in his arms. Well, for her feet. *No,* she had to admit. *It feels amazing to be held by this man.* She wanted to lean in and kiss his jaw. See his eyes on her. Feel his touch on her skin. Pressing her lips together, she battled back the thoughts.

The lone farmhouse came closer into sight, a woman in the yard hanging wash. She saw the two strangers coming across the field and called for her husband. An older man ambled out through the screen door, warily watching them approach.

Vinny stopped at a safe distance so as not to make them nervous. "My wife has hurt her feet while we were hiking and we wondered if we could get some help."

"Oh my goodness," the woman exclaimed. "Well, bring her into the kitchen."

The man stepped back allowing them access into the house, pointing to the kitchen table. Vinny set her down carefully, then bent to take off her shoes. The quick treatment he had given her had helped, but he knew she needed her bandages re-done.

The woman took a look at her blistered feet and

immediately got a large plastic pan and filled it with cool water. Vinny took the heavy pan from her and set it down on the floor.

"Ya'll been hiking?" the old man asked.

Annalissa's eyes stayed on Vinny's, allowing him to give whatever story he wanted to.

"We wanted to go for a drive in the country and then decided to take a little hike. Next thing we know, we get lost and thankfully ended up at the edge of your farm. We thank you for your hospitality and promise that as soon as I can get her feet cleaned and re-wrapped, we'll be on our way."

"Nonsense," the woman said. "You're not any trouble. We're Mable and Alfred Johnson, by the way."

"Pleased to meet you, ma'am," Vinny said with a smile. "I'm Walter and this is my wife, Delores."

Annalissa tried not to grin at the names Vinny had given them, earning her a stern look from him.

"Are your feet ticklish, darlin'?" he asked.

"Y…yes," she answered, stifling her smile.

Soon, he had her feet soaked and re-bandaged. Standing, he was about to thank them when Mable walked back into the room.

"Here are a pair of thick cotton socks, sweetie. You traipsing around in little canvas shoes with no socks is gonna keep wearing blisters on your poor feet."

Vinny accepted them graciously and slid them over the bandages before placing her feet back into the sneakers. Looking into her eyes, he asked, "Better?"

"Oh my God, yes," she answered, her eyes less pain-filled. She smiled at him, mouthing, "Thank you."

Leaning over, he kissed the top of her head, before standing again. Turning to their hosts, he said, "We appreciate this more than you can know. If we could trouble you for some water to put in our canteen, we'd be grateful and will be on our way."

Alfred nodded toward his wife and she returned his smile. "We'd be happy to have you two share our lunch and then I can drive you to the nearest town, 'bout fifteen miles down the road."

Vinny glanced at Annalissa, seeing hunger and fatigue written plainly on her face. Turning back to the kind couple, he agreed. "We'd love to, thank you."

CHAPTER 10

SEVERAL HOURS LATER, after good conversation and a lunch of cold fried chicken, potato salad, green beans, and sweet tea, Vinny and Annalissa were ready to leave. With hugs goodbye to Mable, they climbed into Alfred's old Ford pick-up truck with him, and pulled onto the road heading to the little town.

It consisted of a local grocery shop, gas station, diner, several stores and a few other buildings. Stopping at the gas station, Alfred let them out. "Eugene here has some old cars in the back that he'd let you borrow to get where you're going."

On cue, a man in oily coveralls came ambling out from the garage. Greeting Alfred and nodding to his passengers, he listened as the older farmer described the plight of 'Walter and Delores'. Eugene smiled at the couple, nodded, and said, "Sure, I've got a decent old car. It's not much to look at but it'll get you where you want to go with just a little more work."

Saying goodbye to Alfred, they watched as he drove off and they turned their attention back to Eugene. Vinny said, "We'd love to buy the car off of you. Our car died a ways back and we really need to get on our way."

Eugene rubbed his chin, eyeing the car. "Well, I was just gonna loan it to you, but if you wanna buy it, I don't hardly know what to charge you. It ain't worth very much. It's old, but if you give me a few hours I can get it running real good. We ain't got a hotel in town, but I got a little apartment above the garage that if you can stay tonight. I'll have the car ready for you first thing in the morning."

He and Vinny quickly came to an agreement on the car and Annalissa helped to take their backpacks up to the small room. She moved over to the sit on the edge of the bed while Vinny called Tony explaining the next step of their journey.

"We can get to Huntington, West Virginia tomorrow. Is there an airport we can get to?"

"Jack's contact that was going to pick you up at the previous airstrip is already there and will wait for you."

Gabe got on, checking to see how they were doing and Vinny could hear the tension in his voice. "What's eatin' at you, bro?"

"Annalissa's father, agent, and manager are all gettin' on our last nerves. How the hell does that girl put up with them?"

Vinny looked over to see if she was listening, but she had moved into the bathroom. "I don't know, other than the three of them practically run her life."

"We've told them that the two of you are taking a cross-country trip to relax and enjoy yourselves."

Vinny chuckled, saying, "Not too far from the truth."

Finishing up their next day's planning, Vinny hung up just as she was coming from the bathroom. He watched, mesmerized, as she walked over to the bed wearing only one of his t-shirts that he had given her. It hung to her mid-thighs and off one shoulder. And he'd never seen anything sexier in his life. Once again, he willed his dick to behave, but the sight of her fired his blood.

She pulled back the covers, laying down on the old, but clean bed. Her head had barely hit the pillow when her eyes shut. He stood up and walked over, looking down at her. *She's had very little sleep in the last three days. And fuck, if she hadn't been one helluva trooper.* He looked at his watch seeing it was early evening. *She'll probably sleep for hours.*

He quickly took a shower also and then crawled into bed as well. Rolling over toward her, he curled his large body around her smaller one, pulling her in close. Her hair smelled of shampoo and he let it fill his senses. It was fresh. Untainted. Closing his eyes, he fell into a deep sleep once more.

ANNALISSA WOKE, UNSURE of where she was, but knew the arms around her. The same arms that had held her, carried her, cared for her, and protected her for the past several days. Smiling, she rolled over to watch him sleep. He was perfect – thick hair cut close, strong jaw, his nose slightly bent from probably being broken, a muscular arm holding her tight.

She began to feel her body's response to his virile masculinity. Her breasts felt heavy and her nipples pointed to peaks. Leaning in, she placed her lips on his, willing him to wake up kissing her. Slowly at first, she kept her kiss light, but finding the jolt moving down to her core, she licked his lips and plunged her tongue in as he opened his mouth on a moan.

He immediately rolled over on her, pressing her body deep into the mattress. She wrapped her legs around his hips, feeling his erection against her stomach. Lost in the sensations, she moved her hips upwards in an attempt to seek whatever her body was desperately crying out for. He grabbed her hands in his and with laced fingers, pulled them up over her head. He held them with one hand as the other moved to the hem of the shirt she was wearing. Sliding his hand up her abdomen, he stopped as he cupped one luscious mound, tweaking the nipple.

She wanted to touch him but his hand held hers fast. He pushed her shirt up until her breasts were bared to his view. Moving his mouth from one to the other, she gave in to the feelings of passion. Moisture pooled between her legs and she felt the connecting jolt from her nipples to her core. As his mouth continued to assault hers, he slid his free hand down to her drenched folds. Inserting one finger inside, followed by another one, he began to move them in a scissoring motion, driving her wild. Pumping herself on his fingers in an age-old dance, she felt herself climbing toward…something…she just did not know what. Her insides were coiled as tight as a spring and when his thumb pressed on her engorged clit, she shattered into a million pieces, her head thrown back and crying out his name.

He looked down at her face as her orgasm roared through her. *Fuckin' beautiful.* He had never watched a woman climax just for the pure enjoyment of the act. He always made sure his partner was satisfied but for more selfish reasons. If they had been well sated and lubricated, it made him getting off and then getting out of there a helluva lot easier. *But this? This is different. This is…everything.* He continued to look at her face, eyes closed with her thick lashes resting against her sunburned cheeks. Slightly chapped lips. Dark circles underneath her eyes. *What the hell am I doing?*

Warring with himself between wanting to claim her as his forever and waiting until she was safe had him clenching his teeth so hard he thought they would crack. He looked back down, this time seeing her green eyes staring up at his. Filled with questions. Doubt.

She opened her eyes after the tremors had subsided, her whole body glowing. Only instead of a look of passion in his face, she saw…indecision. He leaned back over to kiss her, sending her doubts away but when she began to move underneath him, he pulled back. His expression, agonized. Regretful.

He moved out of the bed and grabbed his dry jeans off the floor and pulled them on. Trying to smile, he said, "I'll go see if the car's ready and then we can hit the road." Turning, he walked out of the door, pulling on his t-shirt as the door slammed.

ANNALISSA LAID THERE, the euphoria of her orgasm gone. Replaced by the cold reality that he did not want her. From what she could gather, he had had sex with just about anyone...*so what's wrong with me? Did I not do something right?* Bitter tears of embarrassment pricked her eyes. The rush of memories flooded back. Her father telling her she made a mistake in a concert therefore had not practiced enough. Todd telling her what to say when interviewed so that she looked more polished. Sharon telling her that her makeup was not good enough for public appearances and to let her re-do it. Gordon telling her what she needed to do for her career. *On and on and on. And now Vinny.*

Sliding out of bed, she grabbed her stiff jeans and pulled them on as well. Her bra was dirty but dry and she quickly donned it as well, then jerked his t-shirt off as though it were contaminated. Reaching for her sweater from yesterday, she pulled it over her head wanting to be dressed when he came back.

Vinny paced outside of the building, his cell phone pressed to his ear. *Fuck, where's Jobe when I need him?* Jobe had always been the friend that gave them true, honest advice when it came to women. *Well, not me 'cause I never wanted it. But he was spot on when helping Gabe and Tony.*

Finally, Jobe answered.

"I've only got a moment and then have to talk to Tony, but I need...well, it's just that...oh hell, Jobe."

Jobe laughed, "Damn, don't tell me that the great Vinny has fallen?"

"What makes you say that? I haven't even asked you anything yet," he quipped.

"You don't have to. The blushing stammer is coming across loud and clear."

"Goddamnit! Look I don't have time for this, but you've always helped everyone else. I just thought maybe you had some advice for me."

"Damn, Vinny. I don't just pull this stuff outta my ass. I don't even know what's going on, but I can guess that since you've never had a decent conversation with a woman other than 'strip, spread, and thank you ma'am', you are completely outta your league."

"You make me sound like a royal prick," Vinny complained, rubbing the back of his neck.

"Look, you're one of the best soldiers I've ever worked with and by far, the best shot. You've got nerves of steel and an eagle eye. I always figured that one day, someone special would come into your sight and you'd totally fuck it up."

"Are you just going to bust my chops, or are you gonna tell me how to make this right?"

Jobe chuckled. "So what did you do? Go too far too fast?"

"No," Vinny almost shouted. "That's the problem. She's innocent. And actually willing. I just can't...it's just not right to...it needs to be perfect."

"Good God, the great Vinny finally met a woman that he doesn't want to bang and run," Jobe said, astonishment in his voice. Then sobering, he continued, "Man, I'm glad for you. So what's the problem?"

"She thinks I don't want her. She knows a bit of my reputation and I think that she...well, she's upset that I just walked away from her."

"Have you explained what you want? If she thinks you're just stringing her along, no wonder she's pissed. From what we've learned about her over the past few days, she's always got someone telling her what to do. And now you are. Maybe just meet her where she is. No making decisions for her. And then see where it all goes."

Vinny sighed. Jobe made it seem so easy. *Could it really be that easy?*

SUITABLY CLOTHED AND ARMORED, Annalissa watched as he came back into the small room. She turned her back to him and began quickly shoving things into her backpack once more. With a final zip, she slung it over her shoulder and faced him. "Is the car ready?" she asked, trying to still the tremor in her voice.

"Um…yeah. I…thought we'd eat some breakfast first and then leave."

"We really ought to hit the road. I just want to get home," she said with uncharacteristic force. Moving past him, she started through the door but he grabbed her arm as she was about to pass him.

"Babe," he said softly, but she refused to look up. "Look, I thought it was best to—"

"No worries, Vinny," she said quickly interrupting him. *The last thing I need is for you to tell me that I'm your job. Or your mission. Or worse, it's not you, it's me. Yeah, right.*

She slid past and walked down the stairs. Giving Eugene a hug, she thanked him for his kindness.

"Oh, no need, miss. Your man paid me well for the car and the night's lodging, although I'd have thrown that in for free. But he insisted."

Nodding, she tossed her bag into the back seat and climbed into the passenger side. *It's been a hell of a few days…I just want to get home.*

Vinny stood outside the car and watched Annalissa buckle up, her body as stiff as a board. Nothing like the soft, pliant woman that had laid under him just thirty minutes earlier. *I am such a fuck up. I just wanted to do the right thing and all I've managed to do is drive her away.* Climbing into the car, he pulled out and began the next leg of their journey.

Trying to make conversation, he said, "I called Tony." Getting no response, he continued. "The contact that was going to meet us at the last airfield is going to meet us in Huntington, West Virginia. That should be early afternoon."

Still no response. Rubbing his hand over his face, he plunged in, not knowing how to make any of this right. "Babe, we gotta talk about what happened back there." Already Vinny was in unchartered waters with no idea how to swim in them. Talking to a woman about feelings was as foreign to him as anything he had ever done.

She turned her face from the window to look at him, lifting her chin slightly. "There's really nothing to talk about. I suppose correct behavior would have been for me to thank you profusely for your...limited...um...services this morning. How remiss of me."

Whoa, she's pissed. Limited services? What the hell does she mean by that?

"Babe—," he started.

"Under the circumstances I think from now on, you should drop the endearment."

"What did I do that was so wrong?" he pleaded.

"Nothing. From what you have told me you're a man used to getting...what he wants from just about any woman that comes along and I was willing to let that next woman be me. I'm just not...willing anymore," she said, her voice breaking near the end.

"I don't know wh—"

"Friendship...Vinny. That's all...I'm willing to give. Nothing more."

The silence that followed was deafening. The only sound was the highway as it rolled on by.

AFTER SEVERAL MORE HOURS of driving through the eastern part of Kentucky and into West Virginia, the mountainous terrain provided a different scene for Annalissa to look at. Dozing on and off helped pass the time and gave her an excuse to not make conversation; she felt the car slowing and opened her eyes once more. Pulling up to the designated airstrip, Vinny moved out of the car while telling Annalissa to wait in the car. She waited obediently for which he was grateful. He saw a man fitting the description walking toward him. Tall, dark hair cut in a military haircut, jeans and a leather jacket. The man pulled his sunglasses off as he approached. Sticking his hand out, he said, "Vinny? I'm Marc. I work for Jack Bryant. I understand you've had quite a mission?"

Vinny shook his hand, laughing. "Yeah, you could

say that. We appreciate you helping us out. It's taken us two full days to get this far and stay under the radar of whoever the hell is after her."

He noticed Marc's eyes glancing over to the car and light up appreciatively. A white-hot flash of jealousy shot through him. Marc's gaze moved back to him and Vinny knew he had not covered the unfamiliar emotion. A slow grin spread over Marc's face. "Well, alright," he drawled. "Let's get the two of you back to Virginia."

Annalissa watched the two men as she sat quietly in the car. Not normally a vain woman, she noticed her sweat-stained clothes, scratched arms, sunburned face and she lifted her hand to tuck an errant curl behind her ear. *Whatever. Just please get me home.*

Vinny walked over to the car and opened the passenger side. "It's okay. He's from our friend Jack's company. He'll fly us back home." Seeing her nod, he held out his hand to assist her but wondered if she would take it.

She only glanced at it for a second before sliding her hand into his. He wrapped his fingers around hers and the tingling jolted all the way up her arm. Trying to ignore it, she gave him a cool nod.

Marc walked over and shook her hand introducing himself, as Vinny grabbed their bags...and glared at Marc, jealousy hitting him again. Walking over to them, he shoved one of the bags toward Marc, forcing him to drop Annalissa's hand. Smirking, Marc said,

"I'm in the small hanger over there."

She looked around at the large hanger on one side of the airport, finding herself checking the area. It seemed strange to be so exposed after two days of running and hiding. Following Marc around the corner of the building she saw the plane inside. The small plane. She stopped dead in her tracks, causing Vinny to run into the back of her.

His eyes immediately darted to her, seeing the pale, wide-eyed expression on her face. He followed her line of vision and noted the four-seater Cessna. *And she hates flying.* He felt her press her back into his front, as though instinctively seeking his protection. As much as he hated for her to be scared, knowing that she unconsciously turned to him...*fuck yeah.*

She whirled around grabbing the front of his shirt. "I can't do it, Vinny. I can't go in that. Can't we just drive? It won't take too long. We could be in Richland by late tonight if we drive."

He dropped the bag he was carrying and placed his hands over hers as they clutched his shirt. "We can do this. Marc will get us there and get us there safely. We won't have to worry about someone finding us on the road."

Tears pricked the back of her eyes, as she battled them back, not wanting to cry in front of them.

Vinny pulled her closely, wrapping his hand around the back of her head, pressing it to his chest. Sharing a glance with Marc who just nodded before bending and grabbing the dropped bag, Vinny whispered in her ear. "Girl, you got this. In the past three days you have walked through miles of woods, crossed a small river, slept in a tree, climbed out of windows, gone without sleep, and never once fell apart. Babe, if this scares you then know that I'm right here and I won't let anything ever hurt you. We can do this...together."

He held her gaze for a moment as she sucked in a huge breath, letting it out slowly. "You...you'll be right with...me?" she asked.

"Babe, there's nowhere else I'd rather be in the whole world, than right by your side. And I'm not just talking about this flight." He continued to hold her gaze, watching the fear recede slightly, only to be replaced with a questioning expression. "You under-stand what I'm saying?"

She glared at him, giving him a small nod. *He wants to be with me. Me? Well, he sure has a funny way of showing it.* "Don't lead me on, Vinny. It really is cruel." Her eyes full of doubt, she started to turn away.

Dammit! He followed her as she trailed along after Marc over to the aircraft. Knowing she was shaking inside, he admired her nerve. Marc smiled at both of them, giving Vinny a slight head jerk. He had placed their bags on the front passenger seat, allowing them to take the two back seats. As he offered his hand to Annalissa, assisting her trembling form into the plane, he assured her, "You're gonna be fine, Ms. O'Brian. I promise to take care of both of you while you're on my plane."

She nodded nervously and sat in the seat indicated. Vinny hopped in next to her and made sure she was buckled. "You know, in the movies," she said as Marc slid into the pilot's seat, "the heroes always travel in one of those luxury aircrafts with a bar, couches, attendants in skimpy outfits, and even bathrooms."

The two men laughed, glad that she was able to joke. Marc replied, "Afraid my aircraft isn't quite what they show in the movies."

She grinned nervously, leaning back in her seat, finally allowing Vinny to hold her hand. Taking a deep breath as they taxied to the end of the runway. Feeling the pressure of his fingers linked with hers sent another tingle through her arms. *I got this. With him...I got this.*

SEVERAL TERRIFYING HOURS later, the small Cessna began landing at a small local airport near Richland. The flight had been without difficulties, but Annalissa felt as though her stomach had spent most of the time in her throat.

Vinny sensed the panic in her, so he tugged on her arm, pulling her toward him. Thinking of what Jobe told him, he said, "Look at me, babe. Keep your eyes on me." She held his gaze, fear in her expression.

Not taking his eyes off of hers, he said softly, "Annalissa, do you know what I thought when I first met you? I heard the sound of a harp and swear to God, I knew then what the angels play. Then I saw you, only I didn't know it was you. I had no idea you were the mission. I just knew that you were the most beautiful thing I'd ever seen. And it wasn't the makeup or the princess dress. I felt that anyone as pretty as you who could bring so much music to life, was someone I wanted to know."

She sat mesmerized, hanging on to every word. He continued, "Yes, you started out being a mission from Alvarez Security. But as I got to know you, everything changed. You became my mission. Mine. Mine to protect. Mine to guard over. Mine to..." he hesitated. "Care for." *Love. It's really love, isn't it?*

He leaned toward her, slightly pulling on her hand. Meeting him halfway, her lips were ready and willing. He kissed her softly, at first, before taking the kiss deeper.

"We're here," Marc's voice cut into their moment, a smile on his face. She jerked her gaze from Vinny's and saw that they were taxiing on the runway.

She looked back at Vinny's grinning face, narrowing her eyes. *Was he just saying all of that to take my mind off of landing?*

He saw her question and immediately pulled her back close to him. "Meant every fuckin' word, baby.

Every. Word."

Her smile spoke volumes. It made her beautiful face exquisite. It filled his heart with hope.

CHAPTER 11

AS SOON AS THEY exited the plane and thanked Marc, Vinny looked up at an approaching man and greeted him enthusiastically. Grabbing him in a bear hug, he said, "Glad you're the one greeting us, bro."

Gabe laughed then sobered as he saw the slim, pale woman standing to the side. He walked over immediately, reaching out his hand. "Ms. O'Brian, welcome back to Virginia. I'm Gabe. You've had a difficult couple of days and Alvarez Security wants to make sure that we can do whatever's necessary to ensure your safety."

She placed her delicate hand into his large one, noticing that he gave a gentle squeeze...like his brother. Her gaze had not left his face until Vinny walked up to stand next to his twin. *Oh my God, two of them!* Almost identical, she smiled seeing their subtle differences. Gabe was handsome...but Vinny? *Only he made her hand tingle when he touched her.*

Settling into the comfortable company SUV, they began the quick drive into Richland.

"Are you taking me home?" she asked, tired and

hungry.

Gabe and Vinny exchanged looks through the rear-view mirror. "Babe, your apartment is still a crime site."

Sighing heavily, she nodded sadly. "But I need to see my things." Not getting a response, she added, "So where are we going?"

"Alvarez Security, Ms. O'Brian," Gabe answered.

She looked toward the man in the front seat. "Please, call me Annalissa." Smiling, she leaned over toward Vinny, closing her eyes. Soon, she was sound asleep.

Vinny looked down at her face, peaceful in slumber once again. Looking up, he said, "Bro, we've had nothing to eat since last night. Any chance there could be some food when we get there?"

"No problem," Gabe said easily, placing a call.

A GENTLE SHAKE pulled Annalissa from her dreams. "Come on, babe. We're here," Vinny called. Opening her eyes, she felt his hands assist her up. She looked out of the windows, seeing that they were in an underground garage. Gabe was already out of the SUV and had moved to the back to grab their bags.

Vinny opened the door and leaned in to pluck her from her seat. "Whoa, I can walk, you know?" she called, throwing her arms around his neck.

"Yeah, but I'd like to have you in my arms anyway," he said. "Plus, I want to make sure your feet are all right now."

They walked up the stairs leading to a small lobby, and down a hall through double doors into a large area that could only be described as the hub of the agency. Tables, desks, computers, large screens on the walls, maps and more equipment than she had ever seen adorned every space.

She was startled when behind them the clapping began. Vinny turned around and stood proudly with her in his arms, staring at the faces of his friends and brothers-in-arms. Tony, Gabe, Jobe, BJ, and Lily were all there. Plus Lily's husband, Matt, and his partner, Shane. Vinny was surprised to see Tony and Gabe's wives, Sherrie and Jennifer, as well.

Completely overwhelmed, Annalissa simply clung to Vinny's neck, wishing the floor would swallow her up. She knew what she looked like...*death warmed over*. The men created a wall of masculinity. All tall, built, and looking like the kind of men you want to have your back when things get tough. And the women? Beautiful. With warm eyes and friendly smiles.

Vinny noticed her tightened grip on his neck and could see the blush cross her face. Tony stepped up as Vinny gently set her on the floor, keeping his arm protectively around her. He did not miss the looks that passed between the men and the smiles that passed between the women.

"As you may have guessed, this is the amazingly

talented Annalissa O'Brian. Annalissa, this is Tony Alvarez, the man in charge."

After the rest of the introductions had been made, Vinny turned her around so that she was focusing on just him. "Babe, they've got some food for us and I know you're hungry. Do you want to get cleaned up first?"

"Oh yes. I look and feel absolutely disgusting."

Chuckling, he nodded. "Go with the ladies; they'll take care of you and then bring you right back here to me."

Sherrie and Jennifer took her hands, leading her down the hall to a ladies' room that was more like a small locker room, which included a shower. Sherrie pulled out a small bag filled with shampoo, conditioner, body wash, and moisturizer. "I brought anything I could think of when Tony called."

"Thank you," Annalissa said. "I'm sorry you had to come out tonight."

"Oh, honey," Sherrie said with a smile. "Tony and the others have been here almost round the clock since you two had to go rogue. This gave me a chance to see my husband."

Jennifer pulled out some clean underwear, along with navy yoga pants and a pink t-shirt. "We brought some clean clothes as well. Go on and get in the shower and we'll be right here in case you need us."

The warm water sluiced over her bruised and scratched body, washing away the dirt and sweat.

Annalissa could not remember when washing her hair felt so good as she scrubbed her scalp. She could have stayed in the shower for much longer, but knowing the two women were waiting for her had her hurrying. Wrapping a towel around her hair, she quickly put on the clothes they had brought. As she walked out of the shower area, she saw the two women sitting on a bench with a cosmetic bag between them.

Jennifer held up deodorant and Sherrie's hands were filled with different scented body lotions. Annalissa rushed forward, saying, "Oh my God, you're lifesavers." She grinned as the others handed her the bag so that she could finish getting ready.

"Were you really hiking in the woods and had to camp out overnight in a tree?" Sherrie asked.

Nodding, Annalissa said, "Yes, and I have to tell you, I was terrified. I've never been out in woods before and I kept staring down looking for snakes."

Jennifer stood, giving her a hug, saying, "Well, I think you're very brave. Gabe kept me informed as the past three days have dragged on and I know he was worried too."

"Gabe was worried? But Vinny was fine. It was nothing to him," Annalissa explained.

Giggling, Jennifer continued. "Oh, he wasn't worried about Vinny. We all knew he could take care of himself. But it was you we were worried about. We knew this would've been hard for you."

Annalissa looked at the two women, staring at her

with...*concern?* "But why would everyone be concerned about me? I'm just a stranger."

Sherrie and Jennifer shared a look, smiling. Stepping up to place her hands on Annalissa's shoulders. "At first you were just the mission, and we would've been concerned no matter what. But then you became Vinny's mission. And that was when we knew you were part of us."

Blushing, Annalissa pulled in her lips, not knowing what to say.

"Go ahead and finish getting ready," Jennifer said. "You've got to be exhausted and the group will want to talk to you tonight." Walking over, she gave Annalissa a hug. "Look, if you ever need to talk...about anything...just let me know."

The women finished and headed back out into the main room. She was wearing flip-flops that Sherrie had provided because Vinny had left specific instructions to not have anything on her feet until they could be looked at again.

She walked into the room, seeing everyone around a large table, now filled with take-out Chinese alongside their computers and equipment. The tantalizing smell of the food drifted toward her, propelling her into the room full of strangers.

Vinny stood, smiling, and stalked directly to her. His hair was damp from his own shower and the scent of his body wash filled her senses. Having no idea of the rules now that she was safely back in Richland, she stood nervously watching him come closer. He did not stop until he was directly in front of her, wrapping his arms around her, pulling her tightly into his chest. Her face hidden from the others…smiled. She had to admit, *this felt right.*

VINNY KNEW EXACTLY WHAT he was doing. This very act of affection, was also a proclamation. She was his. His own personal mission. Kissing the top of her head, he stepped back, taking her hand, leading her over to the table. As he seated her next to him, he glanced down at her red feet. "We need to get your feet checked out."

Gabe scooted his chair back and went to get the medical kit, walking back with it in his hands. "You want me to look at them, bro?"

Vinny had been the backup medic, but knew that Gabe's experience was more than his, so he agreed. She looked up at him, questioning in her eyes.

"Let him check 'em out, babe. I got them cleaned and bandaged, but I'd feel better if someone else took a look."

She watched him sit next to her, leaning down to place her feet in his lap. Gabe knelt down and applied antiseptic to her broken blisters before wrapping them in soft gauze. "That'll keep 'em clean while you're here, but take it off tonight when you go to bed and let them air out."

"No problem," Vinny answered, absentmindedly rubbing his hand on her leg as Gabe finished.

Biting her lips, Annalissa felt like she had entered the twilight zone…once again. A gorgeous man had his hands on her feet while Mr. Alpha himself had his arm around her…in front of his friends. Five other handsome men and their women were sitting around all smiling at her. *And Vinny called me 'babe' in front of them all.*

Settling around the table several minutes later, they all began eating and talking. Matt looked over, saying, "Ms. O'Brian, I'm assuming that you want to know about your apartment." Seeing her wide-eyed nod, he began. "When we got the call from Tony about what was happening, we went to your place to see if there was any trouble there. And it had already been broken into."

Shane added, "We won't know until you take a look at everything to see what might have been taken, but it was probably someone searching for the drugs. Things were tossed around, but it looked like your more expensive items were left there."

Staying silent, she just nodded, not knowing what to say. *I guess I'll see it tonight, when I get home.*

Tony took over the reporting at this point. "Here's what we know so far," he said, looking at both Vinny and Annalissa. "We're working with Jack Bryant's group on this. His DEA contact has told us that the bag was filled with cocaine. They're looking at the security tapes from the airport, but everything we're hearing indicates that this was not just a couple of low-lifes at the airports trying to send drugs. Once they figured out that you had not landed and they had not missed you at the airport, they put things into motion. It was known that you were traveling by land. And then there were the attacks on you two. This indicates big money, big backing, and high stakes."

"But if the drugs were in Easnadh's case, why did they trash my apartment?" she asked.

"Well, Ms. O'Brian—"

"Please call me Annalissa," she interrupted shyly.

Tony nodded before continuing. "Annalissa, we are considering that whoever was supposed to get the drugs on this end may not have realized right away that your plane was delayed. They may have thought that they missed you and went to see if you were home with your harp."

"So…someone broke into my house? But what if I had been there? What if we had taken another flight and I'd…I'd been home?" she asked, her voice rising.

Silence met her for a moment, so she jerked her head around. "Vinny?"

With one arm around her shoulder, he moved his other hand to cup her face. "That didn't happen and baby, it's not gonna happen."

She looked around the room at the fierce looks from all of the men and the determined expressions on the faces of the women. Licking her lips, she said, "I...I don't know what to do with all of this."

Once again Tony nodded. "That's why we're here, Annalissa. Our job is to keep you safe and work with DEA and the police. We also have to assume that you were the specific target for carrying the drugs. Which," he continued as he watched her carefully, "means that you have probably been used to carry drugs before."

At this proclamation, Vinny cursed as she visibly paled.

"Who would do that?"

"Whoever it was has resources. This isn't just someone who wanted an easy way to get drugs through security. This is someone with the ability to find out what hotel you were at, what rental car you had, and could get someone on the road following you."

Matt said, "Annalissa, we're going to need to have a long interview with you, but we can wait a day. We know you're exhausted right now, but we'd like you back here tomorrow. We can do our interviewing here so that Tony's group will be involved. Jack's DEA contact will be here as well."

She only nodded, not knowing what else to do. Everyone stood up, the women coming over to offer hugs and assurances that they would see her soon. As they filed out with calls of seeing them tomorrow, she turned to Vinny. "I don't have a way home. Can you take me?"

He held her gaze for a moment, a strange look in

his eyes. Slowly nodding, he just smiled. "Yeah, I'm taking you home."

Lifting her chin slightly, she forced a smile. Hearing Tony call out her name, she turned to him.

"I know this is hard for you, but everyone you know right now is suspect. Your manager and agent have been calling. We've told them nothing about where you were or what was happening. Your father knows only what we had you tell him and that your harp was picked up by one of us. At this point he assumes that you have the harp."

"Yes, well Easnadh is very important to him…although I actually own it." Seeing Tony and Vinny's look of surprise, she added, "He enjoys the notoriety from having the antique harp played at the symphony and loves for me to travel with it. It gives him something else to have Todd release to the press when I am playing."

She walked over to grab her purse and backpack missing the look shared by the others.

The words she just said swirled around their heads: *he wants me to keep traveling…* Perhaps, her father may need to move up to the top of the list of suspects.

ANNALISSA WAS QUIET once she and Vinny were in his truck leaving Alvarez Security. Her mind was filled with thoughts that swirled around until she was exhausted. Not noticing where he was driving, she was surprised when he pulled into another parking garage and turned off the truck.

Before she could question where they were, he turned to face her. "Babe, we're home. My home."

"But…why are we here? What about my home?"

"Right now, your home is still trashed and until I can go with you, I'm not having you there by yourself. And…I want you with me."

Biting her lip in indecision, she quickly realized that he was right. *Where else am I going to go right now? Not dad's.* Sucking in a deep breath, she agreed. "Okay, but just for tonight."

Grinning, he moved to her door and assisted her out of his truck. Tagging her hand, he led her through an impressive lobby, greeting the concierge, and into the elevator. Seeing her face, he laughed. "Yeah, I live here. Gabe used to also, but he and Jennifer and her little brother live in a house now. Jobe still lives here. There's a gym and an indoor pool. Which by the way, we're going to start using. I owe you swim lessons."

By the time he finished his explanations, they were on the fourth floor and at his door. Stepping in, she was stunned. She had expected a bachelor pad, complete with beer cans in the window sill, pizza boxes on the counter and a guitar on the sofa. She gazed around the room, seeing the large open floor plan with the living room flowing into the dining room. He had decorated in dark tones with a few accents of bold color. The gray L-shaped sofa was big enough to hold several of his friends, all as large as him. Two leather recliners flanked the sofa and faced a wide screen TV. The rug and lamps were in a dark green.

The dining room furniture was dark wood with green chair cushions and his kitchen had stainless steel appliances with green accents on the walls. She turned to him, curiosity written on her face. "Did you…decorate this place?"

Laughing, he said, "I'm not a complete Neanderthal." She giggled and the sound hit him in the gut. *I want to hear that sound every day for the rest of my life.* Taking her hand he gave her a quick tour. The second bedroom was set up as a study and she wondered where she would sleep. Before they could move down the hall further his phone rang.

Looking down, rolled his eyes and said, "I gotta take this. It's mom and I'm sure she's been blowing up Gabe's phone for three days."

She let go of his hand and watched him move to the balcony to talk. Suddenly, every ounce of energy drained from her and she knew she was crashing. The events of past days overwhelmed her as she walked to his sofa. Lying down, she watched him laugh while on the phone with his mom. *I could so love that man.* That was the last thought that floated through her mind before completely shutting down.

Five minutes later as Vinny came inside, he saw her asleep on his sofa. Completely out. He stood there for a moment staring into the face he had grown to know so well. Thick dark hair, now shiny and curling on the pillow. Her pale face now sun-kissed, with freckles across her nose. She looked like a china doll. One that his mother had on her nightstand that had been given to her by her mother many years before.

Her slim body was familiar to him, each curve noted and longed for. All the other women he had ever been with, slid from his mind. Only she filled his vision and his heart.

Bending down, he gently scooped her up from the sofa and carried her to his bed where he lay her down on the soft sheets. He slid her yoga pants down her legs and pulled the covers up some. Then he slid her t-shirt off and unsnapped her bra, sliding it off as well. Determined to be a gentleman, he pulled one of his t-shirts over her head and covered her beautiful breasts. Then he pulled the covers up to her chin.

Within a few minutes, he stripped to his boxers and joined her on the bed. Rolling over to her, he pulled her unconscious body into his, wrapping himself around her protectively. He had never brought another woman to his apartment. To his house. Never. Until Annalissa.

Nothing's ever felt so right.

CHAPTER 12

THE SUN BEGAN peeking through the slats of the vertical blinds that covered Vinny's tall bedroom windows. Annalissa blinked, trying to recognize her surroundings. A heavy arm lay across her stomach and a tree-trunk leg rested over hers. And something, hard and prodding, was pressed into her ass. Her eyes flew open as she jerked her head around, seeing the smiling face of Vinny. *I'm in his bed? We slept like this?*

Before she could question, he saw the look of surprise on her face. *And the look of interest in her eyes.* "Mornin' beautiful," he greeted, leaning over to kiss her. The kiss started slow. A greeting. Then morphed into something more. Passion. Heat. Desire. Angling his head to control the intensity, he slid his tongue into her warm mouth, exploring every crevice. Tasting her. Memorizing her essence.

He swallowed her moan as she twisted her body around to face his and he pulled her tightly into him. His massive erection was painfully pressed between their bodies. One hand slid down to her firm ass, massaging the globes, while his other hand stayed tangled in her silky hair.

She began to move her hips as she slid one leg over his, pressing her core against his cock. *Please don't turn me away,* she thought, knowing this was the man she wanted. Needed. Trusted.

He leaned back peering into her eyes, looking for permission, seeing nothing but passion and acceptance. Smiling, he moved back in, his tongue sliding from her lips to her neck as he tasted and kissed her smooth skin. Gently sucking the dip where her pulse beat erratically, he latched on leaving his mark as she scored his back with her nails.

Suddenly at a loss, he wondered what to do. *Never made love to a virgin. Hell, never had a virgin. Nor made love to anyone. All others were just a fuck and move on. This? Jesus, what the hell do I do?*

She sensed his reticence and was determined to not let him talk himself out of what she wanted to happen. Sliding her hand down between their bodies and into his boxers, she wrapped it around his cock. The skin was soft over the steel core and she felt it jump in her hands. He was much larger than the few experiences she had in college, but she instinctively moved her hand up and down.

"Baby?" he rasped, voice like gravel. "Are you sure?"

"Mmmmm," was the only answer he received, her lips traveling along his jaw, licking the morning stubble.

Pulling back away from her, he repeated, "Baby girl, I've got to hear it."

Her eyes, still filled with passion, cleared as she smiled at him. "Yes. I want this. With you. And only you."

"Thank God," he groaned, continuing to kiss her as he slowly slid his hand into her panties, finding her folds slick and ready. *A virgin. A virgin,* kept rolling through his mind. *She's got to be ready.*

He maneuvered her up just long enough to pull off her t-shirt, freeing her body to his perusal. Jerking off his boxers his cock stood at attention, already leaning toward her with a mind of its own. *Gotta wait, boy. Gotta take this slow and make it perfect for her.*

Lying back down, he slowly inserted one finger into her tight channel, fingering her gently to bring her pleasure without pain. Crooking his finger deep inside, he hit the spot he wanted to find as her moans increased. Lowering his head he pulled one taut nipple into his mouth, sucking hard. Giving it a nip before soothing with his tongue, he felt her juices increase against his finger.

She felt every nerve. Every tingle. Every caress and suckle. And thought she would die with need. *This feels like flying. Hurling toward the end of the runway, knowing that you'll soon take off.* With one last tweak of his finger her core, tightly coiled, burst with electricity pulsating in all direction. He sucked her nipple as her head fell back against the pillow, a moan filling the spinning room.

He felt her inner walls grab his finger and his cock

jumped again. *God, I want that on my dick.* He watched her pant through her orgasm and realized he had never seen anything as beautiful as a woman he cared about being pleasured. *'Cause I never cared about anyone before.*

She lifted her head as her eyes shimmered, watching him watch her. "Please, Vinny," she begged softly. "Make love to me."

Smiling, he brushed her hair back away from her face, kissing her lips gently. "Anything for you, baby," he promised. Letting go of her just long enough to roll on a condom, he moved back over her body. With her legs spread for him, he stared down at her glistening folds and seated himself at her entrance.

Uncertainty filled his expression. "I...I don't want to hurt you."

"I don't know that we can help that," she replied nervously.

"I'll go slow." He began to push his way in. *Oh, damn, she's tight.* Her inner walls squeezed as he pressed in. While his dick was reveling in the feeling, he was terrified of hurting her.

Never having known a feeling of such fullness, she tried to breathe to ease the passing. *Lamaze, right? That's what they do, I think.* While the feeling of gentle pressure was building, she realized it was not painful as she attempted to relax.

Aware of the tumultuous thoughts flying through her head as he watched her face carefully, he willed his dick to move slowly. Torturously slow.

"Just do it," she panted.

Nodding, he forced his erection to the hilt, stopping as her sudden gasp met his ears. Her face, slightly contorted in discomfort, stilled him immediately. *What the hell do I do now?*

"Go," she begged. "Do something."

He moved in and out slowly, allowing the moisture to slick her inner walls, easing the passage. As her core began to accept his aching cock, he pumped in and out faster. Feeling her relax slightly underneath him he kissed her, his tongue moving in unison with his dick. Her moans filled his mouth as he moved faster and faster with ease.

Knowing he was going to blow soon he slid his hand down between them, resting his weight on his other bent arm.

She had always wondered what the fuss was all about and now she knew. The feeling of the man on top of her, joined with her as one, was overwhelming. The discomfort had dissipated, leaving her hurling once more down the runway. The feeling of friction deep inside had every nerve tingling again, desperately wanting the explosion she knew was coming.

Moving his mouth down to suck on her nipple while his fingers clamped down on her swollen clit was all it took to take her over the edge. With her fingernails digging into his back he watched as she screamed out his name, her tight inner walls clamping down on his dick. He had never liked a woman's fingernail marks on his back before, not wanting any woman to have a claim once they parted, but this? He wanted to wear her marks for all to see, as he looked down at the love bite he had given her earlier. *Both marked. For each other.*

With only a few more thrusts he threw his head back, a grimace on his face as his neck corded with the force of his orgasm. Deeper and deeper. Finally with every drop wrung out he collapsed to the side, rolling with her in his arms, keeping her tightly in his embrace.

Bodies slick with sweat, breaths harsh and panting, they lay euphoric in the aftermath. Minutes passed as conscious thought slowly returned.

Christ, how is she?, he thought leaning back to peer into her eyes. Terrified of seeing regret or worse, what he saw punched him in the chest. A smile that lit her face and sparkling eyes. A well-sated look on her face pleased him, but not in the way it always had. He wanted her to be as moved as he was.

"Babe?" he inquired, not knowing what he was even asking.

"I'm good, Vinny," she replied looking down at his chest. Face flaming, she was embarrassed.

He lifted her chin with his fingers. "Oh no. You get outta your head, baby girl. That was the most amazing thing I have ever felt, but I gotta know you're alright. Did I hurt you?"

"It kind of started out uncomfortable because I was

so tense, but it got better." Seeing the worried look on his face, she amended, "It got a lot better. Like really-good kind of better."

He threw his head back laughing as he admitted, "I like that. Really-good kind of better." Sobering, he touched her lips gently as he slowly withdrew from her. They both looked down and saw a slight smear of blood on the condom.

"Stay here, baby," he ordered softly as he moved off of the bed. Once in the bathroom, he quickly disposed of the condom and wet a washcloth with warm water. Stalking back into the bedroom he knelt beside her, gently washing between her legs.

In the light of day her nudity seemed inappropriate, but she noticed his confidence as he swaggered naked from the bathroom and then took care of her. *Confidence.* Sucking in a deep breath as he gently cleaned her, she blushed beet red.

"I so want to appear sophisticated right now, but am failing miserably," she blurted out.

Touching his lips to hers before sliding back in next to her and pulling her body flush against his. "Why sophisticated, babe? I never want you to be anything except exactly who you are."

"It's just this was...um...special...to me, that is."

He cocked his head to the side, looking at her face for clues as to what she was talking about. "It was special for me too." Her smile speared his heart and he cupped her jaw bringing her closer for another kiss, before tucking her tightly against his chest. "More than special," he admitted, whispering into her hair.

VINNY COOKED BREAKFAST while Annalissa showered and prepared for the day. Throwing some bacon into the frying pan, he thought about what he was doing. *Breakfast. I'm cooking breakfast for a woman I spent the entire night with. In my own bed.* He grinned as he stirred the scrambled eggs and popped the bagels into the toaster. *Not just any woman…the woman.*

His mind then wandered to the reason they were there. The morning afterglow left as soon as he mentioned that Todd, Gordon, Maurice, and her father had all called the evening before. He hated seeing the look on her face at the thought of having to face them.

"Babe," he said, as she walked into the room, freshly showered and looking more beautiful than ever, "You don't have to talk to or see anyone you don't want to. Especially not without me around. In fact, now that I think about it, I don't want you to see them without me."

Her chin lifted slightly and he realized he had stepped on her toes. He started to open his mouth, when her hand came up in his face.

"Vinny, I'm perfectly capable of talking to my father and manager. And I've got to go see Maurice today. I'm sure he's worried sick about me."

He noted that she did not say that about her father. Standing with his legs apart and his hands on his hips, he glared down at her. "I didn't say you weren't capable. But for all we know, one of them is guilty and you're not talking to them without me."

This time her chin lifted even more as she held his glare. "I'm not cowering away from everyone I know and I'm just going to talk to them on the phone while you're gone."

He stood for a moment, not knowing what to say. Before he could ponder the situation any further, she stepped right up to him, placing her hand on his chest.

"I know we have to wonder who planted the drugs, but I refuse to be afraid of everyone. Let's eat and then we can plan our day."

He agreed but was going to make sure that someone was with her, whether she liked it or not. *After all, she's my responsibility even if she doesn't get that yet!*

After breakfast, he pulled her in close, her shampoo wafting in the air as he bent his head to hers. "Babe, I'm sorry. I'm kind of new at this, so you gotta cut me a break. I've got to go in for just a little while, but Jobe lives in this building and he's going to stay around today in case you need something."

She started to protest, but he kissed her silent. Taking the kiss deeper, it was long, hard, and wet. When she came up for air, her lips were swollen and her eyes were half shut.

"So you'll stay here while I run to work?" he asked,

still nuzzling her nose.

"Ummm," she moaned, as his lips slid down to her neck. As he pulled back, she watched him walk away. "You won't always win every argument just by kissing me, you know?"

He turned, his cocky grin spreading across his face. "I know, baby girl. But I've got a lot in my arsenal to use if the kisses don't work."

He ducked as she tossed a pillow at him just as he walked through the door. Smiling to herself, she walked over to look out his window. The city of Richland with the river in the background was beautiful from this view. Turning, her gaze roamed around his apartment. *What now?* She sighed. *Are we a couple? When do I go back to my apartment?* Finding no answer to her relationships questions, she walked over to the sofa and picked up the cell phone he had left for her to use. *Time to get back to my life.*

"WHERE ARE YOU and you'd better tell me that you've got Easnadh with you."

"Dad, I told you that I'm staying with a friend for right now until my apartment is released." Tony had allowed her to tell others that her apartment had been burglarized, but to not give any details. She had made it seem like teenagers broke in and the manager was going to repaint the apartment.

"Friends? What friends? Who are you staying with?" Stewart O'Brian asked.

"I...I'm staying...with one of um...Mr. Alvarez's men," she said, knowing what was coming. And she was right.

"You're staying with some man you just met. Tell me you haven't gone half-mad and convinced yourself you've fallen for some rescuer?"

"Dad, I'm...not going to discuss this...um...situation. I'm safe and getting ready to call Maurice. I'll be back to practicing in no time." *Please let that satisfy him.*

"Speaking of practicing, do you have Easnadh?" he demanded.

"No, but I was told that I may have it later today. Mr. Alvarez—"

"Don't give me excuses," he interrupted. "You sent Easnadh on a different plane and Alvarez Security hasn't heard the last of me yet."

"I told you that I was too scared to get back on a plane then," she said, but knew he would never understand.

After a few more minutes of listening to her father's tirade, she finally managed to get him off of the phone. *No 'gee I'm so sorry you had to go through this'. No 'wow, honey, I sure am glad you're okay'.* She tossed the phone onto the coffee table, leaning forward placing her head in her hands. *Has it always been this way?*

Picking the phone back up, she dialed Maurice.

"Hey, I'm back," she said.

"Oh, my goodness, you have no idea how I've been worried and waiting for you to call," the older man exclaimed. "Are you all right?"

"Yes, yes," she laughed. "I'm fine. Just taking a day to recuperate, that's all."

"My dear, when I heard that you had been delayed because of an airplane problem with a rough landing and then that you had to travel with the security man…well I just couldn't believe it. All I could think about was that you must have been scared."

"It was really fine and it's over now. I'm hoping to be able to practice today if she's returned to me."

"Do you want to come to my studio? I would love to see you and have a chance to check Easnadh out."

"I don't know when I'ill get my hands on her and," she hesitated, thinking about Vinny's warning. "I really should stay in today. But I'll plan on seeing you tomorrow, if that's okay."

"Absolutely, my dear. You stay in and rest today. Are you at your apartment?"

"Um, no. I'm staying with a friend."

"Oh, that's good. You enjoy yourself," he said.

"I…um…will, I'm sure," she replied, her face blushing at the thoughts of this morning's enjoyments.

Disconnecting with that phone call, she realized for the millionth time how comforting it was to be able to have someone in her life who seemed to really care about her. Smiling, she looked back down at the phone. *One more call to make.* Dreading this call almost as much as her father's, she quickly punched in the numbers before she changed her mind.

"Todd Levine, Musical Management Services. How may I direct your call?" came the efficient voice of his assistant.

"Hi Erica, this is—"

"Oh my God, if it isn't the little-lost lamb finally returned," her snotty voice came back. "Do you have any idea how much your vacation has cost Mr. Levine?"

"Va…vacation?" Annalissa asked, not understanding.

"Trip detour, going off on your own, not being able to be reached. You know, the least you could have done was kept the man who made your career in the loop."

"Is he available or not, Erica? Sparring with you after my…my…vacation is not what I want to do," she asked, hands shaking in anger. She heard voices in the background and then was connected to another line.

"Annalissa?" Todd asked. "Are you back? Do you have your harp? I had arranged for you to play for the Governor's wife. She's having a little soiree and thought your music would be the perfect entertainment."

"Um, hi Todd. Nice to hear from you too," she said, sitting up straighter.

"Yes, yes, I'm glad to hear from you," he parroted. "But it's not as though you were lost…just traveling around with that security man."

"Traveling around? You and Erica sound alike. We traveled by car after our harrowing experience with the first flight. I just wasn't comfortable flying again and he was nice enough to suggest that we drive."

"Now, let's not get temperamental on me. I'm the one trying to get things back on track. Now, about that soiree—"

"I can't," she interrupted. "I don't have Easnadh back yet. Someone is delivering her to me today," she lied.

"You don't have her?" Todd asked. "Where is your harp? I assumed it was with you at your apartment." When she did not answer right away, he continued, "I know you prefer her, but any harp will do. Just meet me at the—"

"I can't," she interrupted once more. "I have to stay here and um…rest today."

"Who says? And where are you staying?" he bit out.

Sighing, she answered. "Todd, I appreciate all you do for me, but I'm staying with a friend and will spend the day resting. I cannot possibly do the Governor's wife's soiree today, but I will call you tomorrow and we can see what events I feel like I can do."

With that, she hung up, smiling. *I hung up on him first. I don't think I've ever done that.* Giggling to herself as she stood up and walked back to the kitchen, she admitted, *that felt great!*

EARLY IN THE AFTERNOON, Vinny called. "I wanted to let you know that Jobe will be bringing a surprise for you. I wish it could have been me but I'll be home as soon as I can."

When Annalissa heard the doorbell she opened the door, hoping she knew what the surprise was going to be. She was not disappointed. Jobe stood there, a harp case in his hand. Clapping her hands she screamed joyfully, ushering him in.

"Oh, it's lovely," she exclaimed, showing him where to set the case down.

"I thought it would be larger," Jobe said, watching as she opened the case and pulled the instrument out.

"You're thinking of the large concert harps. Easnadh is a Celtic Harp and in particular, she is a much smaller one."

She sat down on one of the dining room chairs, immediately plucking the strings, tuning as she went. He watched, entranced by the music, before moving to leave. She looked up, her fingers stilling on the strings. "Do you need to leave now?"

Jobe smiled, shaking his head. "No, is there something that you need?"

Laughing, she replied, "Not really. I'm just...well, it feels weird...being here. Alone."

"Are you scared?"

Rushing to assure him, she said, "No. Not afraid. It just seems like I should be in my own apartment. Have you seen it?"

He saw the concerned look on her face. Sitting down on another chair, he faced her. "Well…" he started slowly. "The door did not look damaged, but there were marks around your lock so someone had worked to get in. I can't say what might have been taken, but things were tossed around as though someone was looking for something."

He watched her carefully, wanting to gauge his words by her reaction. The only outward expression of concern was her lips tucking in. "Your drawers were pulled out and dumped and your books were all on the floor where someone must have been looking behind them."

The silence hung between them for a minute as she thought of her apartment. Her safe haven. Away from her father and her manager.

"Do you think they were looking for the drugs before they knew I never left Kansas City?"

"I don't know, but I think it's a real possibility," he answered honestly.

She nodded slowly, her mind still churning. Sighing, she turned back to him and smiled. "Thank you so much for this," she said, patting her harp. "I was going crazy not having her with me for the past few days. And to be honest, being here with nothing to do was making me a little nuts too."

Jobe stood and walked toward the door, Annalissa right behind him. He turned and looked down, saying softly, "You're safe here, you know. Not just from someone from the outside, but with Vinny as well."

She peered at him, trying to understand the meaning of his words.

"He's never, and I mean never, brought a woman here to his home."

At that, she could not hide her surprise. And pleasure. "Thank you for that, Jobe," she whispered, smiling.

After he left, she walked back to the windows to look out over the city. *A man like Vinny would have had women. Probably lots of women. But never brought one here.* Sucking in a huge breath, she wondered what that meant. *Does he just think of me as someone to save and keep safe?* As she pondered, she realized that he was too honorable to lead her on. *So what does he think of me?*

Finding no answers while looking at the Richland skyline, she moved back to the dining room chair and picked up Easnadh. Her fingers flying over the strings elicited the music her heart craved. Inside the music, she could forget. About being chased. Drugs. The police. Her father. Everything negative floated away as the music filled her soul.

And an hour later that was how Vinny found her.

CHAPTER 13

VINNY STOPPED OUTSIDE of his apartment door. The sound of music filtered out into the hall; soft and haunting. There was something about the harp that always brought him to a stop. His eyes closed as his mind rolled back five years. The music. Filtering out through the night. Then...*no*.

Taking a deep breath he leaned his head against the door, hearing the very different music that Annalissa played. He opened the door quietly so as not to disturb her. She was sitting with her back to him, her harp resting against her shoulder. Her dainty, yet strong, fingers were nimbly moving over the strings. The sounds floated around his apartment, filling it with an energy that had never been there before. The sounds of life. And perhaps...*love*.

She did not notice that he was there. Absorbed in the music flying from her fingers, he watched her face. Eyes closed, a smile playing about her lips. She appeared to be one with her harp. One with the music.

As he walked closer her eyes flew open, her fingers stilled, and her smile widened. "Vinny, I didn't hear you come in."

Quickly closing the ground between them, he leaned over kissing her lips. "I heard the music from the hall and thought angels were playing," he murmured.

She laughed thinking he was joking, but sobered as she saw the look on his face. Cocking her head to the side, she asked, "Are you okay?"

Kissing her once again, he nodded. "Perfect, now that I've come home to you and your music."

"Well, aren't you the gallant flirt?" she teased.

Standing to his full height, he winked. "Well, you gave me such a nice surprise when I got home. I've got a surprise for you." With that he headed into the bedroom while she bent to place her harp into its case.

"Come on, babe," Vinnie called out from the bedroom.

Annalissa walked in to see him standing naked in front of his closet, pulling on swim trunks. "Are you going—"

"Not me. We. We're going swimming, so get your bikini on," he interrupted.

"Um…I…um…I don't have…"

He stalked over stopping right in front of her, lifting her chin with his fingers. "Well, we can't go skinny-dipping in the pool downstairs, as much as I would love to."

She had to giggle at that thought. "I mean I don't have my things from my apartment."

He walked over to a large canvas bag that was sitting just inside the door. "I sent Gabe and Jennifer over to your place today. I knew Jennifer would know what you'd need and Gabe was there to make sure she was safe. And," he winked mischievously, "I specifically told her to hunt for a swimsuit."

Embarrassed, she dug through the bag and saw what she was looking for. Looking up, she said, "I have a boring, old bathing suit for when I sit in the sun, but I don't even do that very much. So why don't you just go for a swim yourself."

"Whatever you've got will be fine. Just hop in it and let's go. I'm teaching you how to swim." Seeing her about to protest again, he placed his fingers on her lips. "Now, baby," he ordered gently.

Turning away from him, she pulled out the one-piece bathing suit that she had had for years. He had seen her naked, but now she felt self-conscious. Moving to the bathroom and shutting the door for privacy, she pulled it on. Red, with little blue flowers on it, she blushed as she gazed at her reflection in the mirror. *I look like I'm ten years old. And I'm going to drown. Great. A ten-year-old, drowning kid. Just how I want him to see me.* The knock on the bathroom door shook her out of her thoughts.

"You ready?" he called.

Pulling herself up, she grabbed a towel and wrapped it around herself. Throwing open the door, she said, "Yes, let's go and get this over with."

He took her arm as she attempted to pass him by and gently pulled her in for a hug. "What's going on, babe?"

Sucking her lips in, she just shook her head. "Just nervous, that's all." She pulled herself out of his embrace and slid her feet into flip-flops as she walked toward the door.

He looked as she walked away, his brow knit in concern. Grabbing his own towel, he followed her out of the door.

Several minutes later she had to admit that the pool was not like what she expected. The indoor facility was beautiful and the water was a pleasant temperature. There were a few other people swimming laps so she had dropped her towel and slipped quickly into the water at the shallow end. Moving her hands around she loved the feel of the water as long as her feet were touching the bottom of the pool.

Vinny slid into the water behind her, noticing her nervousness. But her rockin' body was holding his attention. Down boy, he reminded himself, knowing his swimming trunks were beginning to tent out.

"Okay, princess. Give me your hands," he said, moving toward her. As she reached out her hands, he took them gently as he walked backward slowly toward the deeper water. She walked along, holding his hands until the water reached her shoulders and he felt her stop.

"Oh, no. No further. If you're going to teach me to swim, then we can do it right here," she claimed.

Smiling, he agreed. "Now just remember, I got you.

And I promise not to let you go."

She looked at him, wondering if his words held a double meaning. Licking her lips, she looked at the other swimmers nervously. One had just exited the pool and the other was still doing laps. Sucking in a huge breath, she said, "So what do I do now?"

For the next several minutes, he had her float on her back with one of his hands under her back and the other at the bottom of her ass. He walked around giving her a chance to feel what it was like to have the water support her and not have her feet on the pool bottom.

She opened her eyes and saw him smiling down at her. She leaned up, losing the balance of floating and her head went under the water as Vinny's arms immediately plucked her up. Sputtering, she clawed her hands toward him.

He moved them closer to the edge as he felt her panicked grasp. "I got you, babe. You're fine," he reassured. "You were doing great floating along."

She clung to the edge and, realizing that her feet would not touch, began scooting her way toward the shallower end again.

"Hold on," he said, halting her progress. "Hang on the side and practice kicking your legs." He showed her several different kicks and she began to relax again, feeling comfortable holding on to the side of the pool.

Admiring the way her ass wiggled back and forth as she practiced her kicking, he once again had to force his dick to behave.

She smiled at him and then noticed his strained expression. "Are you alright?" she asked hesitantly.

He moved behind her, stilling her legs, and caging her in with his massive arms on either side of her. Slowly floating inward, he pressed his front against her back until there was no mistaking the evidence of his desire.

"Oh," she said with a giggle.

He moved away and growled, "Let's finish up the lesson for tonight and get upstairs, baby. Seeing you lookin' all sexy as hell in this bathing suit is killing me."

Twisting around, she looked confused. "This? Vinny, I look like I'm a kid in this old thing."

With her now facing him, he pressed in again, this time his swollen dick nestled against her core. "You don't look like a kid, Annalissa. You're fuckin' hot in this and all I can think about is peeling it off of your delicious body." Moving in for a kiss, he captured her lips as he plunged his tongue inside. The kiss had taken on a life-force of its own before he pulled back.

Her wet hair hanging about her shoulders, the ends floating all around. Her eyes still closed. Her lips kiss-swollen. *I've never seen anything so beautiful.* Knowing he needed to stop before he took her in the pool, he moved away keeping her hands firmly in his, pulling her along.

Her eyes popped open as he gently ordered, "Kick your legs, babe. Just like if you were still hanging on the side."

She kicked along, feeling the force keeping her lower body high in the water as he pulled her along from the front. His hands were firm and strong. Moving all over the pool, even in the deep end, she knew he would never let go. *Safe. Secure. Cared for. Loved?*

Slowly they made their way to the shallow end of the pool where he assisted her out. Taking the towel from her hands, he dried her off before wrapping her in a large, dry one.

She lifted her face toward his, smiling. "I was kind of swimming, wasn't I?" she said proudly.

"Absolutely, babe. We keep doing this and you'll be swimming laps before you know it." He met her lips, taking the kiss deeper. Pulling back, he tagged her hand as they headed toward the back elevator. Quickly entering his apartment, he hustled her into the warm shower.

And then he did exactly what he'd been wanting to do for an hour. He peeled the bathing suit slowly off of her body, exposing all of her beauty to his eyes.

Then he worshiped her long into the night.

THE NEXT MORNING found Vinny and Annalissa arriving at the Alvarez Security building. Moving into the large work area, they found everyone gathered. The others greeted her warmly and Tony motioned for them to sit down.

"I've got a friend that was able to pull up the security camera feed from the airport in LA. I want you to watch them as carefully as you can to see if you recognize anyone."

She sat for the next hour, carefully watching everything on the screen, but came up empty. She looked at the men, saying, "I'm sorry. I just don't see anyone I know."

Tony nodded and then moved to the file in front of him. "Don't be sorry, Annalissa. It's not your job to have to identify anyone. We just want as much input from you as we can get."

She visibly relaxed, sinking back into her chair. Vinny's hand slid from the edge of her chair to her shoulders, noting how tense they were. His eyes cut over to the others and silently signaled for a break.

"We'll take a break, get some food in here and then we'll resume checking into your contacts, all right?" Tony inquired politely.

"I'm fine, really." Cutting her eyes over to Vinny, she said, "You don't have to coddle me, you know. I'm not going to fall apart."

Grinning, he touched his lips to her forehead. "I know, babe. You're a helluva lot stronger than you even know. But we're tired, so let's take a little break."

She cocked an eyebrow as she looked at the men around the table. "Hmmm, you expect me to believe that a group of former Special Forces soldiers are tired from sitting at a table?"

Laughter rang out as they shook their heads. "All right, Tiger. We'll keep going," Vinny said. "But how about we order some lunch."

Several minutes later they began looking at the list of people she knew who had been in LA with them.

"I just don't see why it had to be someone I know?" she complained.

"Well," Gabe answered slowly, watching her reactions. "Your harp is always in your possession except for a very few minutes and even then it is close by. So that would indicate that someone close to you could have had the opportunity."

"Yes, but what about motive?" she retorted. "Why would someone want to do this to me? I'm nobody. I'm not a threat to anyone."

"We don't know that anyone did it specifically *to* you. It may have just been that you were the convenient carrier," Jobe replied.

She leaned forward, rubbing her temples, trying to force back the slight headache that was building. The men shared a look again. Just then, Sherrie appeared carrying barbecue sandwiches and chips from a little restaurant down the street. Her eyes scanned the room seeing the look on her husband's face, she quickly moved over to the table.

"Hey everyone! I hope you don't mind but I brought lunch over figuring ya'll needed a break." She looked at Gabe and said, "You may want to go help Jennifer. She's lugging up the drinks."

Gabe hopped up to find his wife as the others spread out the food. Annalissa looked at the lunch, realizing how hungry she was. As they ate, talked and laughed, she also realized how different this group was. They needed each other, but there was no pressure. No trying to force one or the other to do something for them. *How unlike my life this is. Someone is always pushing or pulling me to do something.*

As the meal was finished, she looked at Tony with renewed determination on her face. "All right. I'm ready."

The others recognized her steely resolve and nodded as they pushed the empty plates to the side. Jennifer and Sherrie quietly cleaned up the table, but both stayed close wanting to hear what their new friend had to say. Tony and Gabe grinned, knowing their wives were nosy.

She looked at the list of people that had been around her harp and asked, "What do you need from me?"

"We have the list, but I'd like you to just talk about each one. Who they are. What they do. What your impressions of them are. Even what you know about them. Just talk and we'll listen and take notes. You may say something without even realizing it that we find useful."

Glancing to the side to see Vinny's concerned expression, she squeezed his hand. "I've got this, Vinny. I'm okay." Seeing his reassuring smile, she began.

The first name on the list was Todd Levine. "Todd's my manager. My father hired him a year ago to chart out my career. He was supposed to take the shy harpist and turn me into a public figure." Seeing the incredulous looks from around the table, she shrugged. "I know it sounds ridiculous. Most symphonic musicians are very anonymous. But sometimes a principle player is supposed to be the show-stopper. That was supposed to be me. So Todd took me in hand, hired a make-up artist and stylist to design for me and to travel with me. He schedules press releases and photo shoots."

She looked down at the file with Todd's name on it. "I hate it," she confessed. Looking up quickly, she said, "Not him. I don't hate him. Well, I don't exactly like him either, but I don't hate him. I just don't like being on show. I love playing the harp in front of an audience, but not the forced status that is shoved down my throat."

"Tell us what you don't like about him," Gabe prodded as Vinny moved his hand again to rub her shoulders.

Screwing her face up in concentration, she said with a half-hearted shrug, "He just doesn't listen." Looking around, she realized that for the first time, she did not hate talking about herself. This seemed like she was talking to friends…not the press judging her every word.

"I know I'm an introvert. I'm shy. That doesn't mean there's something wrong with me that needs to be fixed. I'm not some poor little girl that needs someone to lead me around. It's just very hard for me to stick up for myself when someone is determined to overrun me. Todd has a job and he's determined to do it. What I want doesn't matter to him."

They had been joined by Lily and BJ, who were busily typing in searches as she talked. The others were jotting down notes, but Vinny just kept his hand on her shoulder, listening as he took in what she said. Smiling up at him, she looked at the next name on the list.

"Okay, Gordon Fisher is my agent. He does the actual booking of the concerts. He works with Todd, but he's actually the one who makes the arrangements with various symphonies or shows. He makes the arrangements as to which cities I will play in and then has his staff make the arrangements."

"So Gordon is the one who actually decides if you will play in LA or New York or wherever?"

"Yes," she said slowly, understanding the implication. "But that doesn't make sense. He represents other musicians and bands. Believe me, if he wanted to move drugs, he'd have lots of better opportunities than me. I don't travel much and certainly don't tour. I'm located here with the Richland Symphony and just travel as a feature musician for certain venues.

"Next is Sharon Turner and Parker Williams, my makeup artist and stylist." Stifling a giggle, she said, "Parker is my one true friend on the trips. He's funny and nice. He actually listens and keeps Sharon in check."

"How so?"

"She wants to do makeup for movie sets and I know she wishes that I would travel more. She used to apply the makeup with a heavy hand, making me feel like a drag queen, but Parker is the main stylist, so he pulls her back. She's fun to talk to and understands that I don't like crowds. She and Gordon seem to get along really well, but I don't know about Todd. I think he irritates her too."

"And Parker?" Gabe prodded again.

"He knows how I want to look and he works with that. He listens to what I like to wear and the colors that I like. Sometimes I think that if he wasn't on a trip with me, I'd lose my mind. I definitely know it's not him because he really likes me."

"You can't make that assumption, babe," Vinny warned, only to be greeted with a frustrated look from her.

"I can't just suspect everyone I work with. That's not right!" she huffed, crossing her arms in front of her.

Wanting to keep Vinny from bearing her wrath,

Tony jumped in. "Annalissa, right now, you can't trust anyone you know. Anyone could have had motives that you don't know about."

She held his gaze a moment before leaning over the table, resting her head in her hands.

Sherrie brought a bottle of cold water over to her and wrapped her arm around her shoulders. "I know this is hard, honey."

Annalissa looked up gratefully, giving a small smile. Looking down at the files again, she recognized others from the stage set up. "These people don't travel with me. They're hired by the concert halls for each city's symphonic orchestras. They would have no idea of who I am or where I go. Someone would be responsible for bringing my harp to me after the concert is over. I don't carry it with me. After the final bow, I exit the stage and Easnadh is left there on her stand. Once the curtain goes down, the person in charge would make sure she was cased and brought to my room."

"Could someone slip in unnoticed in all the confusion of a full orchestra and stage hands moving about?"

Scrunching her face in thought, she answered, "I suppose. They all have name badges that they wear around their necks, but...I guess anyone can make up a badge."

The others grinned at her innocence, knowing that each of them had used fake badges, licenses, and identifications on multiple occasions. Tony turned to

Lily, saying, "Check the stage crews for the last year of concerts for Annalissa and see if there are any crossovers."

Turning back to the file in front of her, she flipped the page and stared at a picture of her father. Looking up sharply, she asked, "Why is this here?"

Tony, his gaze steady on hers, said, "We have to look at everyone."

She sat still, no longer feeling Vinny's touch even though he was still caressing her shoulder. *My father. He's no drug dealer…just…* Suddenly feeling very vulnerable, she stood up saying, "I'm sorry. I've given you all I can today."

Vinny jumped up with her, pulling her in for a hug. "Babe, you did really good. Let me take you home."

She leaned back, her eyes flashing. "Home? What home, Vinny? My home has been broken into and trashed. Right now I don't even have a home."

He looked down at the dark circles under her eyes and the trembling of her chin telling him she was holding on by a thread. *I should never have let this go so far.* Calmly he said, "I know and I'm sorry. Let me take you back to my place so you can rest or practice if you would like."

Jennifer moved over, knowing that the group would want to continue to work and process all that Annalissa had told them, saying gently, "Hey, why don't you, me, and Sherrie go out for a little while for some girl time."

Annalissa looked over at the faces of the two women she was fast considering as friends. "I think I'd like that," she admitted.

Vinny leaned down and kissed her...on the lips...a simple kiss but one that spoke volumes to those who knew him. He had claimed her. The big man had fallen. As the three women left the room, the others sat in silence.

The twins shared a look and Gabe gave a nod of approval as a grin spread across his face. The others sat back down, smiles on their faces as well. Lily beamed at Vinny, saying, "I knew it would hit you one day and I kept saying that I wanted to be around when it did. Who knew that you'd fall for such a quiet, talented sweetheart?"

Vinny, actually blushing, agreed saying, "Yeah, I guess my behavior before meeting Annalissa wasn't so good." Shaking his head, he continued, "When I was getting to know her as we were running through the woods and hiding out in trees—well, let's just say that I was falling for her but didn't think there was any way in the world I deserved someone like her."

"Oh yes you do," Lily effused. "You just needed to find the right one." She looked around the table at the men she worked with and cared for, her eyes stopping on Jobe. "Now, we just need to find someone for you."

Jobe smiled, but she noticed it did not reach his eyes. Shaking his head, he said, "Nah. Had it once but threw it away. Don't think that'll come again."

"You don't know that," Lily said. "Look at BJ here. He found his love four years after they'd broken up. If it happened to him, it could happen to you." She caught the looks between the former brothers-in-arms, recognizing a story. One that she did not know. And one that would only be shared when Jobe was ready.

The group went back to studying the files as Vinny filled them in on Annalissa's father, remembering what all she had told him on their trip.

"This just doesn't make any sense," Gabe groused. "She doesn't travel that much and so she can't be someone's main source of smuggling."

"I'm sure that someone she knows is using her," Vinny bit out, as they sifted through the suspects. "But which one?"

"Don't know yet, but we'll just keep working the problem," Tony replied. "Jack's DEA contact said that there were no fingerprints on the bags of drugs, the case, or the harp."

"I think it's been done before and would have worked this time if we hadn't had to miss our flight," Vinny said. "So you're right. We keep looking and in the meantime, I intend to keep her watched."

Tony grinned. "Already got a rotation set up to be with her."

Nodding, Vinny settled back. *Now to convince Annalissa to stay with him. Not only for her safety...but for as long as she would have him.*

CHAPTER 14

THE NEXT DAY, Annalissa caught a cab to her teacher's studio after Vinny left for work. Walking up the steps of the old brownstone with her harp case in her hand, she knocked on the door. As it opened, she saw the look of surprise on his face. As he threw his arms out wide, she rushed into them, feeling the comfort he offered.

"Oh, my dear, what a time you've had. Come in, come in and tell me all about it."

She picked up her case and followed him down the hall to his studio in the back.

"Mrs. Baxter, some tea for us, if you please," he called out to his housekeeper. By the time they had settled into chairs, she was already bustling in with a tray of steaming tea and a platter of cookies.

Placing it on the table in front of them, she hurried over to give Annalissa a hug. Pulling her into her bosomy embrace, she effused, "Oh dearie, you gave poor Mr. Feinstein such a fright." Making herself right at home with her employer, she settled her girth on the settee and poured the tea.

Annalissa had to laugh; Mr. Feinstein and his

housekeeper had been together for so long they seemed more like an old married couple, even though they had never been interested in each other that way.

The next hour passed with her regaling them with tales of her trip. She told in great detail the plight of the man having the heart attack and how Vinny saved him. She followed that with the harrowing landing in Kansas City and once again how Vinny took charge. "I just couldn't fly again so soon," she lied, feeling horrible at the necessity of keeping the truth hidden. "So Vinny suggested that we book Easnadh on the next flight and we drove instead."

"But why not just keep Easnadh with you?" Maurice asked, his brow furrowed.

Remembering her practiced explanation, she said, "It would be too crowded in our little rental car. And it was much safer for us to ship it and have one of the Alvarez Security men pick it up at the Richland Airport."

"So it came directly to Richland and not through Dulles?" he asked.

"Yes, we could get a direct flight from Kansas City to Richland for it."

He nodded thoughtfully, while Mrs. Baxter's head bobbed enthusiastically.

"It sounds like you not only had an adventure, but perhaps had some fun as well?" she said, desperately wanting more gossip.

"Yes," Annalissa grinned. "I did have fun since I

never get to travel by land and Mr. Malloy was perfect company."

As they finished their tea, Mrs. Baxter hustled the dishes away after giving Annalissa a kiss and another hug.

Annalissa opened her case and removed her harp. "I thought instead of just practicing at home to relax, I'd come over and practice with you."

Smiling, the older man nodded as he moved to his instruments in the corner of the studio. Choosing another Celtic harp, they sat and played companionably for another hour. The music filled the room, allowing her to finally and completely relax. With a few of his windows opened, the tones drifted outside.

Jobe sat in his SUV, the windows down, listening to the music. He had already called in her location to Vinny since it was his time to follow her. *Not a hard duty*, he thought as he allowed the music to settle over him. *I can see what she has done to Vinny. Her music is bewitching. And for a man like him…*he smiled thinking of his friend. Leaning his head back, he maintained his vigilance while his mind rolled to what Lily had said earlier.

They've all found it…the forever kind of love. His friends Shane and Annie, Lily and Matt, BJ and Suzanne. And now his brothers-in-arms, Gabe and Jennifer, Tony and Sherrie, and now Vinny. The last of the professed bachelors was fully, completely in love with Annalissa.

Sucking in a huge sigh as the haunting melody

floated out to him. *I had it. And I goddamn threw it away. Thought I was being noble. God, what a prick.* Giving himself a shake, he forced his mind back to the case and off of the past.

As Annalissa came out of Maurice's house, she was walking down the steps when suddenly Jobe loomed before her. Taking the harp case from her hands, he nodded toward his vehicle.

"Did Vinny send you to spy on me?"

"No ma'am," he replied with a wink. "You have the protection of Alvarez Security. One of us will be with you when you aren't with Vinny."

"Oh," she said, a concerned look on her face. "I don't mean to be a problem," she admitted.

He placed her harp in the back of the SUV before rounding to her side to open the door. "No problem. It wouldn't matter if we were working on your case or not. You're one of us now. We protect our own," he said simply.

As she settled in for the ride back to Vinny's, she smiled. Belonging. Friends. *Just what I've been looking for.*

THAT EVENING, SHE slipped easily into the pool, holding on to Vinny's hands as he led her around, and kicked her legs.

"Feel how the movement of your legs propels you

along?" he asked, trying to keep his eyes off of her ass as it wiggled just above the waterline.

"Yes, but that's only my bottom half. What am I supposed to do with my arms?"

"You don't want to keep holding my hands?" he joked.

"I'd love to but I don't think that will help me swim on my own," she sputtered trying to keep her head above the water.

Moving back to the shallow end, he let go as she stood on the bottom of the pool. "Okay, let's work on the arm movement." He spent the next fifteen minutes teaching her how to circle her arms in a paddling motion. After she was comfortable with that, he supported her with his hands on her tummy as she kicked while moving her arms.

"You promise not to let go?" she asked as they moved toward deeper water.

"I promise, baby. I'll never let you go."

Once again, she wondered if there was a double meaning in his words. After several minutes of working to get the rhythm correct, he pulled her in close to his body. She wrapped her legs around his waist and her arms around his neck, luxuriating in the feel of floating in the water holding on to him.

With her breasts pressed tightly to his chest and her core firmly nestled against his throbbing cock, he kissed her as they continued to move through the water. Her back finally landed against the side of the pool and he pressed even closer. The kiss became desperate. Needy. Just like his desire for her.

"Princess," he growled. "We've gotta get upstairs. I fuckin' want to take you here and now, but I'm not about to chance someone coming in."

Panting into his mouth, she nodded. "I need you now," she cried.

With an easy lift, he set her on the side of the pool and pulled himself out effortlessly. Reaching down, he plucked her up, carrying her in his arms. Bending as they rounded the side, he grabbed their towels as he carried her to the elevator. Once inside, he continued the kiss that had been interrupted in the pool. As the elevator doors opened, he set her down and grabbed her hand as they quickly walked to his apartment.

Another man came out of a door, his eyes noticeably appreciating the view. Vinny looked down, seeing Annalissa's nipples clearly poking through the worn bathing suit material. Throwing a towel around her chilled body, he growled at the neighbor who quickly paled at the sight of the large, muscular, and obviously pissed-off man.

Giggling, she felt herself gently pushed inside his apartment as Vinny kicked the door closed behind them.

"I can't believe I let you walk around in that bathing suit on our way up here," he exploded. "I must be crazy."

"Vinny, really?" she asked, tapping her foot on the

floor. "Are you telling me that you've never been at a pool party or beach with other women in skimpy bikinis?"

He stopped and looked at her, his eyes still flashing irritation.

"Well?" she prodded. "You've never ogled a woman in a bathing suit? You've never been with another woman at a pool who was wearing a lot less than this old one-piece?"

"That's different," he spluttered.

"How, for crying out loud? Please tell me how you and your friends hanging around a pool trying to pick up girls in skimpy bikinis is any different than that man catching a glimpse of me in this outfit? Which, by the way, covers most of me?"

He stood there, perplexed as to how to answer her. She was right. He had spent a lot of time hooking up with skimpily clad women and not caring what his own dates were wearing. If his friends got a glimpse of the tits or ass of a hookup of his, he never cared.

Running his hand through his dark blond hair, making it stand up on end, he looked down at the beauty in front of him. *But this was different. He had wanted to gouge his neighbor's eyes out.* Sighing, he knew he could not lie to her.

"Because I never cared about anyone before you. Because I've fallen in love with you. And because the thought of anyone else seeing a part of you that's only for me, makes me crazy," he confessed nervously.

"You…you love me?" she whispered, forgetting to breath.

"Yeah, but I know a man like me doesn't deserve someone like you," he said, his eyes gazing deeply into hers. *Give me a chance, baby. Please.* He watched her own eyes tear up. Stepping closer, he reached his hand out to touch her cheek. "Breathe, baby," he reminded.

She gasped as she leaned her face into his hand. The warmth of his touch melted into her.

"Tell me I've got a chance. I know I've live wild and rough, but please tell me that you might feel something for me too."

Her smile lit up his world. Dark, wet hair tangled behind her, still dripping water off of the ends. An old, faded, red bathing suit designed for practicality instead of sex appeal. No makeup. *And the most fuckin' beautiful woman I've ever laid eyes on.*

"I think I fell in love with you somewhere between Indiana and Kentucky," she said, still smiling.

Struck speechless, Vinny stared at the woman who had stolen his heart. And was handing it back to him along with hers.

Suddenly, the two reached for each other, hands grasping as they quickly pulled off their swimming attire. He scooped her up in his arms, her naked body inflaming his, as his aching cock swelled.

Making it to the bedroom in record time, he lay her on the bed reverently. *She loves me.* Determined to worship her body slowly, he lay next to her as his lips sealed over hers. Moving his hand down, he felt every curve, from her breasts that just filled his hands to her flat stomach all the way to the gentle swell of her hips.

She turned on her side to face him and his hand slipped between her legs. Tangling in the strip of curls, he moved through them to her drenched folds. Sliding two fingers in, he reached a place and a rhythm that had her writhing on the bed.

His tongue danced with hers as he captured her moans. His dick was painfully pressing against her stomach, eagerly seeking entrance. *Down boy. This one's for her.*

Her body felt as tight as a bow ready to snap but could not quite reach the breaking point. He sucked her tongue into his mouth and the sensations zinged from her throat to her nipples down to her aching core.

He reached the spot that finally threw her over the edge, the explosion causing her inner walls to contract and weep over his fingers. Eyes closed tight, she saw colored lights sparkling behind her eyelids as she floated gently back toward earth.

He kissed his way down her body paying special attention to each breast as he sucked one nipple deeply into his mouth before moving over and nipping the other. Continuing his downward path, he slid between her legs, lowering his mouth to replace his fingers. Her juices were like nectar as he feasted on her drenched folds before plunging his tongue into her sex.

Absolutely fuckin' nectar. He loved her innocence.

No pretense. No faking. Every movement, every sound from her was real. True. Heartfelt.

Moving from between her legs, he kissed his way back up her body, displayed for him. For his eyes alone. He closed his eyes for a moment in silent reverie, thanking God that he was lucky enough to have found her. When he opened them again, her green eyes were gazing intently into his.

"Are you all right?" she asked, gently reaching up to caress his cheek. His strong jaw filled her hand as her eyes moved over his muscular chest and thick arms, with the Malloy Celtic tattoo on them. Her gaze lifted back to his, pleased to see him now smiling.

"Yeah. I'm great." He hesitated a moment and then plunged ahead with something that had been on his mind. "Can I ask you something?"

"Anything," she replied.

"Would you consider getting on the pill? I'm clean and I swear I've never, ever gone without a condom." Seeing a look cross her face, he continued, "Honest, babe. Never without a condom. But we had to have physicals all the time in the military and for Tony as well. I've got the paperwork."

Her pink tongue darted out, licking her lips. "I've thought about it but just never did anything. I...I can go to see my doctor."

"If it's not what you want, then you don't have to do it. I'll keep a sheath on," he assured her.

"No. No, I don't mind," she admitted shyly.

"I...I'd like to see what you...um...feel like."

Bearing his weight on his arms, he leaned down to kiss her again. "Good, 'cause I want to feel your walls squeezing me without any barriers and baby, I've got to tell you, I can't wait to fill you."

Moving away just long enough to roll on a condom, he moved over her again placing his eager cock at her entrance. Looking down into her eyes, he felt her grasp his shoulders before he plunged inside.

Her body welcomed his as she felt the tight stretching when he filled her. Her hand slid from his shoulders to his back, feeling the muscles ripple and move underneath her fingertips. *Such power,* she thought. *All this and he could have anyone. But he wants me. He loves me.* The warm friction was building inside as he rocked in and out, still bearing his weight on his forearms. Her head was supported by his hands on either side, as their gazes never wavered.

She watched him and all the emotions that played across his face as their bodies were joined as one.

Looking down at her, he felt a myriad of feelings. Love, certainly. But also protectiveness. Pride. Awe. And the desire to feel all of these forever. Right before his body's needs took over all rational thought, he was left with the realization—*I want this woman in my bed and in my heart for the rest of my life.*

Powering through his own orgasm he felt her body contract around him, squeezing as he poured himself into her. Refusing to take his eyes off of her, his thick neck strained as he gritted his teeth, the orgasm sending shocks down to his toes.

Underneath all of his strength and power, she flew apart again, her core clutching at him. Feeling him release deep inside, she knew this was a connection she wanted to experience forever.

Their eyes finally closed, he lay his head down on the pillow next to hers, their ragged breaths heaving from their bodies. Legs tangled, arms wrapped tightly, hearts beating as one.

He loves me, she thought with a smile.

She loves me, he realized, knowing he would protect her with his life.

JAWAN WONDERED IF THINGS could possibly get more fucked up. His contact had just called to say that the harp had never passed through Dulles and the handler had gotten nervous. Not only that, but instead of searching carefully, he had trashed the harpist's apartment and now was on the police's radar. Sighing heavily, he placed another call.

"I need a hit," he bit out.

"You got it," came the response.

Jawan felt his blood pressure slowly drop as he received the answer he desired. Tired of bumbling fools making a mess of things, it was satisfying to have someone he could count on to take care of things. And this would surely make Don happier with him.

Giving the name of the handler and his address, he disconnected.

Now, placing another call, he reported to Don. "We're making progress. It never went to Dulles and we're eliminating that problem. It will be easier to train and place new employees there than to leave him as a threat."

Not hearing Don reply he continued, "We know where the drugs are. They've got to still be with the harp."

"And why hasn't it been confiscated? How difficult is it to get it from the carrier?"

Jawan recognized Don's icy tone. Licking his lips, he plunged ahead, "She's not living alone. It appears that she is living with her security escort from Alvarez Security."

"So the drugs have been discovered? Is that why they're still involved? Are the goddamn police and DEA involved as well since it appears the whole fucking world is?"

"No, no," Jawan hurried to explain. "It seems like no one has discovered what is inside the harp yet. She's just living with him. I guess they started fucking on the trip and are still involved. But don't worry. She'll be on her own soon. He's got a reputation for not sticking with one woman, so he'll soon tire of her."

Silence once again greeted him.

"Don, I've got this. She can't keep the harp secluded forever. It'll come out and when it does, we make our plans. I'll get the drugs back. That's a promise."

"You'd better. Cousin or no…I don't accept failure."

Sighing after Don hung up on him, he called his contact. "Are you keeping tabs on her? I want to know where she is and who she's with. And we need that fucking harp."

"Look, all my other runs for you have been successful—even the ones with lil' miss princess. I've got this. I'm keeping an eye on her and as soon as I can, I'll get the stuff back for you. I can still make it to the buyer on this end."

"I'm sending someone to take care of the baggage handler. No problem to me if he does another job for me. You get what I'm saying?"

Licking their lips nervously, they bobbed their head as they rushed to agree.

CHAPTER 15

SEVERAL DAYS LATER VINNY dropped Annalissa off at Maurice's home for practice. Kissing her goodbye, he checked to see when her lesson would be over with. "I'm having Terrance pick you up when you're done, babe."

"I'll be here for several hours. Should I call when I'm finished?"

After he agreed she went inside, greeting her teacher. Moving to the back room, they began to practice for an upcoming concert with a visiting symphony. The first hour went by quickly until they were interrupted by a visitor.

Mrs. Baxter walked into the studio with Todd right on her heels. Annalissa's heart sank. She had hoped to continue to avoid seeing him for a little while longer.

"Maurice. Annalissa," he greeted.

"Todd," she said listlessly, lifting her face as he came over to air-kiss her cheek.

"What are you two working on?" he asked greedily.

Maurice motioned for Todd to have a seat as he answered. "The pieces are for the small contingency from the New York Philharmonic that you've scheduled for next month."

"Perfect," Todd exclaimed. "Look Annalissa, I know you've had reservations, but now's the time to strike while the iron is hot." Pulling out his Ipad, he quickly found what he was looking for and turned it around. "Look at the press from the concert you just did in LA. They loved you."

Before giving her a chance to read it, he turned it back to himself and read it aloud. "The director claimed that you were the most talented harpist he has ever worked with. Let's see, yadda, yadda, yadda. Oh, here it is. 'The lovely Annalissa O'Brian wowed the crowd at the symphonic concert last night. Her musical interpretation is brilliant, making her possibly the country's most notable Celtic harpist. Considering her youth, she can expect to have a long and distinguished career ahead of her and here's one reporter that will be looking forward to having her grace our fine city once again.'"

She was pleased that her performance was well received, but knew that Todd was not finished.

Pulling out a sheaf of papers, he said, "Here's what I've been working on. The contingency from New York is just a preliminary contact that we have with them. This concert will build our reputation and they have already agreed to have you play with them in six months in New York. Before then, there is an excellent opportunity for you with the Phoenix orchestra and I can pair that with a trip to Chicago and then Minneapolis." Shuffling through the papers in his file, he showed her more concerts that he was proposing. "I've worked closely with Gordon to make sure he can book these."

"Todd, that has me traveling for a week every month for the next year. You know I don't want to travel that much," she protested.

"I've talked to your father and he agrees—"

"No!" she said vehemently, coming to a stand. "I don't want to travel that much."

"Look, this is what can make your career. I'm working on a CD deal, but you need to make sure you have a name for yourself and a following. That's what these concerts will do for you."

Her eyes swung over to Maurice, looking for support. He sat quietly, staring down as he rubbed his hands together. Sighing deeply, he lifted his gaze to hers.

"I know you want to teach, Malyshka," he said, using his native Russian's endearment. "But it is hard to make a living at this unless you have something to go along with it." Leaning forward, he reached over to take her hand. "If you want to ever be free of your father's dominance, then having this career will do it."

Her unwavering gaze held his as she plopped back down in her chair.

"Travel some for a few years and then…when you have a bigger name and a bigger following, then you can slow down and teach more."

Todd eyed the couple in front of him greedily. He knew she would listen to the old man. She always did.

Her thoughts, a whirlpool of emotions, filled her mind threatening to overwhelm her. *It all seems so easy to them. Travel, live out of a suitcase, be surrounded by people who pull me in different directions all of the time. Practice nonstop until my fingers can't move. And I hate flying...unless Vinny is with me. Vinny. They don't know about him. And me. And us.* Her eyes closed, trying to block out the voices in her head.

"My dear, you're tired. Why don't we call our lesson for today over and you go back home to rest. Think of what I've said." Maurice leaned in closer, saying, "And think of your father. Yes, traveling will make him happy since this is what he wants for you, but it will give you freedom. Away from him. And then financial freedom so that you can have your own life, apart from his."

Maurice knows me so well. Tempted to sign the forms from Todd immediately, she hesitated. *But I want to know what Vinny thinks. Or am I just exchanging several men's opinion of how I should live my life for another's?*

Standing up again quickly, she packed up Easnadh. Turning to face Todd and Maurice, she forced a smile and said, "I appreciate all you do for me. I really do. I'm going to think about these Todd and will let you know." Reaching her hand out, she took the file of possible bookings from him and slid them into her music bag. Bending to kiss Maurice, she whispered, "I'll be back after I practice those difficult passages."

He patted her back, giving her a kiss on the cheek. Todd moved in for another air kiss and she followed Mrs. Baxter to the front door.

Once on the sidewalk, she realized she had not called Vinny, but desperately wanted to be alone for a little while. *I'd love a walk* but…she looked ruefully down at Easnadh's case in her arms. Lifting her hand, she hailed a cab. Giving the address of her apartment, she sent Vinny a text letting him know where she was. Settling back in the seat, she decided that it was time to take charge of her life again. And the first thing on her list? Take a look at her home.

THE CAB DRIVER let her off at the entrance to her building. The old, red-brick apartment building was located in a decent part of town—not expensive by any means, but not in a scary location. The apartments were mostly filled with university graduate students. They did not seem to mind her practicing and she ignored their occasional parties.

Lugging Easnadh up the front stoop, she entered the building and made her way down the first-floor hall. Her apartment was located in the back of the building, her windows overlooking a small courtyard. Letting herself in, she stopped dead as the doorway swung open.

Oh my God, Vinny wasn't kidding. Her apartment looked like something from a movie. The cushions were off of her old brown sofa and the shelves were empty of her books and CDs. They too had been strewn onto the floor. Her chair and music stand next to the window were the only things still in place in the entire small room. Stepping carefully, she set her case down and walked the few steps to her kitchenette. The cabinets were empty of their contents and even the refrigerator had been searched.

Her heart sank as she looked at the destruction. Moving around the breakfast bar, she stepped into the small hall that led to the bedroom and bathroom. Seeing the bathroom first, she could see where her medicine and sink cabinets had been emptied. Even her towels were tossed on the floor. The bedroom was last.

Stopping at the door, she gasped. Her drawers were pulled out of her old dresser, the contents strewn about as well. Her underwear. Her nightgowns. Her personal items. Tears stung her eyes as the thought of someone rifling through her belongings. The bed had been stripped and the mattress slashed along with the pillows.

Her hand covered her mouth as she stifled a scream of rage. Her body shaking, she peeked into the tiny closet, seeing her clothes all on the floor and the plastic boxes that had been on the upper shelf tossed as well. *Who would do this to me? I'm nobody. Other than a drug carrier. Oh Jesus.*

Finally the reality of what everyone had been telling her sunk in. Someone used her. Used her as a carrier for drugs. And they wanted them back.

Tears ran unchecked down her face as she slunk to the floor, next to the closet. Her knees bent, she wrapped her arms around them and rocked herself as the sobs took over.

VINNY AND JOBE walked down the hall of Alvarez Security, ready to leave for the evening. Doug, a new employee who was on the security detail, stuck his head out of the surveillance room.

"Vinny. Thought you'd picked up Ms. O'Brian. She left the music teacher's location about an hour ago."

"Where the hell is she?" Vinny growled.

"Her GPS has her at her apartment building. I thought you'd taken her there."

"Shit," Vinny bit out, turning to run toward the garage.

Jobe, on his heels, called out, "I'm driving."

The two of them raced down the road, Vinny calling her cell phone continuously. No answer. He saw her text on his phone, growling that he had not heard it.

"Why the hell would she go there?" he agonized.

"Anyone could have gone back to look again."

"Vinny, this is our world. Not hers. I don't think it's sunk in yet."

Pulling up to the building, Vinny was out of the vehicle before Jobe could park. He pounded up the stoop and through the door. Racing down the hall, he felt Jobe's presence behind him. Her front door stood open, her harp case sitting just inside. His eyes swept the area, seeing no change from when he looked at it when they had arrived back in town.

Pulling out his gun, they moved carefully toward the bedroom. Nodding to each other, Vinny moved in first, seeing no one. Hearing a slight sound coming from the closet, he cautiously stalked forward. The sight nearly took him to his knees.

Annalissa was crouched in the closet, tear-filled green eyes large with fright and her hand clamped over her mouth.

"Vinny," she cried as she jumped up, hurling herself at him. He caught her in mid-air, feeling her arms clamp around his neck and legs encircle his waist. Jobe slid up next to him, taking and securing his weapon so that he could grasp her with both hands.

Moving backward, he sat on the bed with her still wrapped tightly around his body. "Baby, are you all right?" Not hearing anything other than her crying, he pulled her back slightly so he could peer into her eyes. "Are you all right?"

She nodded and tucked her head right back into his

neck once again. Jobe nodded at him and discretely left the room to report in to Tony.

"Why are you here? Why didn't you wait for Terrance?"

With her tears spent, she murmured, "I needed to get out. I…needed to see my place. Now it seems…not mine."

Jobe walked back into the room, his eyes seeking Vinny's for reassurance that she was fine. As usual their non-verbal communication was all it took for Jobe to nod and leave the room again.

"Princess, we can put this place back together again. The guys and their women will all meet and we can have this place put to right in one quick day. But I know that Matt and Shane wanted to know if anything had been taken. I never meant for you to come here without me. Jobe's called them and they'll be here soon. Can you do that for them?"

Nodding against his neck, he heard her sigh deeply.

"Yeah, I can do that." A moment passed before she leaned up saying, "I hate feeling this way, but can I stay with you a few more days until this place can be cleaned up? And I want to get new locks on the doors and windows."

His eyes held hers as his hands came up to cup her face. "Babe, as far as I'm concerned you never have to live anywhere else but with me. But I don't want to rush you. You want to stay here, we'll fix it up and Tony's men will get it secure."

Sucking in a deep breath, she glanced around at the trashed bedroom. "I don't know. I...just don't..."

"Don't make a decision now when you're emotional."

Jobe stuck his head back into the room. "Matt and Shane are here. Gabe's here too."

Allowing Vinny to assist her to a stand, she wiped her face with her hands and smoothed her hair back from her face. Lifting her chin, she said, "Okay. I'm ready."

Fuckin' adorable. And fuckin' strong, he thought.

BY THE TIME MATT AND SHANE had taken her accounting, she was exhausted. They had her go through each item and room, cataloging what should have been where and what looked missing. Nothing was missing. Not one thing. Just everything tossed around in a hasty manner.

Gabe and Vinny stood to the side with Jobe, as she moved about with the detectives. Vinny kept his eyes on her the entire time, watching for signs of a breaking point. But the more she looked over her items, the angrier she became.

When they left, she turned to face the men still in the room. Seeing her shaking, Vinny stalked toward her, enveloping her in his arms.

"I'm so angry right now," she said, her voice muffled in his chest.

He lifted his eyebrow in surprise, having never heard her curse before. "I know. Let's get some of your things and get out of here."

While Gabe and Jobe got trash bags from the kitchen, she began moving about the room picking up things that she wanted to take. Collecting her sheet music, she was startled by a voice at the still open door.

"Lissa? What the hell happened here?"

Turning she saw her neighbor and fellow musician standing there with grocery bags in his hands and a surprised look on his face. She approached him only to be stopped by a growl at her back.

"Who the hell are you?" came Vinny's bark.

Turning to glare at him, she said, "He's my neighbor, Vinny." Turning back, she smiled and apologized. "I'm sorry, Les. I was gone and my place was broken into. We're here to get some things for me to take."

Les started to step into the room, but was stopped when a wall of large men created a barrier. Annalissa looked up to see Vinny, Gabe, and Jobe shoulder-to-wide-shoulder blocking the entrance. Her eyes wide in irritation toward them, she made the introductions.

Receiving reassurances that she was fine, Les headed off to his apartment after inviting her to play with his band that weekend.

Closing the door behind him, she turned to face the wall. Of men. All glaring. Putting her hands on her hips, she said, "What? What is wrong with you all?"

"Did he know where you were going to your last concert?" Vinny growled again.

"Yes. Several of my friends know when I'm out of town." She looked confused momentarily, then her eyes widened in understanding. "Oh, my God. You think he's a suspect? Well you're wrong. I know other musicians that I play with and there's no way they would have been involved. No way."

"We need their names," Jobe said softly.

"Oh no," she began to protest, putting her hand up.

Vinny, losing patience, said, "Don't you get it, babe? Anyone who knows you could be a suspect. You don't think some other musician could have done this?" he said, sweeping his arm out across the trashed room.

Standing, lips pursed, chin quivering, she refused to cry again. Lifting her chin, she looked over at Jobe. "I'll make a list of my friends who knew I was traveling. It won't be a long list. I don't have many friends and it seems that you all are determined to take even them away from me."

Vinny watched as she moved from the living area back to the bedroom and he stood, rubbing his hand over his face. Sighing, he looked up at his twin and friend. "How the hell do you do this?" he asked Gabe.

"What?" Gabe asked back, a grin on his face. "Fall in love or keep the love or keep the woman you love happy?"

Jobe chuckled, nodding in understanding. "She'll

be fine, you know. She's tougher than she looks."

Gabe slapped his twin on the back, saying, "Bro, you've never spent more than a few hours with some chick. Falling in love and creating a relationship takes time and energy. And yeah, there're fights and misunderstandings."

"So what do you do?" Vinny asked.

"Just take care of her, man," Jobe said. "And never…never let her go. Even if for some fucked up reason that seems like the best thing to do."

"Let's go," Gabe said to Jobe, deciding to leave Vinny with Annalissa. "She can give the list of friends to you and we'll have Lily and BJ run them tomorrow."

As the two walked toward the door, Gabe turned with a smile. "Oh and Vinny? The makeup sex is phenomenal."

"I can hear you all, you know!" Annalissa shouted from the bedroom.

Laughing the two men left the apartment, leaving Vinny to decide if he should stay put or wander in to face her wrath.

CHAPTER 16

ARRIVING BACK AT VINNY'S apartment, they began the task of moving her things to his place. Grabbing a cart from the concierge's closet, Vinny and Annalissa loaded it with the bags of clothes, a few books, all of her music, her violin and Easnadh, as well as her laptop. Another suitcase filled with clothes and toiletries completed the pile.

"This looks like I'm moving in," she said softly, eyes avoiding his.

"Look at me. Please, baby," he added. Seeing her gaze move up to his, he continued. "I told you the truth earlier. I'd love for you to move in permanently, but know that your world has been turned upside down." Stepping closer, he towered over her, lifting her chin to keep her eyes on his. "I'm sorry, babe."

Nodding, she said, "I'm sorry too. I shouldn't have taken my frustration out on you and the others."

"It's okay. Let's get your stuff upstairs and then eat. After that we can talk more about who we need to check out."

They made an easy dinner of enchiladas with leftover rotisserie chicken, sautéed peppers and onions and tortillas. Afterward he walked into the bedroom, seeing her hanging up her clothes. He stood in the doorway for a moment watching her in the closet, trying to keep her things to a small corner of his large closet. He waited for the moment of panic or unease. Nothing. *Never even brought a woman to this apartment. Never wanted someone knowing where he lived and showing up unannounced. Never wanted a woman to leave any of her shit around. This was his space. His retreat.* Smiling, he continued to watch as she bent over to the bag, pulling out an article of clothing and then hanging it in the corner.

Never wanted any of this…until now. Seeing her things hanging next to his felt right. Good. Normal.

Walking up behind her, he reached around her body and scooted her hangers out over more of the bar. "Babe, I don't need this much space for my shit. You're here now, so take as much room as you need."

She turned, his arms still around her, and looked up. Words left her so she stood on her tiptoes and kissed him instead. His arms left the clothes bar and slid to her back, pulling her in tightly. Allowing her to take the kiss where she wanted it to go, he gave her control.

She felt his gift, understanding what it meant for a man like him to give her the power. But she was not interested in just a kiss of thanks. Or a kiss of now. She wanted to give him the kiss of forever.

She opened, welcoming his tongue. Sucking on it,

she pulled it deeper into her mouth. This time she captured his moan. Her tongue tangling with his sent sparks through her body as her breasts were crushed against his chest. Moving her hips, she pressed her pelvis closer to him as she rubbed her core against his jean-clad leg.

That was all the invitation it took before he assumed control. Grasping the bottom of her shirt, he pulled it over her head, their lips parting only for the passing of the material between them. Her lacy bra pushed up her breasts like a feast for his eyes...and mouth. Dropping his lips from hers, he trailed a path down to the tops of her tits with his tongue. He grabbed the material with his teeth and jerked it down, exposing her rosy tipped nipples already hard for him. Sucking deeply on one, he rolled the other between his forefinger and thumb. Moving between her breasts he teased each one, nipping then soothing, sucking deeply until she pressed harder against his leg.

Her hands moved between them finding his jean button. Unfastening it as quickly as she could, she maneuvered the zipper over his massive erection. Palming him with one hand, she pushed his jeans down with the other.

His hands left her breasts and quickly divested her of her pants and panties as well. Soon they were both naked, hands caressing as they explored each other's bodies. Her lips traced the tattoo on his chest before pulling his own nipple into her mouth. Hearing his sharp intake of breath, she smiled knowing she retained some control.

Suddenly, she found herself hoisted up in his powerful arms as he stalked to the bed. As he set her down, his gravelly voice commanded, "On your knees, babe." Up to now, sex had been phenomenal, but missionary. Hoping to take it to a slightly more creative level, he moved behind her pulling her ass up as high as it would go. Leaning down, he licked her folds as his hands reached around, pulling on her nipples.

The electric charge sent shockwaves throughout her body as she writhed in need. "Hold still. No moving." Following his command he gave her ass a small spank, barely leaving a pink mark.

She gasped, the slight sting quickly replaced by a warmth that had her longing for more. His tongue continued to lap her juices, reveling in the taste of her, but for every movement she earned another spank.

Holding perfectly still, she panted as her orgasm neared. The sensations of his tongue probing her sex as his fingers pinched and rolled her nipples threatened to send her into oblivion. But at the moment, that was the only place she wanted to be transported. *Sweet oblivion. With him.*

Replacing his tongue with his fingers, he reached deep inside to tweak the place he had learned was the exact spot that really triggered her release. Not to be disappointed, she threw her head back just as he moved his other hand back to press his fingers against her rose button entrance.

Screaming his name, her orgasm rocked through her, hurling her farther and longer than she could have ever imagined. She had read about ass play, but never considered herself one to enjoy that. *Just that tiny taste and I want another orgasm like that again.*

Watching her come so hard and fast, he almost came himself before even entering her. Quickly sheathing himself, he plunged into her entrance from behind, feeling her walls stretching to accommodate his girth.

No longer able to consider anything slow, he moved quickly, rocking in and out as hard and as deep as he could. Glancing at the mirror to the side, he saw her pert tits bouncing in rhythm to his pounding. She had turned her head and he captured her gaze in the reflection.

As tightly wound as he was, he knew it would not take any time for his own orgasm to explode. "Touch yourself," he growled, then watched in fascination as her hand moved tentatively to her clit.

"Spank me, please," she begged and he grinned.

Don't have to ask me twice. His hand came down on her ass and her gasp had him grow even harder. After each spank, he soothed the warm skin with his palm. After five spanks, he felt his balls tighten. "You ready?" he bit out, trying to maintain control. Moving his thumb to her rosebud entrance again, this time he slid it in just barely, but enough to add more pressure to her already aching core.

Fingering her clit once more, she felt the sparks rush to all her extremities as her inner muscles clamped harder on his cock than she had ever felt.

As she screamed his name, he roared as his release poured into her. Pressing as deep as he could, he continued to let her milk him until every last drop was gone. Falling on top of her, he rolled to the side as he pulled out and moved her so that she was facing him.

Her breathing ragged, she felt like the winner of a long race. Exhausted, but elated. Her limp body lay next to his as he tucked her in tighter.

For long minutes they said nothing, allowing the air to cool their bodies and time to slow their breathing. After a few minutes she began realizing what she allowed him to do. Knowing it was very tame compared to some people's sex-play, nonetheless a blush crept from the tops of her breasts to her face.

He looked down, seeing her embarrassment. "Babe, are you okay? We don't have to do any of that again, if you don—"

She silenced him with a touch of her fingers on his lips. A shy grin appeared on her face. He watched her carefully, but the grin spread to a twinkle in her beautiful green eyes.

"It was…um…I liked it," she admitted.

His heart lighter, he asked, "You're sure? I don't ever want you to be uncomfortable."

Giggling, she said, "I never imagined that it would feel so…um…good."

"Good? That's all you've got to say is that it was good?" he joked, a pretend hurt look on his face.

"Um…great? How about amazing, fantastic, hot, and orgasmically phenomenal?" she asked, her blush deepening.

Throwing his head back in laughter, he said, "Orgasmically phenomenal? I'll take that, princess. I like that."

Pulling the covers up over their cooling bodies, he tucked her in tightly. With her head on his chest, her arm across his stomach and leg across his thighs, he ran his hand through her silky hair.

As she drifted off into a sated slumber, he could not believe that this amazing woman was in his bed. In his arms. In his life. And he knew…this was forever.

CHAPTER 17

V INNY SAT AT the large conference table rubbing his hand over his face in frustration. The list of people that knew Annalissa's schedule had grown, and yet no one was standing out in their search. Listening to his co-workers around the table only made his frustration worse.

"BJ and I are working the financial angle on the list that we have to go on, but so far there has been no unusual financial changes in anyone's status," Lily reported. "But, as we know, that can be hidden so we are digging deeper."

"Jack's contact says that the DEA is looking at a large scale drug smuggling ring, taking the angle that this is something that goes on in airports all of the time and that she was just one of many who unknowingly transported drugs. I'm just not feeling that," Tony said, holding the attention of those present. All knew Tony's knack for analytical problem solving, but his former men knew that he was never wrong when it came to a mission that did not feel right.

"You still think it's personal?" Jobe asked.

Vinny watched Tony carefully as he answered. "I

don't know that it is *personally against* Annalissa, as though someone wants to target her for trouble. But yes, I think she was specifically chosen and my guess is that it had happened before and would have happened again if she hadn't discovered it."

"What about the goddamn neighbor?" Vinny growled.

"Lester McCleod?" Lily asked. "He's a graduate music student. Plays in a local band called The Turners that can be found at a lot of local pubs on the weekends. Annalissa has played the violin with them and sometimes her harp."

"I didn't like that guy. Keep looking," Vinny ordered, his foul mood deepening.

Gabe looked at his twin knowingly. "Bro, just because the guy knows her and has played in a band with her doesn't mean—"

"I fuckin' know what it doesn't mean. I just think if we're looking at the people who know her in the symphonic orchestra then we need to look at his local band as well."

Tony nodded at Lily, silently communicating for her to keep digging.

The group meeting was interrupted by Terrance entering the room quickly. "Boss, Doug and I combed through hours of video from Dulles to see if we could identify anyone. We finally came across a video of the handlers taking the luggage off of the plane. Looks like one of the airline handlers was searching for something and kept going back and forth between the baggage trucks and the conveyor belt. After about ten minutes, he pulled out his cell phone and made a call."

The group listened intently at the first break they had had in the case. Tony barked out, "Good work. Now isolate that video and send it to Jack and feed it into Lily and BJ here."

"You got it," Terrance answered as he left the room.

Several minutes later, BJ pulled it up on their screen so that everyone could see. Sure enough, as the luggage came off of the trucks from the plane, one handler seemed to search for something specific.

"Can you isolate his face and bring it up closer?" Vinny asked.

With a few clicks of the keyboard, BJ was able to show a clearer, but still fuzzy, photograph of a middle-aged, Caucasian male with dark hair. His badge was unidentifiable and Vinny cursed as he looked at it.

Within twenty minutes, Tony received a call from Jack. The conversation was short but Tony was not smiling when he got off the phone. "Jack's FBI source has an identification. The airline worker is Milo Richards. He's only been working for the airline for about a year. He lives in D.C. and Jack just checked him out. He's dead."

The group sat stunned for a moment as Tony continued. "Milo was found dead in his apartment by his girlfriend four days ago."

"Damn," Vinny spit out, as the others cursed around him.

Lily piped up, "Annalissa flew to Los Angeles eight months ago and again four months ago. Same airline. She also flew to New York two months ago. In and out of Dulles Airport and same airline."

Tony, calm as ever, said, "I think we can assume at this time that Annalissa is definitely a targeted carrier, but may not be the only one. Although with the amount that was found in her harp case, someone wouldn't have to make many trips to keep someone local supplied and dealing."

"So it could be a dealer on a small scale or someone who is part of a larger gang?" Jobe surmised.

"Yep." Tony looked around the room and added, "We need someone on Annalissa at all times when she's not with Vinny. If the person thinks that she has figured out who they may be, they may decide to deal with her directly."

Vinny jumped up, heading out of the room. Tony looked at Jobe. "Follow him." Jobe nodded and left as well. Tony then looked at Gabe and added, "Set up a rotation for when she's alone."

The meeting broke up much the same as it had started. Frustration all around.

DON JUAREZ LOOKED out on the Los Angeles skyline,

his mind wandering over his empire. A slow smile crossed his face, as he felt untouchable. Who knew the most powerful drug lord in California sat in a million dollar office, his legitimate businesses flourishing. And laundering his drug money. He never dirtied his hands with the seedier side of the business. That was why he paid a great deal for those under him to handle all of the transactions…and the problems.

His cell phone rang and he glanced at the number. Answering curtly, he asked, "Anything?"

"The baggage handler was taken care of," Jawan reported.

"That's hardly what I would call progress," Don's voice bit out.

"I know. I'm in constant contact with my person on the inside of her group. We'll have it soon, I promise."

"If not, you'll end up like the handler."

With that, Don hung up. His angry gaze now glaring at the skyline. Taking a deep breath, he relaxed. Jawan will take care of everything.

On the other end of the disconnected phone call, Jawan paced his office. Calling his contact, he growled, "What have you got for me? I'm telling you, you'd better come up with something. You and your little helper."

"I'm trying to get her to commit to another trip. That'd be a perfect time to have the harp alone."

"Why the hell can't you get the harp when she has

it out now?"

"It's too chancy. Too many witnesses. Listen, I've got this. Promise."

"You'd better or we're all dead." Jawan hung up this time, still pacing his office.

ANNALISSA WAS DREADING the meeting. She was at the Richland Concert Hall practicing for her next performance with them, but needed to meet with her father afterwards. She had gone to see him a couple of days after she had gotten back, but found that after the initial "you look fine and how's Easnadh" there was little he had to say.

Earlier, when she had been walking around the stage, she felt ill at ease. As the sound technicians and stage hands greeted her, she smiled, but secretly wondered if they were involved in the transferring of drugs.

As other string members of the orchestra came into practice together with her, the same feelings rose to the surface. *I hate this! I'm beginning to see everyone as a threat.*

Backstage was a hub of activity. Musicians, hall personnel, costume designers working on the next play performance, sound technicians, lighting technicians…they all began to blur. Some even looked at her suspiciously…*or is that my imagination?*

Moving to one of the practice rooms on the lower

floor, she and a string quartet that she had performed with before, settled in.

"You seem tense," one of them commented.

Forcing a smile, she lied, "I just didn't sleep very well last night."

"No worries," the first violinist said. "It's just not like you to make any mistakes. Let's continue."

An hour later, Annalissa was glad the practice was over. Her talent and professionalism had been called upon to play her very best, but it was difficult when all she wanted to do was try to figure out who had used her. Exhausted, she left the practice room, carrying Easnadh's case.

Walking up the stairs to her father's office, she hesitated at the door. She remembered coming here as a child when her mother was still alive. It was so different. She and her mother would skip up the steps calling out chords as they went. *She could make anything fun,* she thought. *I miss you mom. You would have liked Vinny so much.*

Steeling herself, she entered. Stewart O'Brian looked up as she made her way over to him. A distinguished man in his mid-fifties, his dark hair was only slightly graying at the temples. His sharp eyes scanned her up and down, before nodding toward a seat.

Before she could speak, he began, "Todd tells me that you're reticent to accept his proposal for the next year's tours."

Pursing her lips, she lifted her chin slightly. "If my

manager cannot keep my confidences then perhaps it's time for me to find another manager."

"I pay half of his salary, my dear, so I don't think that now's the time to be making demands that you cannot meet."

Sucking in a deep breath, she said, "Father, I don't want to travel for a week every month. I would like to take on teaching here in Richland and then only travel when necessary."

"Annalissa, you need to develop a name for yourself. I've gone to great expense to make sure that happens. Teaching is something you can do when you're older but for now, performing is what your focus must be. That is where you'll gain more of the financial freedom you so crave."

She cringed. *He has me and he knows it. I barely make ends meet on my salary, but he pays for the expenses of being a performer.*

"I'll look over the schedule carefully with Todd and see which ones I feel that I can make."

He eyed her suspiciously. "Where are you staying, by the way?" he asked.

This was the moment she had been dreading.

Taking a deep breath, she looked her father in the eyes and stated firmly, "I'm still staying with Vinny Malloy. He's the employee of Alvarez Security that was hired to escort me back from LA."

The silence in the room resounded all around as though a bass drum was pounding in her ears.

"Staying?" he asked, the one-word question hanging in the air between them.

Licking her lips, she lifted her head slightly. "Yes, father. Staying. My apartment was trashed and Alvarez Security is concerned about my continued safety."

"Are they really? That's interesting since they've been paid in full for the escorting service from LA to Virginia. Our contract is over so why are they continuing to perform security services?"

"They're not. That is to say, they aren't providing security services for me other than what they provide for...um...people that...um..."

"Come now, daughter. You were so brave a few minutes ago. What is it that you are hiding?" he asked sardonically.

"I'm not trying to hide anything, father. I'm just trying to tell you something that I know you don't want to hear."

His raised eyebrow was the only change in his expression.

"I'm involved with Vinny Malloy. As in we now consider ourselves to be a couple."

"A couple?"

Her father's habit of asking a question with only a word or two had never bothered her before. But now? It was pissing her off.

"Yes, father. A couple. You know—when a man and a woman decide to be together for more than just a night or two. When feelings are involved. When there's care, concern, emotions."

"Now you're being facetious, Annalissa. I don't care that you have a boyfriend as long as it doesn't interfere with your career plans."

This statement had her confused. "I...I don't know what you mean."

"If you think to turn down traveling for concert engagements because of Mr. Malloy, then think again."

Not able to think of a reply, she sat stoically.

"I will have no problem contacting Mr. Alvarez and letting him know that his employees seducing clients while on the job will not look good in the press."

Heart pounding a tempo in her chest, she stood quickly. "I can't believe you're so callous. I've done nothing but bend to your will and your goals for my career." Tears sprung to her eyes and she hastily brushed them away, cursing the sign of weakness. "Why can't you understand? I'm not turning my back on performing. It's just not everything to me the way it was for you."

Knowing if she stayed for another minute she would fall apart, she bent to pick up Easnadh's case and walked toward the door. Back straight, head held high. With her hand on the knob, she turned and looked her father directly in the eye.

"I'm in love. The kind of love that mom had for you." At this she saw a flicker in his eyes; pain or annoyance, she could not tell. "I'll look over the contracts from Todd, then I'll decide what's best for me. You try to bring this to Alvarez's door, you'll lose me. Forever."

All of her bravado gone, she hurried down the stairs and outside, seeing Jobe waiting for her. He saw the look on her face and bolted out of the SUV. He caught her as she ran toward him, holding her close with one arm while making a call with the other.

"Tony? Jobe. Get Vinny to meet us as soon as we get in."

Pushing herself away, she wiped at the tears saying, "Jobe, I'm so sorry to be so much trouble."

He shushed her then hustled her inside, carefully securing her harp in the back. The drive to Alvarez Security only took fifteen minutes and as soon as they parked, she jumped out of the vehicle. Jobe jogged up the stairs with her and as he slammed through the door they were met with Vinny, Tony, and Gabe.

Vinny grabbed her in his arms, feeling her legs wrap around his waist. *She does this when she wants close.* She was not crying, but he could feel her body shaking. The four men made eye contact with each other.

Pulling her back slightly, Vinny peered into her eyes, searching for the cause of her distress. Giving him a small smile, she moved to have him put her down. She surprised him when she turned to Tony, wringing her hands.

"Tony, I'm so sorry. I think my father may make trouble for you and I...I...don't know what to do."

Ushering her to a chair, Tony gently pushed her

into it, pulling another one up in front of her. Vinny immediately sat next to her, his arm around her shoulders. Gabe and Jobe stayed behind Tony, ready to do whatever was needed.

"Annalissa, I can assure you that there's nothing that your father can do to hurt me or the company. Tell us why you think that."

"He's angry that I won't agree to more traveling and that I've told Todd that I want to stay here more and also teach. Then, he wanted to know where I've been staying." Licking her lips, she glanced around nervously. But all she saw were friends. Supportive friends.

"I told him about us," she said looking at Vinny. "He said he didn't care who I was with as long as it didn't interfere with my concert traveling. And then," she continued, turning her gaze back to Tony, "He said that he would go to the press about your company's employees seducing clients."

Sucking in her lips, she waited for the explosion. Or anger. Or cursing. Nothing but silence.

"What did you tell him?" Tony asked, curiosity clearly written on his face.

She looked over at Vinny, whose expression was unreadable. "I told him that I love you. And if he interfered with you or Tony's business, then he would lose me."

The room was quiet for a second before Gabe and Jobe burst out in laughter. Tony followed their response.

She looked on in confusion, first at the laughing trio in front of her, and back toward the man next to her, seeing his smile split his face. His beautiful smile.

"Oh, babe. You're tough as nails and that's no lie," he said, leaning in to kiss her. *She fuckin' stood up to her old man for me. And for the agency.* Moving his lips over hers, he felt her tremble and pulled back to see tears shining in her eyes.

"Annalissa," Tony said, drawing her attention. "Don't worry about your dad. Hell, if he let out that rumor then my business would probably triple!" Hearing a snort of laughter from behind him again, he smiled. "Your father has no threat to hold over us and so get that right out of your mind."

She looked at him dubiously, but a small smile played at the corners of her mouth.

Vinny raised his fingers to her chin, gently turning her face toward his. Wanting to kiss the frown off of her face, he leaned in and said, "Baby, you standing up to him for yourself is amazing. You standing up to him for Tony's company is wonderful. But you standing up to him for us? Fuckin' hot!"

Then he pulled her the rest of the way in, capturing her lips in a kiss that told her just how hot he thought it was. Someone finally clearing their throat separated them.

"Hate to break this up, but I really need to ask you if there was anyone at the Hall that you saw today that you thought might be suspicious," Tony asked, ignoring Vinny's shit-eating grin.

Blushing furiously, she shook her head. "No, although I hate suspecting everyone. I feel like I'm second guessing everything that everyone is saying to me." Looking at her watch suddenly, she jumped up. "Oh, I have to go. I'm playing a little impromptu concert at Jennifer's elder care home in an hour."

"I'll take you, babe," Vinny said.

"I'll tag along too," said Gabe. "Then I can ride home with my wife."

The three of them left, leaving Tony and Jobe in the conference room. "What are you thinking, Captain?" Jobe asked.

Shaking his head, Tony said, "I'm thinking she's got a lot of people in her life that are determined to keep her traveling. And that includes her own father."

"Anything special you want?"

"We've got some more surveillance to do." Turning toward Lily, who had walked into the room. "Add her father to the list of people I want you to dig into."

"You got it, boss," she replied.

CHAPTER 18

THE LIVELY IRISH TUNES floated through the air as Annalissa's fingers quickly plucked the strings of Easnadh. She sat in the front of a large room filled with elderly men and women, all entranced with the music. Some tapped their feet and others nodded their heads to the rhythms. At the end of her selections, she asked if there were any requests.

A few song titles were called out and she began playing one that she was familiar with. In the back of the room stood Gabe, Jennifer, and Vinny. Jennifer, a social worker for the city, helped run the elder-care center and loved seeing the smiles on the faces of those she cared for. Gabe, enjoying the music as well, was more interested in both the woman playing the harp and his brother's reaction to her.

Vinny stood mesmerized, his eyes never leaving the dark-haired beauty weaving her musical magic. Jennifer looked over at Gabe, seeing where her husband's attention lie. She then glanced at Vinny and understood the interest. It was obvious that Vinny's heart was with Annalissa. She and Gabe shared a smile before turning back to the music.

Annalissa loved performing for this group. The chance to play for those who often do not have the opportunity to come to a concert hall, yet appreciate music, was humbling. At the end of the little recital, the elderly residents flocked to her, their praise and enthusiasm showing on their faces.

When the residents finally left the room for dinner, Annalissa packed Easnadh in her case as Jennifer walked over, hugging her new friend.

"That was amazing. You're so talented and they really loved your performance," she gushed.

"I loved playing for them", Annalissa said. "I only wish I could do it more."

"I'm envious of your talent. I am so not musical," Jennifer bemoaned.

As the two women chatted, the twins stayed at the back of the room watching them. Gabe turned to Vinny, saying, "She pretty amazing, bro. So this is it? She's it for you?"

Without taking his eyes off of her, Vinny nodded. "Yeah, Gabe. From the moment I first saw her looking like some goddamn fairy princess and heard her play, I think I fell in love. Then I saw how she was pushed and pulled by everyone around her and all I wanted to do was step in and protect her. Then when we were on the run," he turned to look at Gabe, "Swear to God, she shocked the shit outta me. She held in there like a trooper, never giving up and never giving in." Looking back at the women, he watched as she threw her head back in laughter at something Jennifer said. "Fuck, bro. I'm a goner."

Gabe chuckled, slapping his twin on the back. "Well, I just got two things to say to you," he said, gaining his brother's attention. "One, thank God, because it's about time you found someone worthy and she's definitely it."

"And the second thing?"

"You'd better take her to meet mom and dad, 'cause when Jennifer tells them all about her, which will probably happen tonight, mom'll skin you alive if you don't let her check her out!"

Vinny laughed as he agreed, gaining the attention of the two women. Annalissa stared at the picture of male beauty standing at the back of the room. Gabe, leaning against the doorframe, his large arms crossed in front of his chest with one tree-trunk leg crossed in front of the other. His dark-blond hair neatly trimmed, eyes sparkling as they looked at his wife. And next to him, identical in most ways, Vinny. He stood with his jean-clad, muscular legs apart, his hands on his trim hips. His dark navy shirt that stretched deliciously across his chest and arms. And his face...square jaw with a hint of stubble that tickled when he went down on her. Perfect lips that teased and tormented hers. And the same sparkling eyes as Gabe's...only his were staring right at her.

"I could stare at him all day," Jennifer said, startling Annalissa out of her musing.

Quickly looking over at Jennifer, realizing she was referring to Gabe, she had to giggle. "Yeah, me too. With Vinny, that is," Annalissa clarified.

The two men, in unison, stalked over. "You ready to go home, babe?" Gabe asked his wife, taking her in his arms.

Vinny looked down at Annalissa, opening his arms and loving that she walked right in. Wrapping her in his embrace, he kissed the top of her head.

As the four of them walked out of the center, Jennifer looked up at Vinny. "Um, you know that your mom is going to have a fit if you don't take Annalissa there soon."

"I was thinking of rectifying that situation this Sunday," he answered.

"And just when were you going to tell me that?" Annalissa asked, glaring up at him, while secretly thrilled that he was planning on taking her to meet his parents.

"Hey, I work on a strictly need-to-know basis," he joked, earning a poke in the ribs.

"Well, I wanted to invite all of you to Third Street Bar tomorrow night. Some friends and I are playing there," Annalissa added.

"Oh, we'd love to," said Jennifer, already planning on asking some of their friends, while Gabe nodded.

Vinny, frowning at the thought of her playing with her neighbor, looked down at her. "And just when were you going to let me in on that little tidbit?" he growled.

Smiling up at him, she batted her eyes, saying, "Oh, didn't I mention? You're on a strictly need-to-know basis!"

Patting her ass, he said, "Let's go before I'm tempted to do more than just give you a swat."

The four headed out of the building, Gabe's laughter ringing in their ears.

THE BAR WAS crowded by the time the group of friends gathered. Vinny had gotten there early, presumably for securing a table large enough for them and for keeping an eye on Annalissa. He hated to admit that he might be jealous, but he intended to keep an eye on Les as well.

The waitress took their orders as Shane, Annie, Matt, Lily, Tony, Sherrie, BJ, Suzanne, Gabe, Jennifer, and Jobe, along with his date, found their seats.

The women included Jobe's date in their conversations, but she was as quiet as all of his other dates.

Jennifer leaned over to Sherrie, asking, "What's up with her? Every time Jobe brings someone along they look as though they would jump at the slightest noise."

Sherrie discretely whispered back, "I've asked Tony, but he says that Jobe just looks for someone who is…forgettable."

"Forgettable?"

"Yeah. You know. Not loud or boisterous. Not in-your-face. Just someone simple who will go out and then not be a pain if you don't call again."

Lily leaned over hearing their conversation, and said, "Jobe's a total sweetie. I wish he would find someone more… substantial."

"Tony says that Jobe had someone once. Back when they were overseas. I have no idea what happened, but ever since they've been here he just goes for someone who's kind of blank. That's all Tony will say right before telling me to stay out of his men's love lives!" Sherrie giggled.

"Well, I think he needs a woman with backbone. You know? A real tiger. Someone who'll not only stand up to him, but take care of him as well."

The women's conversation was interrupted by the musicians moving to the stage. They watched excitedly as Annalissa, wearing a hunter-green sleeveless dress with a short, flared skirt, sat in a chair pulling Easnadh onto her lap.

Lester took center stage introducing their song before putting the fiddle to his chin. Another young man played the drums and the fourth member played another fiddle. The quick Irish jig tempo immediately had the audience tapping their feet or clapping to the rhythm.

Vinny could not take his eyes off of Annalissa. Her eyes closed, she moved her fingers over the strings eliciting the most delightful sounds. The quartet's instruments blended perfectly, each complimenting each other. Les moved excitedly around the front of the small stage, dancing a bit while fiddling.

The expression on Annalissa's face was enchanting. Moving to the music, her body rocked gently back and forth as her fingers made it all look so easy. A delicate smile played upon her lips. Even without the long gown and theatrical makeup of a symphonic performance, she was the most beautiful woman he had ever seen. Her beauty was simplistic. His eyes roamed over her outfit and as his dick began to press uncomfortably against his jean zipper, he found himself cursing her short skirt and scoop-neck bodice.

As they neared the end of the jig, her eyes opened and immediately found his. Locking on her gaze, all others in the room fell away leaving only the two of them bound by the swirling tones. Realizing he was holding his breath, he gulped air as the last chord was played.

The audience went wild and Les introduced the musicians. When Annalissa's name was called, her friends' table cheered the loudest. She blushed, never having had a group of people there to see her. Looking at Vinny, she could not believe that the most gorgeous man in the room was there for her.

Their next song was a slow ballad, showcasing her harp skills. As the haunting melody floated over the quiet bar, Vinny felt it in his soul. He closed his eyes for a moment, going back in time. A time of sand and dust. A time of war and destruction. He saw the woman playing her instrument, her sound much different from what was playing now, but her passion the same. Then, suddenly, the vision of her broken body and bloody harp filled eyes and he jerked them open, searching for the scene in front of him.

But all he saw were his friends, their eyes on him— the brothers-in-arms knowing exactly where his mind had taken him. His gaze moved to the stage, seeing Annalissa there. Calm. Serene. Letting the music flow from her fingertips to his heart. Soothing his soul.

Sucking in a deep breath, he slowed his breathing, his eyes never leaving her. She was looking at him, a questioning expression on her face. Giving her a smile and a wink, he leaned back in his seat to enjoy the rest of the performance.

As THE MUSICIANS stepped off of the stage, they were flooded with admirers. Les eagerly encouraged the women who had moved forward, but to Vinny's ire there were men moving toward Annalissa. With his height, he could see her anxious expression and began nudging people out of the way to get to her.

As her eyes met his, her smile lit up her face. *Fuckin' beautiful,* he thought. Putting his large hands around her small waist, he lifted her easily from the stage and set her on the floor directly in front of him. Their gazes held as he leaned down to touch his forehead to hers.

"Baby, that was amazing. I could listen to you for-ever."

"I hope so," she whispered against his lips.

Before he could kiss her, she was shoved from the crowd behind and his arms instinctively wrapped around her, protecting her as he growled. "Let's get you back to the table before we're crushed."

"Vinny, wait," she protested. "I can't leave Easnadh up there."

He lifted her back up on the stage and watched over her as she quickly secured her harp. Carrying it with her, she allowed him to take the case and then offer his hand to assist her down. Moving to their large table, the group slid chairs around to accommodate her and her instrument.

The group enthusiastically congratulated her on her performance and then settled in to enjoy each other's company. Vinny, with his arm around her, could not remember feeling so content. As he eyes moved from her beautiful face to some of the women hanging around the bar that used to be the type he banged, he gave himself a mental kick in the ass.

"Hey Lissa," Lester called from behind. "We just wanted to say goodbye and thank you for playing with the guys tonight."

Annalissa and Vinny turned at the same time, see-ing Lester with his arm around a pretty red-head and Vinny saw the way they looked at each other. *Thank*

God he has a girlfriend.

Annalissa stood, hugging first the girl and then Les. Vinny accommodated by shaking Les' hand as well.

"You got any more concerts planned?" Les asked. "I like to mark 'em on my calendar so I know when you might play with us."

Just as Annalissa was about to answer, Vinny interrupted, "She'll let you know if she's available."

Les held Vinny's stare for a moment before nodding and walking away with his girlfriend.

Annalissa turned, sharply saying, "That was rude. Why did you answer him that way?"

The men at the table shared a knowing glance and looked at their friend with sympathy. He was right to suspect everyone that inquired about her travels, but they knew she was not going to like it.

"Don't be getting your panties in a bunch, babe," he quipped. "No reason for anyone to know when and where you travel."

"My panties in a bu—"

A kiss interrupted her mini-tirade. Hot, wet, and completely served its purpose. When he raised his head up, her eyes were hooded and her lips were kiss-swollen. Vinny shifted uncomfortably in his chair, his dick swelling at a painful angle in his jeans. She glanced down and grinned.

"Serves you right," she muttered with a smile.

The evening continued with good friends enjoying each other's company. As the group began to disperse for the night, Annalissa realized how long it had been since she had had so much fun with a group of friends. Not since her college days, when her father's reach did not interfere with some of her nights out with friends, had she been so relaxed. Shane, Matt, BJ and their wives had left, all needing to get back to their babysitters, leaving just Tony's crew. Jobe and his date left soon after, she looking bored and he looking like he wished he were somewhere else with someone else.

Vinny moved to the bar to settle the tab when he was accosted by two women. He could not remember their names, but remembered them vaguely as a past trio-fuck. *Goddammit!* The thought of who he used to be before Annalissa made him ashamed, and the fear that she would see them made him turn to throw down his credit card on the bar. "Settle up quickly, please," he barked to the bartender.

The two women slid up to either side of him, hawk-like expressions on their faces. "It's been a dull crowd, Vinny," one purred, circling his bicep with her fingers, nails like talons. He glanced down at her long, dyed-blonde hair and a body that he used to go for—all tits and ass. And most of that showing in a too-low top and too-short skirt.

"You up for another romp, handsome? Like last time, we can all have a good time," the other said, a carbon copy of the first.

"Not interested ladies—"

"He's off the market," came a voice from behind.

Soft, but strong. He closed his eyes for a moment, a smile touching his lips. It hit him as sure as a punch to the gut. *She doesn't see the fuck-up I was, even with all this staring her in the face. What the hell did I do to deserve something this good? No pouting, no screaming, no making me feel guilty. Just...pure goodness.*

He turned quickly, wrapping his arms around Annalissa, but noted her uncertain expression. *Her words had been strong, but she's got doubts in her eyes.*

The two women on either side of him looked back and forth between the gorgeous man and the woman they recognized from the performance. Understanding flashed through the eyes of one and she pulled her less intuitive friend along with her.

"Princess," he said softly. "I'm sorry—"

She face-planted into his chest, no longer feeling brave. When she saw the women approach him, she felt jealousy and the innate desire to stake her claim. But after the words came out of her mouth, she felt nervous. Shaky. Unsure.

"Babe," he murmured against her hair. Her only response was to shake her head against his chest. He lifted his head, catching the gaze of Gabe, making a motion toward her harp still sitting at the table. Gabe nodded and pulled Jennifer back into his lap, keeping an eye on the instrument.

Taking his fingers and lifting Mackenna's chin, he confessed, "I can't change my fucked-up past and I'm so sorry about that, but you gotta know you're it for me."

She peered up into his eyes, searching for truth…and finding it. A small smile curved the corners of her mouth as she accepted his apology and his promise. "Let's go home," she whispered against his lips as he lowered his mouth to hers.

His answer was his kiss. Deep, hard, wet. And a very public branding of who she belonged to and who he had now given himself to. The hoots around them broke them apart, grinning as they made their way back to the table. He leaned down to grab Easnadh's case with one hand with the other arm around her. Winking at Gabe and Tony as Annalissa hugged Jennifer and Sherrie, they all headed out into the night.

CHAPTER 19

ANNALISSA DREADED THE TRIP the next day to meet Vinny's parents, until they pulled up outside the quaint stone building near the riverfront just outside of town and saw Gabe's truck parked outside.

"I didn't know they were going to be here!" she exclaimed, relief evident on her face.

"I wasn't sure either," Vinny stated, "But this'll put mom in a happy coma."

"A happy coma?"

"You know. Her two sons showing up at the same time, now both with women. Jesus, it may actually kill her with happiness."

She giggled, but felt her nerves return as soon as he helped her down from the truck. She smoothed her long, navy, jersey dress and tucked her hair behind her ears.

"You look gorgeous, baby," he whispered as he ushered into the pub.

Her eyes had to adjust to the dimness of the insides of the building, but as she looked around, she was enchanted. A stone fireplace was in a gathering place to the left, with old, comfortable sofas surrounding it. She could smell the slight smokey scent of the fireplace that gave the pub a homey scent. Along the right wall was a long, polished bar with mismatched stools lining it. In the corner was a dart board with a chalkboard to the side for keeping tallies. Toward the back were empty tables and booths, awaiting the lunch regulars.

"Vincent," boomed a voice from the back. A large, muscular man headed toward them wearing jeans and a **Malloy's Pub** t-shirt. A Celtic tattoo on his bicep peeked from the t-shirt, matching the one she knew so intimately on Vinny. *I would know this man anywhere—he looks like an older version of Vinny and Gabe.* The man bear-hugged first Vinny and then turned to her.

"Maeve, get out here woman," he shouted with a smile.

A beautiful, petite, dark-haired woman came out of the kitchen as well, wiping her hands on her apron. Jennifer followed closely behind, next to a young boy.

After hugging Vinny, his mother turned to Annalissa as Vinny made the introductions. Placing his arm around her, he turned back to his parents. "Mom, dad. I'd like you to meet Annalissa O'Brian. Annalissa, I'd like you to meet Patrick and Maeve Malloy."

Maeve stepped in front of her and took both of her hands in hers. "Oh, my darling girl. You're absolutely beautiful and you've no idea how happy this makes me."

Annalissa noticed tears in Maeve's eyes as she was

pulled into another hug.

"Thank you for loving my son. I've prayed so long that he would find someone," Maeve whispered.

"Don't mind my Maeve," Patrick said, putting his hands on his wife's shoulders. "She cries when she's happy."

Patrick stepped up to Annalissa and she had to lean way back to look into his cheerful face. "Good to have you here, darling. Maeve and I've heard a lot about you and are tickled to finally meet the woman that tamed one of my boys."

Jennifer giggled before accusing her in-laws of saying the exact same thing when she met them last year. The young boy ran over to fist-bump Vinny.

"This is my brother, Ross," Jennifer introduced. "He and Vinny are great friends."

"Hey buddy," Vinny greeted. "I'd like you to meet Annalissa."

Gabe walked through the back carrying a tray of beers on tap. "Let's celebrate," he called out.

Maeve and Patrick had their servers bring out platters of fish and chips and the rowdy group settled in to eat. Patrick regaled the women with tales of Vinny and Gabe growing up on the river and the shenanigans they used to get into. Maeve beamed at the gathering and Annalissa felt her eyes on her several times.

Finally, she leaned over to Vinny and whispered, "I think your mom wants to say something, but she just stares instead."

"She wants you to play your harp."

Her eyes widened as she bemoaned, "But I didn't bring Easnadh."

Vinny winked as he moved from his chair. "I'll be right back." A few minutes later he returned with her harp case in his hand. "I stowed it in the back. I just knew Ma would want to hear you play an Irish tune."

Maeve clapped her hand in delight. "Oh, my dear. Please do. Ever since Vincent told us you played the Celtic harp, I just knew you were the one for him."

The group moved to the sitting area in front of the fireplace as Vinny got a chair for Annalissa to sit in. For several minutes she played one Irish ditty after another, interspersed with several ballads.

Once more Vinny sat entranced watching her play, her fingers gliding over the strings eliciting the most beautiful sound he had ever heard. Her eyes were closed as she rocked back and forth, one with the music. Suddenly another sound emerged. His heart pounded in his chest as he realized she was singing. *Singing!* The haunting tones from the harp were now joined by the sweetest voice he had ever heard as the words to the Irish lullaby floated over the pub.

As her fingers stilled, Annalissa opened her eyes realizing that she had been singing in public—something she never did. And the gathering was silent. Perfectly silent. *Oh Jesus, what have I done?*

Maeve burst into tears as she sprang from the sofa, rushing over to envelope her in her embrace. "Oh, my.

I've not heard that since my mother would sing it to me and I sang it to my boys."

Annalissa glanced over Maeve's shoulder to see Patrick wiping his eyes, a broad smile on his face. As the older woman released her, she dared to look Vinny's way. He moved over to her, pulling her from her chair and encircling her in his arms. Looking down into her green eyes, he whispered, "Never thought I'd hear anything as beautiful as you playing the harp. But hearing you sing at the same time? Fuckin' amazing."

"I didn't mean to sing," she confessed. "It just sort of happened."

"Happened for a reason, babe."

Soon it was time to say goodbye, this time she was comfortable with his parents' show of affection. They were so much like her mother that she had to fight the tears of remembrance.

As they pulled away from the pub, Vinny turned to her and asked, "You okay, baby?"

She returned his smile as she answered, "Everything's perfect."

THE WARM WATER was no longer frightening to Annalissa as she treaded through the shallow side, slowing making her way into the slightly deeper water. Keeping her head above the water line, she moved her arms while kicking her legs to propel herself toward the stunning man smiling at her as he floated along. He dipped his head under the water, rising up before her like a Viking god. Chiseled abs, with the Celtic pat-terned tattoo around his thick bicep, water dripping from his hair down his square jaw with a hint of stubble.

Good Lord, she thought as her motions faltered. He quickly reached forward, a smirk on his face.

"Babe, keep your mind on the lesson or you'll drown."

Clinging to his hard body, she replied, "How can I be expected to keep my mind off of you when you look like that?"

Laughing, he pressed his erection against her core. "You're not the only one struggling here. Just the sight of your sexy body sliding through the water is keeping me hard."

"Maybe someone else should teach me to swim," she suggested, licking the water off of his neck. "Maybe Jobe is available."

"Fuck, no," he growled, squeezing her ass. "He may be one of my best friends and true to the core, but no one'll ever be this close to you when you're half naked." His aching dick was making the lesson difficult, so he moved her out to arms' length as he floated her to the shallow side.

"Back to business," he ordered, giving her a quick kiss on the nose, admiring her little pouty mouth. "We need to get your head under the water and add the breathing into the strokes."

Determined not to show fear, she stood and followed his motions of holding her breath and lowering herself under the water. Up and down she went, practicing taking a deep breath before plunging, blowing bubbles under water and then rising again.

Having conquered her fear of being under the water, he then stood behind her moving her arms as she turned her head. Her attempts to put arms, legs, and breathing together were awkward and resulted in swallowing water.

Sputtering and coughing, she lifted her head in frustration. "I'm never going to get this! There's too much going on for me to remember how to do it all."

Once she had caught her breath, he pulled her close allowing her to wrap her legs around his waist again as she locked her hands behind his thick neck.

"Babe, you're doing great." Seeing her start to interrupt, he continued. "How long did it take you to learn to play the harp?"

Knowing where he was going, she grinned ruefully. "Okay, okay. I know, I have to practice. But it's not like I'm ever going swimming by myself. And I have no intentions of ever trying to cross a river again."

"You never know, babe. After all, when we have kids and they're playing around the docks at my parents' place, you'll want them to know how to swim and be able to swim with them if you need to."

She stilled, bringing her head from his shoulder to

face him. Her eyes searched his, looking between them. He looked…serious.

"Our…children?" she asked, her heart beating a staccato rhythm in her chest.

"Don't know where you think this is going, but I see it going all the way," he said holding her gaze, feeling her body tremble against his.

"I…but you've only known me a couple of weeks," she whispered, afraid of him changing his mind and terrified of him being serious.

"Lived hard, baby. Seen things I wish I hadn't seen. Done things I wish I hadn't done. But when something comes along that's right and you know it's right? You don't sit around just twiddling your thumbs."

A nervous giggle erupted from her lips as she said, "I hardly think we've been sitting around twiddling our thumbs, Vinny."

He watched as water droplets made their way down her silky cheeks, dropping onto the tops of her breasts peeking out of the water. Then he lifted his gaze back to hers. "First time I saw you on stage performing, I had no idea you were the woman I was supposed to escort. But I stood there in the wings and knew I'd give anything to know someone who could bring such beauty out of an instrument.

"Then, when you walked into the dressing room and I knew that I was going to be able to spend some time with you, I felt like the luckiest man alive. And babe," he said, making sure to hold her gaze, "There hasn't been one moment in this crazy couple of weeks that have made me doubt my feelings for you."

The sound of water lapping against the edges of the pool was the only noise heard as she clung to his body, her thoughts swirling.

"What are you thinkin', princess?" he asked, his confidence leaving him as her expression was unreadable.

"I'm stunned," she replied truthfully.

"Stunned good or stunned bad?"

Smiling gradually, she said, "Stunned good."

He let out the breath he did not realize he was holding. "Can we work with that?" he asked.

She nodded before saying, "I still can't believe that you're in my life. You, who could have any woman, want me."

With his arms still enveloping her, he began to slowly twirl them around in the water. "You're all I've ever wanted." Deciding not to push her, he maneuvered her toward the side, his mind already on the ring he wanted to purchase.

Lifting her up on the side of the pool, he hoisted himself out as well. She leaned her head way back to take in all of him. His wet hair appeared as dark as the scruff on his strong jaw. Wide shoulders and muscular chest tapering down to his trim waist. His tree-trunk legs spread in a wide stance. And his hand…held out to take hers.

He was doing his own perusal, looking down at the

woman sitting in front of him. She thought the faded one-piece swimsuit looked childish, but there was nothing about her that did not scream all woman. Her long, dark hair fell in wet waves down her back. Her face, devoid of all makeup, resembled a china doll with her porcelain skin. And the body encased in the swimsuit, toned with perfect curves. Nothing lush and overblown...just perfect. *Damn*—his cock was twitching again. Reaching his hand out, he noticed she hesitated in taking it because her eyes were roaming over his body. Smirking, he waited until her gaze lifted to his and grinned at her embarrassment.

"Come on. Let's get you warm, dry...and in bed."

It was her turn to smirk as he assisted her up. "In that order?" she asked coyly.

With a quick slap to her ass, he swooped her up in his arms laughing. Arriving in their apartment, he lowered her feet to the plush rug in his bathroom. Turning on the shower to let the water warm, he moved to stand in front of her again.

Sliding his hands up her arms until he came to her straps, he peeled them over her shoulders until the top of her swimsuit barely hung on her breasts. She placed her hands on his chest, feeling the steely strength underneath her fingertips. Glancing down she noted the tent in his swim trunks and as her gaze wandered back to his face, she noticed his smirk.

"Oh yeah, babe. You do that to me."

Giggling, she purred as he exposed her breasts and

lifted her up in his massive arms, latching his mouth over one nipple. Sucking deeply, he teased and taunted her flesh until the need for movement caused her to ride his abdomen against her core.

He set her down to quickly divest her of the swim-suit, peeling it off to expose all of her beauty to his eyes. With a jerk down, he kicked his swim trunks to the side as well.

Hoisting her up again, he stepped into the shower allowing the spray of warm water to hit his back, and pressed her against the tiled wall. Moving between breasts, he feasted until she cried out with need. He was almost ready to enter when she stilled him.

"A condom, sweetie," she reminded. His look let her know that he hated having to stop. She hastened to say, "I ran to my doctor the other day, but I have to be on the pill for a bit to make sure…"

"Gotcha, baby. I appreciate it." *Stop being a prick,* he told himself. *If she's willing to do this for me, then I can keep him covered until it's clear.*

Stepping out to sheath himself, he re-entered the shower and immediately assumed the same position— her in his massive arms balancing on the tip of his straining erection. His gaze met hers and she nodded her approval. With one swift push, he plunged to the hilt in her warm, sweet body.

For a few seconds, he remained still; the feel of her silky wetness squeezing him tightly was pure nirvana.

Wiggling, she complained, "Vinny, please. Do

something!"

Chuckling, he began to move her up and down on his shaft, eliciting moans from her lips as he captured them with his. Thrusting his tongue in rhythm to the movement of his cock, he felt his orgasm approaching quickly.

One hand under her ass for support and the other pressed against the tile, he moved her up and down, the friction nearly taking him over the edge. He held himself back wanting her to come first.

She felt the pressure building, trying to reach the finish line of a race, knowing that crossing the end would bring euphoria. She was barely aware of him pressing her back tighter against the shower wall until she felt his hand move between their bodies. One tweak of her clit was all it took and she shattered. The vibrations moved from her core outward until she was sure she felt them down to her toes.

Just then, she heard him roar and opened her eyes quickly to watch his face as he came. His head thrown back, thick neck muscles corded in strain, he powered through his orgasm as he pumped his last drop inside.

After a moment, when their breaths slowed, he allowed her to slide down so that she was standing next to him, the warm water covering her body. Leaning her head back, she looked up at the huge man whose arms were still around her.

He wants me. He wants to be with me. A smile curved the corners of her mouth as she leaned forward, placing her lips on his chest. Holding that kiss for a moment she could feel his heartbeat pounding. "I love you," she whispered. His arms tightened around her body.

"I love you back," came his answer, rumbling against her face.

A short time later, tucked in bed, he pulled her body next to his and enveloped her in his embrace once again. *Forever,* he thought. *Mine forever.* With that thought, he followed her into slumber.

CHAPTER 20

V INNY ROLLED OVER and looked down at the early morning sun peaking through the windows of his bedroom, casting a hazy glow over the woman sleeping in his bed. *My bed. My woman in my bed.* The caveman thought could not be squelched even if he had wanted to. After years of meaningless sex in stranger's beds, to have a beautiful woman that he loved sleeping beside him made life worth living.

She rolled toward him, still asleep. Her face, gentled in repose, held his gaze as he thought of the music that flew from her fingers. *And her voice.* He smiled as he stroked her cheek. The ruffles of her nightgown dipped low enough for him to see the tops of her breasts and he feasted his eyes on the creamy mounds.

Then the thought of someone trying to hurt her came to mind, and the smile left his face. Replaced by anger. And determination.

Annalisa slowly woke, her eyes opening to the sight of the most handsome man she had ever seen staring down at her. His expression appeared tight with anger, then immediately softened as he focused on her eyes as well.

"Morning, babe," he murmured, his voice hoarse with need as he slid one hand down her back and over the globes of her ass, pulling her into his swollen dick.

"Mmmmm," she moaned, responding by grasping his erection and slipping her hand up and down over its silky hardness. "I thought we needed to be at Tony's this morning."

"They can wait," he growled, the movements of her small hand driving his need to a fevered pitch. Rolling over her body after discovering that she was not wearing panties, he pushed the nightgown up and entered her quickly after sheathing himself.

Her hands pulled him closer as they roamed over his back and down to his ass. Within a few minutes, she was thrown over the edge of her orgasm as he powered through his at the same time. Laying sated, they smiled as their bodies cooled in the early morning sun.

He moved out of the bed, reaching down to pluck her off of the covers. "Shower, babe. I'll fix breakfast while you get ready."

She turned to pout, saying, "You're not going to join me?"

He chuckled as he gave her lips a quick kiss. "I join you and we'll be a lot later for the meeting. Then you might have to explain to the group why we're late."

Grumbling, she headed toward the bathroom, his eyes following her longingly. His dick twitched again and he willed it down as he made his way into the kitchen. *How can that nightgown be so fuckin' sexy?*

THE GROUP GATHERED around the large conference table at the center of Tony's work area, Lily and BJ on laptops with their screens projected on the wallboards.

The frustration of the group was palatable. So far none of the people on the list of possible suspects had suspicious behavior, nor had Lily been able to uncover any unusual monetary transactions.

"It's too fuckin' clean," Gabe groused. "Not everyone can be that clean."

"I've been working with Jack, since he has DEA contacts. They're working on an undercover operation in Los Angeles where they've found drug smuggling that even gets by airport security," Tony announced.

"Intel has an organized gang, run by those that supply drugs to the rich and famous. Once hooked, extortion is also used to keep their buyers and runners busy. The organization is huge and with runs between LA and other national airports, such as Dulles, and it wouldn't be too hard to find those that travel with large cases. They sell worldwide and one of their many schemes is that they target frequent fliers between D.C. and LA or New York. DEA is after the top guy, but they wonder if he knows how everything works in his own organization. So far, he's been untouchable and he manages to stay clean. Now the many minions that work under him? That's a different story."

"DEA can't get to the subordinates?" Vinny asked.

"They can't all be untouchable."

"They're working on it. So much money passes through the hands of all types of people in entertainment that's off the books, it can be hard to find what's legal and what's not."

"Moving drugs using unsuspecting airline passengers sounds really random...and detailed," Jobe noted.

Lily spoke up and added, "But it wouldn't be that difficult to figure out. All it takes is a comparison of frequent fliers, what luggage they check, how often and when they travel. That's something that any person with enough IT knowledge could organize."

"So I was just a random victim to begin with?" Annalissa asked hopefully, still not able to grasp the concept that she was targeted.

"We're not sure, but still checking every angle. We don't want to assume anything and let our guard down."

"Give me the names of the major distributors and let me see if I can find a connection from anyone on our list," BJ said.

Lily sat quietly, her lips pursed in thought. Her husband, Matt, Looked over. "What's on your mind, babe?" he inquired.

"I keep going back to motive. If we're just looking at the drugs being smuggled in a large container, then a harp makes sense. But if we are looking at something more personal, who would want Annalissa to suffer?"

Annalissa's gaze cut over sharply to Lily. "What are

you thinking?"

"Tell me more about some of the people you work with. What about Sharon and Parker?"

Laughing, Annalissa said, "If there were two people who were definitely not involved, it would be them! They're the only ones that really talk to me, you know like they want for me the same things that I want for myself. Never demanding...always supportive. When I travel, I am surrounded by people who are pulling me in different directions. But Sharon and Parker keep me sane."

"How did you meet them?" Vinny asked.

Her brow crinkled in thought as she tried to remember. "I think either Todd or Gordon arranged for them to be with me the first time I had a solo performance with the Richland Symphony. I'm sure my father made the request," she added ruefully.

"Okay," Lily said. "What about Les and the members of the band that you play with sometimes?"

Feeling Vinny tense up next to her, Annalissa patted his knee. "Lester heard me practicing the harp one day and knocked on my door to talk. He was getting some friends together to play in a bar and wondered if I would ever consider playing with them too. We became friends and when I can, I work with them."

"Any of them party hard?" Gabe asked.

Annalissa looked over at him, confusion knitting her brow. "I...don't know," she answered, not really understanding what he was asking.

Vinny leaned toward her, saying, "Any of them do drugs that you know of?"

"No," she answered vehemently, her eyes flashing. "I mean I don't know them very well, but no…not that I know of. Not in front of me." Turning to glare at Vinny once again, she said, "I really hate this you know. You have me wondering about everyone I know. I had few friends before this mess and I'll have even less now!"

Vinny wrapped his arm protectively around her shoulders, pulling her in closely. "I'm sorry, princess," he whispered. "I know this is tough on you."

"I just really don't think that anyone I know would do this on purpose to me. I must have just been the random, large case at the airport that got picked."

Lily smiled, but remained thoughtful.

VINNY DROPPED ANNALISSA off at Ross' school where she met Jennifer. After having played for them at the Malloy's pub, Ross had told his music teachers about her and she received a call to show some of the students her harp during their music class. Standing in front of the school, Vinny resisted the urge to kiss her. "Either I or Jobe will be back to pick you up in two hours, babe," he said softly, knowing she hated to be reminded about needing security.

"There hasn't been any threat to me for several

weeks," she protested. "Can't I use the cabs again?"

"Not budging," he announced as she huffed. Looking down into her eyes, he added, "Not taking any chances."

Smiling, in spite of herself, she knew he cared. Nodding, she and Jennifer walked into the building.

Thirty minutes later, she sat with Easnadh in her lap playing songs to the fourth and fifth-grade classes. As she finished her performance, she allowed them to ask questions and to pluck the strings of the harp. The teachers allowed the most interested students to stay and she continued her mini-lessons for another hour.

"How do you know which strings to play?" one little girl asked.

"See the red ones?" Annalissa asked. "They're for certain notes and as I play, I can quickly see where I should be by looking at them for guidance."

"Don't that hurt your fingers?" came the next boy, reaching out to feel the wires.

"I usually pluck the strings with my fingernails, but can use the pads as well. Here, try it," she encouraged.

The time passed quickly and she looked up when she heard a noise at the door. Jennifer had returned and was standing there with Vinny. His warm eyes were on hers and the smile on his face took her breath away.

"Miss, miss," a little girl said as she dragged Annalissa's attention back to the task at hand. "If I wanna learn, would you be my teacher?"

Annalissa smiled at the child and answered truthfully, "Right now I'd love to say yes, but I'm still traveling a lot playing concerts. But I tell you what—if I can start teaching soon, I'll have the music teacher talk to your mother."

The little girl ran back to class smiling, and Vinny walked over as she placed Easnadh in the case. He leaned over, snagging the case from her hands as she finished and walked her back to his truck.

"Let's grab something to eat."

"Sure," she replied. "What are you in the mood for?"

He lifted an eyebrow in response, eliciting a giggle. "Didn't you get enough of that this morning?" she asked. Before he could respond, she quickly added, "I know, I know. You're insatiable."

"Only with you, babe. Only with you."

They turned into the parking lot of a little restaurant overlooking the river. After being seated by a window where they could see the river slowly meandering by, they settled for pizza and beer.

"You looked good earlier," he said. "Seeing you with those kids, babe. You're a natural with them. You'd make a good teacher."

Smiling up at him, she stopped mid-bite with a long string of cheese hanging out of her mouth clinging to the pizza. She chewed quickly trying not to choke. He chuckled while patting her on the back.

She sat silently for a moment thinking on his words. *No one's ever accepted that about me. What I want. What I'd like to do.* She closed her eyes, letting his words slide over her. Clearing her throat, she replied, "Thank you. That means a lot to me. It...it means everything to me."

"What do you want to do babe, if you could do anything?"

She thought for a moment before answering. "I'd like to be like my mom," she said. Seeing his questioning look, she continued. "I like performing. I really do. I wouldn't want to give up performing. But I just don't want to travel every month for a week or more. Maybe just five traveling concerts in a year plus what I am doing with the Richmond Symphony. Then I'd like to teach children."

"Then that's what you should do," he claimed.

"Well..." she said, smiling. "I've been planning on telling Gordon not to book the concerts that Todd was lining up. In fact, I'm calling him later tomorrow."

"ANNALISSA, DARLING. HOW are you?" came the smooth voice of Gordon on the other end of the phone.

Rolling her eyes, she replied, "I'm fine. Great actually."

"Good, good. Well, I just wanted to let you know that I was going to be in town for the symphonic gala. At your father and Todd's invitation of course."

"Okaaay," she said hesitantly. "Um…I'm not playing that night."

"I know, but I'll want to see you anyway. I've got some bookings that Todd sent to me and I want to get busy with them. We need to get you back out touring again soon."

"I told Todd that I wanted to slow things down—"

"Nonsense, darling. You've got to keep your name out there if you want the kind of success that we all want for you. Now, I'm looking at renewed visits to New York, Los Angeles, and Chicago. We have a real interesting possible booking in Miami. Todd and I have talked, we think that trips to Florida might be profitable."

Pursing her lips, she sucked in a deep breath letting it out slowly. "Gordon," she said deliberately. "Just stop. I'll see you next week when you come into town but do not book anything yet."

"Look, Annalissa. I'll be patient, but you've got to continue to travel more. If you won't be reasonable, I'll talk to your father."

"Go right ahead, Gordon. In case you've forgotten, I'm an adult and I'll make my own decisions. Granted, I gave control to my father for a long time, but those days are over. I'll be making my own career choices from now on."

"Fine," he bit out. "We'll talk in a week." With that he hung up.

It did not take long for the phone call from her father to come in, demanding that she come in for a meeting. Walking into his small, crowded office that afternoon, she realized that her heart was no longer pounding. No fear. No trepidation. Just the peace that came from knowing that there was someone who loved her. Wanted her happiness.

With a genuine smile on her face, she walked over and gifted her father with a hug. Surprise crossed his face as he patted her back uneasily.

"Hello, father."

He nodded to the chair across from his and as she sat her eyes roamed the room. Music books, sheet music, and instruments filled almost every space. He's been a symphonic conductor for most of his adult life and it's all summed up in this tiny room. Suddenly, she felt sorry for him. Her mother had been his catalyst. The reason they put down roots instead of traveling the world. The reason there were things in their life besides just music. And with her gone…now her father only had his music. *If you would let me in, father, I'd now be able to bring to your life what mom brought to ours. If only…*

"I've heard from Gordon and Todd."

The statement hung out there between the two, creating a wall as sure as if he had built one from bricks.

Sighing she said, "Yes. I told you that I'm now taking charge of my career. I want to teach part time and perform part time. If I can do a CD, then I will. I plan on spending most of my time in Richland and only traveling when necessary or to do several concerts a year."

"It's him, isn't it?"

Smiling, she said, "If you are referring to Vinny, then yes. Part of it is because of him."

"You're letting a man who knows nothing about the classical music industry, one you have known for a few weeks, make decisions for you?" he accused.

"No, I'm not, father. I'm letting a man who would lay down his life for me, one who has saved me, comforted me, discovered what I want. One who has given me the freedom to be who I want and the courage to stand up for myself, even though it's long overdue. And one whom I've fallen in love with. That's the man who I choose to be with." Standing, she looked down at her speechless father with nothing but pity in her heart and continued, "This is me...being me. If you can find a continued place for me in your symphony, and in your heart, then I'll be there gladly."

Turning, she walked to the door but his voice halted her. "Will you at least consider some of the concerts?"

A lovely smile curved the corners of her mouth. "Of course. I'll be happy to discuss any of the possibilities with you. I'd value your opinion." With that, she opened the door and walked down the hall.

As soon as she turned the corner, she ran into a wall. A human wall. Bouncing back, strong arms reached out to grab her arms to steady her. "Vinny!" she squealed, her smile now lighting her face. His customary close-fitting jeans stretched across his thighs and blue shirt that barely contained his muscles were a sight she would never tire of. Lifting her gaze to his strong face, she asked, "What are you doing here?"

"Knew you were coming to talk to your father and thought you might need some support. You okay?"

Green eyes sparkling, she nodded. "Yeah. I'm...perfect."

"You sure are," he chuckled.

Playfully slapping his arm, she added, "No, I mean with my father. I know he's not happy, but I finally realized that I'm not responsible for his happiness. I can't bend my life to his vision if it makes me miserable."

Touching his lips to hers, he offered a chaste kiss. One that he would like to take deeper. Longer. But that was for later. Now, it was just for her. "Proud of you, princess."

"Me too." Sucking in a deep breath, she said, "It feels...freeing."

Throwing his arm across her shoulders as they walked out of the large concert hall, he asked, "So how do you want to celebrate your new freedom?"

"Hmmm," she said, tapping her forefinger on her chin and looking at him through eyes filled with desire.

"Don't start that here or I'll likely go back into that building and find an empty practice room," he warned.

Laughing, she said, "Well, practice makes perfect."

Swatting her ass, he laughed. "Come on, I'll take you to lunch. I think the guys are meeting at a little deli near here and if I know them, some of their wives will be there also."

"Lunch with you and friends…perfect!" she exclaimed, linking her fingers with his as they walked down the sidewalk.

CHAPTER 21

AFTER LUNCH, TONY invited Annalissa to join them back at the agency for a briefing. As they filed in and sat at the large conference table, he began.

"There's a gala next weekend that we've been contracted to provide security for. Should be a minimal security contract. Mostly local and state dignitaries present although, there may be some others that are higher profile. It will be, for all intents and purposes, our standard contract mission. Security outside the building and a detail inside. Those inside, formal dress of course."

"I know what you're talking about," Annalissa interjected. "That's for the annual fund-raising ball for the Richland Symphony."

Tony nodded, "Yes. And that's why I've asked you here. I want to discuss another security contract with you."

Vinny's eyes cut sharply to his boss' face. *What the hell are you talking about?* About to interrupt, he heard someone clearing their voice and he looked over at Gabe. Their unspoken communication told him that he needed to at least listen to what Tony was proposing, but his heart was already pounding.

"Okay," she said, her attention divided between Vinny and Tony.

"If the drugs were planted in your harp before it left for the airport, then just about everyone who's a possible suspect will be at the gala or the vicinity. We'd like to—"

"No way, Tony. You're not using her for bait," Vinny shouted, his face red with anger.

"Bro," Gabe started.

"Man," Jobe jumped in.

Tony eyed the large man, one of his best, who was not the calm, cool, collected marksman of the team. In front of him was an enraged man in love with a woman who was being threatened. He had to fight to keep the smile off of his face thinking of the big man who had fallen so hard.

"Not using her as bait," Tony explained.

Placing her hand on Vinny's arm to calm him, she turned to Tony asking, "Then what do you need from me?"

"Your harp."

"Easnadh?" she asked, her voice cracking. "I'd rather you use me."

"Goddamn it, Annalissa," Vinny bit out. "We're not using you."

Jobe spoke up, "What's the plan, Captain?"

Tony looked around the room, once more in command. "Whoever put the drugs in your harp knew what they were doing and must have trained someone at the airport to retrieve them with no damage or consequences to the instrument. And, as far as we know, they think they're still there.

"Whoever was responsible has got to be feeling some pressure from above to get their hands on it. No gang, no matter how wealthy, wants to take a hit for a half a million dollars worth of cocaine. We've protected the harp, but now this gala provides the perfect chance to get whoever targeted Annalissa."

"But, I'm not scheduled to play at the gala. I wouldn't have a reason to have her there."

Tony nodded, "But would it be difficult to get a chance to play?"

She thought for a moment of all of the possibilities, then realized all eyes were on her, awaiting her response. Blushing, she admitted, "Sorry, I was thinking of the best way to go about it."

"Never apologize for brainstorming a mission. That's exactly what we do," Tony assured.

"My teacher," she stated. "Part of the gala is a tribute to his work in strings since he's been in this country. He's not only a brilliant musician and teacher, but restores antique string instruments. He was one of the first to encourage me to travel."

Shrugging, she said, "I think if I approach him, he would agree with me doing a duet with him, and that would give me a chance to have Easnadh at the concert hall."

"Not liking this," Vinny admitted, his face no longer angry but full of concern. "Tony, I've never bucked a mission, but shit, boss."

"Annalissa's never going to be a target," Tony added. "We need to make sure that it's well known that she'll be there playing her harp. That will be too great a temptation for whoever is smuggling the drugs. They need that retribution to their supplier."

Sucking in a huge breath and letting it out slowly, she agreed. "I think it could work."

Tony nodded as Jobe winked at her. Gabe smiled, but his gaze stayed on his twin, knowing that even the hint of danger to Annalissa was killing him.

"Then let's start planning," Tony announced as the group turned their attention to the concert hall's floor plan that BJ pulled up on the screen.

"MR. FEINSTEIN?"

"My dear, he's in the back," announced Mrs. Baxter, appearing around the corner. "You can go on. He's expecting you."

Gifted with a hug, she sat down as he looked at her expectantly. "You have not brought your harp so am I to assume this is a social call?" he asked, a twinkle in his eyes.

Grinning, she said, "I wanted to see what you thought of an idea. Because of your work on Easnadh, I wondered if you would mind if I played a duet with you next weekend at the gala? Something simple. Something we've done before. I just thought it would be a lovely tribute to you as a teacher and as an instrument restorer." While the words were true, the reason behind them made her feel like a liar. Worrying her bottom lip, she was not sure if she were more nervous at trying to get him to agree or if he would see through her ruse.

"Why, my dear Malyshka," he exclaimed. "I'd be honored to have you perform with me. Oh, what shall we play?"

He immediately began to search his music for the right piece, but she was no longer paying attention. Sighing in relief, she inwardly gave a fist-pump. *I did it. One down, more to go.*

Later that evening, she called Todd. "Hey, I wanted to give you a heads up. I'm going to be playing with Maurice Feinstein at the gala this weekend. I thought you'd want to get some advertising and promotional materials together if you can. You know, famous String player, his student, and the harp that he restored?"

"Can this be the Annalissa that I know?" Todd nearly screamed into the phone. "Fabulous, girl. I'll get right on it."

"Um, can you call Sharon and Parker? I want to go in full costume for the event."

"Oh, my God, I've died and gone to heaven. Now maybe you'll decide to take more of the performances

I've found for you."

"Let's take things one at a time," she cautioned. "So, have Parker and Sharon call me and I'll have them come to the apartment an hour before the gala begins."

Gaining his approval, she then called Gordon.

"Well, if it's not the difficult diva," he said, sounding as condescending as ever.

Ignoring his attitude, she told him of her plans, gaining his surprise and approval as well. "It's my understanding that there will be quite a few dignitaries there, so that should make Todd happy."

"If you'd stop the ridiculous aversion to flying, then perhaps you'd meet a great many more dignitaries," he quipped.

"I was going to tell you that I do plan on flying again soon. Nothing set in stone, but I agree that I need to travel more."

"Well, it's about time you came to your senses. What happened? You have a tiff with that big oaf boyfriend of yours?"

Gritting her teeth, she replied, "No, not at all. He's just encouraging me, that's all. I've got to go, but I'll see you Saturday night at the gala."

Tossing the phone down on the sofa, she leaned over putting her head in her hands. The pounding in her forehead was relentless. *Who knew being stealthy and sly was such hard work?*

Vinny walked over, saying nothing, but holding out two Advil and a glass of water. Accepting her smile of gratitude he pulled her forward so that he could maneuver her into his lap. Rubbing her shoulders and back, he felt her slowly begin to relax.

"You don't have to do any of this."

She sat for a moment letting the feel of his fingers moving on her muscles send her to a place of peace.

"You know that, don't you?" he continued.

She turned to him, cupping his strong, stubble covered jaw in her hand. Kissing him softly she leaned back and said, "I know. But this feels like the right thing to do, Vinny. We need to flush out this person before they do it again to me or someone else. And also…" she hesitated. "It feels good."

He looked at her in confusion. "Good?"

She twisted so that she was straddling him. "You get to rescue people all the time. Your job is difficult but, in the end, you get the good feeling of helping someone. Me? I just play music. So this feels like I'm helping."

He reached up to cup her delicate cheeks, pulling her in close. "Listen up, babe, and listen well. What you do is bring joy and emotion to so many. You heal others through your playing. Don't ever think you've got to be a part of this mission to help someone."

She looked at him, questions in her expression. "Heal? You said I heal others?"

He held her on his lap, cupping her face and rubbing his thumb over her cheek. Tentatively, he said, "Yeah, healed. You healed me."

She sat quietly, knowing that whatever he wanted to share would have to be in his way. In his time.

Bravely holding her gaze, he said, "When I was in Afghanistan, we were on patrol and I heard a woman singing and playing some kind of lyre. She and some other women were alone. Or at least they thought they were alone." He heaved a sigh, then shook his head slightly. "Women weren't allowed to play music or sing, but I guess they thought they were safe."

"The desire to make music is universal," she said softly.

"Yeah. Her music wasn't like yours, but it still felt fuckin' good to hear. Made me think of mom and the songs she used to sing to us. And I felt peace…crouched on the hard ground behind boulders in the middle of a warzone…and I felt peace."

Annalissa stayed still, knowing there was more to the story.

"But the soldiers following us came through and silenced the music." He lifted his gaze back to hers. "Permantly."

"Oh, Vinny, I'm so sorry," she sympathized.

"Anyway, after that I only listened to my loud, hard, heavy music. Until you. And from the first time I heard you play, I felt…peace. Healed."

"Do you remember what you said to me that first night in the limosine?" she asked.

Before he could answer, she said, "You told me that my music was soul-changing. That meant so much to me then and now that I know why, it means even more."

Moving forward, he touched his lips to hers in a barely there, whisper of a kiss. Smiling, she leaned her head on his shoulder. After a few minutes, her body began to relax and she was only slightly aware of him picking her up.

He deftly made his way to the bedroom and, supporting her with one hand, he leaned down to pull the covers back with his other. Laying her down on the bed, he slid her pants down and left her shirt on as he pulled the covers back over her. Her face, no longer etched in pain, looked peaceful and he stood for several minutes just staring down at her. *Has it only been a few weeks that I've known her? How the hell could she have rocked my world in such a short time?* He continued to watch her sleep, rubbing his hand absentmindedly over his heart. *But she has. Rocked my world. Stolen my heart. Given me peace. Given me a future.* Sighing deeply, he moved quietly out of the room, closing the door.

Calling Jobe, he asked his friend to come up. "Gotta minute, bud? Annalissa's sleeping so I need you to come here."

A couple of minutes later Jobe walked into his apartment, his eyes immediately taking in his friend. He saw worry. Concern. Frustration. "Okay, man. Let's have it," Jobe ordered, as they both sat down on the oversized sofa.

Vinny tossed him a beer and for a few minutes they

sat in companionable silence, Jobe allowing his friend to gather his thoughts.

Snorting ruefully, Vinny finally said, "Never thought it'd happen for me, you know. I saw what Tony went through over there when his wife died and never wanted to feel like that. Plus, I was young, stupid, thought I fuckin' knew everything. Cocky. Thought spreading it around made me some kind of man. Then my own twin fell in love and I couldn't believe it." He stood and walked over to his windows overlooking the city, shaking his head.

"Of course, I met Jennifer and realized she was perfect for him. I love her as a sister but even seeing Gabe fall in love didn't make it seem real to me." Chuckling, he looked back at Jobe. "Then Tony. Hell, who'd ever thought the Captain would fall in love again? And with Sherrie? I mean, seeing them together now, it makes sense. They're perfect, but I sure as shit didn't see that coming."

Walking back over to the sofa he sat again, taking a long pull on his beer. He looked up, seeing Jobe's gaze still on his. "I headed out to California a month ago thinkin' I was going to be escorting some big-shot rocker chick back to Richland. You could have dropped me when I was taken to a symphonic hall and saw Annalissa. And then heard her play. Fuckin' shot right through the heart. If you believe in Cupid and all that shit…" he shook his head. "Shot right through the fuckin' heart."

"So you gonna get around to the problem? You got lucky enough to find a woman worthy of you, someone amazing. Someone who made you pull your head outta your ass. And someone, I might add, who loves you back and is currently sleeping in your bed right now." Jobe leaned in, resting his forearms on his thighs, staring Vinny directly in the eyes. "So what's the problem? You're not about to fuck this up are you?"

"No, man, no. I'm just...hell, I don't even know how to put it into words."

Jobe sat back, a knowing smile on his face. "You're scared."

Vinny's gaze jumped to Jobe's. "What the—"

Jobe threw up his hand, silencing Vinny. "Look, you were trained to be the best the Army has to offer and you ended up in the elite squad with others just like you. Fearless, dedicated, tenacious. Ultimate control. Over situations and ourselves. Willing to execute every mission with utmost vigor. Never back down. Never say die. Never give up."

Jobe, having obtained his friend's attention, continued. "But you're finding out what every one of our friends has already found out. First of all, we can't control love. Not when it hits us, nor when it takes us prisoner. And it's impossible to maintain that level of control when the one we love is threatened."

Vinny sat back letting Jobe's words move over him, reaching down deep. *I have been about control. Control of my career. Control of my body. Control of my heart.*

And now? Totally, fuckin' out of control.

Jobe chuckled as he saw understanding pass over Vinny's face. "Sucks to lose control doesn't it? You could, of course, dump her and get your control back," he taunted.

Shaking his head, Vinny groused, "Fuck you."

Both men leaned back in their seats, finishing off their beers.

Vinny looked over and said, "She's worth it. Every worry. Every concern. Every heart-stopping moment."

"Yeah, I know. And I knew you'd handle it when it finally came."

"Now you, on the other hand. I could always see you falling in love and here you are the last of us still single." The silence sat heavily in the room. "You could always try to find her, you know."

Shaking his head, Jobe stood up. "Too much time has passed. I fucked up a long time ago and killed whatever was there."

"Maybe—"

Jobe cut him off by walking to the door. As his hand reached the doorknob, he turned and looked over his shoulder at Vinny. Nodding his head toward the hall leading to the bedroom, he said, "Take care of her, Vinny. Don't worry about the control. That's what got in my head all those years ago and the reason I fucked up with the one I loved. Just care for her. Protect her the best you can. But mostly—just love her." With that, he left, leaving Vinny to think on all they had said.

He finally headed back to the bedroom, quietly moving into the bathroom to get ready for bed. Sliding naked under the covers, he moved closer and pulled her yielding body next to his. Wrapping her in his massive embrace, he kissed the top of her head as he tucked her under his chin. *Sleep well, princess. Nothing's gonna ever harm you.*

IN THE MIDDLE of the night, Vinny woke to the feel of Annalissa's hand on his chest. Moving slowly over his muscles. Gliding up to his shoulders and then down his bicep, tracing the pattern of his tattoo. Her soft touch caressed, and as he turned toward her, he saw green eyes following the trails of her fingers.

Afraid to speak, not wanting to break the spell that she was weaving, he held still watching her face.

Lifting her gaze to his, she whispered, "You're beautiful. Everything any woman would want in a man."

"I don't care about any other woman," he whispered back. "Only in being what this woman wants." He leaned forward just enough to kiss her forehead before capturing her gaze again. "As long as I'm what you want, princess, I'm good."

A smile curved her lips and he felt the piercing straight to his heart once again. Only this time...*no fear.* Giving control over to her, he allowed her to pull his head down to kiss his lips. Warm. Pliant. She licked his lips and he growled his response.

Taking over the kiss, he teased his tongue slowly into her mouth, exploring. Tasting. Tempting. Cupping her face with his hand, he ran his thumb over her cheek, the soft skin silky underneath his finger. The kiss lasted longer than most as he was determined to not rush. *We have all night. We have our whole lives.*

Rolling her slowly to her back, he bore his weight on his forearms resting on either side of her head. Never losing her lips, he maintained the kiss while gently pressing his swollen cock against her pelvis.

Their lips separated only long enough for him to divest her of her t-shirt from the evening before. Bearing his weight now on one arm, he moved his other hand leisurely down her side, rubbing his thumb on the underside of her breast. He held that pose for a few minutes, gently massaging her nipple, feeling her body come alive under his. Continuing his downward path, he slid his hand over the curve of her waist and down her thigh. Throughout this exquisite torture, he held her lips, taunting and teasing them with his tongue.

She spread her legs so that he could settle between them in the natural position that had held men and women since the beginning of time. His cock nestled into her wet folds that beckoned him. He moved slightly so that his hand could explore further as his fingers found the way inside her warmth. He moved them, crooked them, felt her inner core begin to tighten and then slowly pulled them out.

Chuckling at her moan, he moved his fingers up and as he pulled his mouth away from hers, he slid his fingers coated with her juices between his lips. Her green eyes implored him, but she did not speak, both knowing what was happening between them was beyond words.

He reached over to grab a condom, rolling it on quickly. Keeping his gaze on hers, he deliberately slid his cock into her waiting body. Inch by tortuous inch. Not pounding. Not plunging. But so slow he could feel every twinge of her body. Memorizing her feel. Reveling in the sensation of her body accommodating him. *Nothing…nothing has ever felt like this. Pure, exquisite torment.*

He finally reached as far into her as he could go and then began to slide lazily back and forth. The friction built just as quickly as if he had been rocking her body. Both arms were on either side of her head again, and their eyes never wavered. Over and over he moved until finally the fevered pitch had reached its crescendo.

Determined to hold his gaze, she squeezed his shoulders tightly as her orgasm rushed over her, electrifying her body from the core outwards. Tightening her legs around his waist, she pulled him in as he emptied himself into her. His neck was corded with thick, straining muscles until he finally collapsed to the side taking her with him.

Eyes still connected. Hearts beating as one. Legs tangled and arms holding tightly.

"What just happened?" she whispered in wonderment.

He held her close, kissing her lips once more. "Love, princess. Love just happened."

CHAPTER 22

T HE EVENING OF the gala was filled with women in glittering gowns and men in black tuxedos. Earlier in the evening, Vinny had moved to the second bedroom to get dressed while Sharon and Parker worked on Annalissa. Parker was over the moon with a new dress he had procured for her. She had to admit that when he pulled it out of the garment bag she was speechless. The dress had a fitted, beaded bodice that flowed down to a full skirt made of iridescent material that shimmered with blue and green. He helped her into it and then stepped back to admire his creation.

"Oh, darling, girl. You are a vision," he gushed.

Sharon hustled her over to a stool and began working on her stage makeup while Parker then fixed her long curls. Leaving them hanging down her back, he expertly pulled the front away from her face so that they would not interfere with her playing. Fastening bejeweled clips all around, she had the appearance of wearing a crown interwoven in her hair.

Sharon chattered on about people in LA that she was meeting and hoping would get her acting career started.

"You are such a talented makeup artist, Sharon," Annalissa said, laying her hand on her friend's arm.

Giving a little shrug, Sharon said ruefully, "That's nice to hear, but it's kind of like always being the bridesmaid and never the bride." Looking up at Annalissa eyes, expertly applying just the right shade of eye shadow to compliment the dress, she smiled, saying, "Speaking of brides. Anything we ought to know about with Mr. Hunky?"

"Oh, do tell," Parker said, plopping down in front of her too.

"No, nothing to tell."

"Well, you're still living here. Did you ever go back to your place?" Sharon asked.

"I did, but it was so trashed. Vinny didn't want me to go back there, and quite frankly I didn't want to either." Looking at them both, she admitted, "I guess that sounds kind of weird, doesn't it?"

"Not at all," Sharon said. "Hey, when you've got that, who'd want to live alone?" She stood up and walked over to her makeup case, putting her supplies away.

Parker leaned in, inspecting her face. "Beautiful, as always." Capturing her gaze, he added, "Honey, when it's right, it's right. Don't matter if it's ten years, ten days, or ten hours. You got it, you hang on to it."

They shared a smile before he assisted her up. Sharon and Parker wished her well and headed out of the apartment on their way to the event. "We'll meet you there and do touch-ups before the press makes it into the room," they promised.

Nervously, she walked out of the bedroom. Not seeing Vinny, she walked down the hall and when she turned, she stopped dead in her tracks.

He was standing in front of the windows, the evening sunset behind him. His black, fitted tuxedo stood out in stark contrast to the crisp white shirt that he wore. She knew it had to have been specially made—it fit him to perfection. And perfection he was.

Tall, handsome, and that smile. *Dear God, that smile.* His eyes were pinned on her and she felt her breath catch in her throat.

While she had been perusing him from head to toe, he had been staring at the vision in front of him as well. Every inch of her was elegant. The hair. The dress. The makeup. The shoes. Elegant. And perfect.

"Princess," he called softly, holding out his hand.

She glided toward him, taking his much larger hand in hers. "Babe, you take my breath away."

Smiling, she ducked her head, but he lifted it again with his fingers under her chin. He offered her a kiss. Just a touch on the lips. Just a promise.

A knock on the door interrupted their moment and as Vinny called out, Jobe entered. He looked almost as marvelous as Vinny and she smiled as she walked over to welcome him.

Jobe looked her over, his eyes twinkling as he took her hand and lifted it to his mouth to place a kiss there.

She giggled as Vinny gently pulled her back.

"You get the harp and I get the girl," Vinny joking-ly reminded him.

"Just my luck. Well, come on Easnadh," Jobe said, as he carried the case down to the limousine that waited for them.

"WE CAN'T AFFORD to fuck this up tonight."

"You think I don't know that? You think I haven't laid awake every night trying to figure out how to get our hands on that harp?"

"All I know is I've got no plans of this taking me down. And if I make one more call to Jawan, then the next thing coming from California is someone to take care of me—permanently!"

"Shut-up! You're not making this any better. I've got this. It won't fail."

The two continued to argue for several minutes, each hoping that tonight, this entire fucked up situa-tion would be over.

ONCE AT THE RICHLAND CONCERT HALL, Vinny left Annalissa's side reluctantly as she made her way with Easnadh to the ballroom upstairs. The guests were still meandering around as they arrived, hor d'ouevers being passed by the wait-staff. As they made their way to the room where the evening's activities were taking place, Tony's men mingled.

Tony had several men outside providing their regular security service for some of the city's dignitaries. Security cameras had been installed on the inside of the ballroom focusing on the small stage where Easnadh would be for most of the evening. BJ was at the helm of the van outside, monitoring the cameras and training another new hire.

On the inside, Tony placed the men he trusted the most. Terrance and Doug had been working for him for about a year and had earned the right to work security on the inside. Gabe, Jobe, Vinny, and Tony himself considered Annalissa and her harp to be their mission. And one they would not fail.

Once upstairs, she saw Maurice near the small platform stage where they would perform. Making her way over to him, she set her harp down to offer him a congratulatory hug.

"Oh, Mr. Feinstein, this evening is all for you. And I can't think of anyone who deserves it more."

Returning her hug, he smiled warmly down at his protégé. "Malyshka, I am so pleased to have you with me tonight."

Sharon called her over from the side of the platform and Annalissa made her way toward her. "Hey, Parker and I are in a small room back here if you want to touch up. Todd said that we can use this room and you can leave your case here if you need."

She followed her into the room, surprised that it held mostly stacked chairs that were not being used. There was a temporary mirror that Parker had placed on the wall and was already moving her in front of it. Fixing a few pins in her hair, he declared her ready for any performance.

Sharon had stepped through a door at the back and was re-entering, tossing a cigarette behind her. There was a small balcony overlooking the river beyond her. "Sorry," she grimaced. "I just can't break the habit. I know it's nasty and I always go outside so I won't get any cigarette smoke on you."

Parker waved his hand in front of his face, fanning the last of the smoke away. "That's why this room is so good—you can have that outside door if you need it."

Sharon moved in front of her, eyes roaming over Annalissa's face. "Makeup looks good, dearie."

Smiling, Annalissa walked out of the room, setting Easnadh's case at the edge of the platform, near the door. Taking the instrument out on the stage, she placed it next to Maurice's violin, nervously patting it.

"Annalissa," came a call from behind. In no time, she was surrounded by Gordon, Todd, and her father. The guests had moved to the ballroom and she was ushered to her seat at the place of honor next to Maurice.

The dinner passed quickly, although Annalissa had to admit to herself that the conversation was tiresome. An elderly senator, who appeared to be attempting to enter the campaign race a little early, and his wife dominated the conversation. She could hear Gordon from the table behind corner an airline mogul and was trying to hash out a deal for her travel. Todd, at another table, was whining to the waiter about his wine not being the proper temperature.

Just when she wanted to face-plant into her plate, her gaze landed on Vinny. He was staring straight at her as well. With a wink her way he moved around the room, seemingly casual, but she knew he was on high alert.

Finally, it was time for her and Maurice to step up on the platform stage to perform. They settled their instruments, beginning a violin and harp duet. The music flowed from her fingertips once again, weaving a spell over the audience. She closed her eyes occasionally, letting the rhythm move through her. When she would open them, she would glance at her partner, but find that he was as lost in the melody as she was.

Vinny stood in the back of the room, not taking his eyes off of her. *Perfection*, he thought. The moving vibrations flowed over him, finding their healing way deep inside. She had taken his agony and turned it into peace. She looked as though Easnadh was merely an extension of herself. The two needing each other to make the music as beautiful as it could be.

As the first selection came to an end, the gathering erupted in applause. The second piece was just beginning when he heard a voice from behind him say, "And you would keep that gift from the world?"

He turned, seeing her father standing nearby looking at him. The man's eyes were not cold…just evaluating.

He held Mr. O'Brian's gaze for a moment and then turned back to watch the performance. "No, sir," he answered. "I would protect that gift with my life."

He could tell when her father had moved along, but did not care. All that he cared about was the beautiful harpist on the stage. Annalissa and Maurice were on their final selection of the evening and he did not take his eyes off of her, still allowing the harmonies to fill his soul. When the last strain was ended, the crowd erupted once again, giving the pair a standing ovation.

Annalissa set Easnadh down, then turned to hug Maurice, once again congratulating him on his honor. Seeing Gordon and Todd making their way through the crowd, she quickly placed her harp in its case. Looking around she did not see any of Tony's men. The plan had been for her to leave the harp near the stage and Gabe would keep it in sight.

Gordon managed to catch up with her, immediately engaging her in conversation. "I've been networking darling. I've got some people I want you to meet." Seeing her standing with her harp case, he waived it dismissively. He saw Sharon coming out of the small storage room and signaled for her to wait. "Where's Parker?" he asked.

"He's gone for the evening. He said he'd just get the dress from her tomorrow. Why? What's up?" Sharon asked, her gaze moving between Gordon's and Annalissa's.

"Todd's got people she needs to meet and I was going to get Parker to take charge of her harp."

Annalissa wanted to protest, knowing that if her harp was taken out of the building they might never catch who was moving the drugs.

Sharon looked around then said, "Annalissa, what about that storage room? The door's right here and you'd be close."

She noticed Vinny near the back of the room and was glad he was so tall. He gave her another wink and she smiled as a warm feeling filled her heart. She moved into the room with Sharon, setting the case down, then they followed Gordon back out to the ballroom to meet with Todd and some music admirers.

VINNY MOVED CASUALLY around the room, making his way over to where Gabe and Tony stood. The three men made an impressive sight, all over six feet tall and in their tailored tuxes, each with discrete, wireless ear-radios so that they could maintain constant communication.

"Hate this shit," Vinny admitted.

"The job or this particular mission?" Tony asked, eliciting a raised eyebrow from Vinny.

"You know me, boss. I'll take anything you give me—but trying to protect someone you love? Fuckin' hard as hell."

Tony and Gabe nodded ruefully, both having done just that.

"I look at everyone as a suspect and try to keep my eyes on her at the same time."

"You focus on her and let the rest of us watch everyone else," Tony ordered. Not hearing a response, he looked at Vinny sharply. "Do I need to pull you from this job?"

Vinny's eyes cut over to Tony's. His former Captain. His boss. His friend. Shaking his head, he answered, "No, sir. I've got it."

Nodding, Tony moved on around the room leaving Vinny with his brother, who was looking at him with sympathy showing on his face.

"I know it sucks, bro. And honest to God, if we never had to worry about our women it would be great. But we've got this. We've got an eye on the crowd and an eye on her. We know where her harp is and we'll make sure that they're both safe."

Vinny rubbed the back of his neck, feeling the hairs standing on end. He looked into Gabe's eyes and said, "I know we've got it planned out, but I've gotta tell you...I've got a bad feeling. Like when a mission is ready to go to hell."

Gabe clapped his brother on the back before moving away into the crowd again, not acknowledging to Vinny that he had the same feeling.

"WHAT ARE YOU doing? You barely spoke to the Mayor and his wife," Todd hissed to Annalissa. Turning, he then spoke loudly, "Ah, Mayor Fisher and the lovely Mrs. Fisher. Here is our delightful harpist. She was understandably pre-occupied earlier, her mind on her performance." Leaning in toward them, he said conspiratorially, "You know the artistic type." Chuckling loudly, he pulled himself up to his inconsequential height and continued, "But she'd love to talk to you now."

After chatting with the couple, other patrons approached her. She relaxed and began to enjoy herself, talking about her music and Easnadh, as Gordon and Todd seemed to disappear in the crowd.

"My dear," one elderly gentleman addressed her. "We understand from the program that your harp was restored by Mr. Feinstein."

Smiling brightly, she said, "Yes." She glanced around to find Maurice hoping that he could join her for the conversation, but could not see him anywhere. "It was found in a dump and sent to him to see if it was repairable. He was able to restore it and gifted it to me—"

The screeching sound of the fire alarm howled throughout the room. For a second everyone was stunned into silence before the crowd immediately began to rush toward the doors. The meandering patrons of a moment before, wandering with their wine glasses, became an unruly mob all pushing each other, clambering for escape. Crystal could be heard shattering as some knocked into tables to rush to the doors.

Annalissa felt herself being pushed along by the throng, unable to see over the taller bodies nearby. The unnerving shriek of the fire alarm made rational thoughts fly from her head.

Easnadh! Oh my God, Easnadh! Turning, she began to force her way against the tide of people moving in the opposite direction. Managing to wiggle and thrust her way toward the back of the room again, she stumbled out when she passed the last person. She ran around the platform stage to the door of the storage unit, praying that someone had not locked it.

The knob turned easily and she threw open the door, rushing in.

THE FIRE ALARM jolted Tony and the others into action. Not knowing if it were real or not, they had a responsibility to make sure the congregation exited the building as quickly as possible.

Tony barked out orders to his men. "Jobe, front entrance. Gabe, main stairwell. Terrance, back stairwell. Doug, top of the stairs. Vinny, get Annalissa."

Each man hurried to their station, offering assistance and reassurances along the way. Vinny had no need of instruction—he was already on his way through the masses to where he saw Annalissa last. His progress was halted as he felt a jerk on his arm. Looking down sharply, he saw the frightened expression of her father.

"Are you getting her?" he asked, breathlessly.

"I don't care about the fuckin' harp," he growled.

Confusion filled the older man's face...and then guilt. "No, no," he said with pain. "I meant my daughter. Please save Annalissa," he pleaded.

Vinny held his stare for only a second but nodded curtly. "With my life," and he hurried along.

He had lost sight of her group, but being taller than most there he tried to see over the heads of the throng. *Where the hell are you, baby?*

He barked into his earpiece, "BJ. Where is she?"

BJ's voice came back immediately. "She ran around the back of the platform stage. It looks like she is heading toward that storage room where the harp was placed after it left the stage."

Tony, hearing BJ's comment, barked, "Gabe, follow Vinny."

Gabe immediately turned and began moving through the crowd toward the back as well. An elderly woman stumbled in front of him and he was slowed when he stopped to assist her. By the time he was able to hand her off to another man, he saw Vinny just approaching the back and he ran toward his brother.

CHAPTER 23

AS ANNALISSA RUSHED into the room with the shrieking fire alarm ringing in her ears, she stumbled over her high heels. *What the hell?* The small back door was open, allowing the night air to blow into the room from the outside balcony. She teetered forward, grasping a stack of chairs to regain her balance as she looked down at...

Sharon was bending over the open harp case, the base of Easnadh lying to the side, with her hand up inside the body of the instrument. She looked up in surprise, her face a mixture of guilt and...rage.

"You? You?" sputtered Annalissa, unable to believe who was searching her harp.

"You bitch, you found it. You found my stash and took it. Where is it? Where is it?" Sharon screeched, loud enough to be heard over the alarm.

Annalissa rushed forward, bending to grab Easnadh, and screamed, "We have to get out. The building's on fire."

Before she had a good grasp, her arm was jerked around and she missed seeing Sharon's flying hand as she was slapped hard across the face. Her cheek stung, but before she could react, she looked down to see what was in Sharon's other hand. A gun. Pointed right at her.

"You stupid bitch. Who do you think started the fire in the first-floor bathroom? Paper towels and my handy lighter was all it took to make the high-brow crowd run for the exits. And you should have too. I should have known you'd come back for your precious harp."

"Sharon," she said, trying to still her pounding heart. "It's gone. I gave it to the police. They're on to you now. They'll know it was you. You can't get away."

Just then the door slammed open with a bang as Gordon rushed forward, screaming, "Have you got it?" He came to a halt as he saw Sharon holding a gun on Annalissa. "What the hell are you doing? You were supposed to get the shit and get out unnoticed."

Annalissa felt her head spinning, adrenaline rushing through her veins. "Gordon?"

His eyes, round with fear, looked at her incredulously.

Sharon smirked as she held the gun steady, still aimed toward Annalissa, and as she jerked her head toward Gordon, said, "Seems like he got a little greedy with the stuff going up his nose and agreed to let me know your flight schedules. And the flight schedules of others. I had a good thing going until you cocked it up. Now get over there," she barked while jerking her head toward the back door.

"No, no, you don't have to do this."

"Your security stud will probably come through that door any second. You get out there or I blast him the instant he makes it here."

"Fuck, Sharon. This is not what I signed up for," Gordon whined. "You can't shoot her."

"You moron," Sharon barked. "You don't tell me what to do. I've been running this shit for a while now and got a name for myself with some people that can make my movie dreams come true. Now shut the hell up or you can get over there with her."

Annalissa, unable to think rationally, moved toward the balcony, but stopped as she looked down at Easnadh. Bending to grasp her harp, she clutched it protectively, but the motion unnerved Sharon, who fired her pistol. The shot hit the column of the harp, splintering the wood. Shards flew out, deeply embedding into Annalissa's chest and neck. The pain caused her to stagger backward out onto the small balcony, the rail hitting her back as blood flowed over the broken instrument. Easnadh clattered to the floor as she was unable to hold it any longer. Looking down in numb surprise, she saw a large piece of sharp wood sticking out of her upper arm, blood flowing down.

The cool night air washed over her and she could hear the river two stories below now that the inside alarm was less piercing. She turned her hazy gaze to the specter in front of her. Sharon, her face a mask of rage, moved toward her with the gun raised again.

"I was stuck making others look glamorous. That money, that money was going to get me noticed. It was my ticket out. And you had to ruin it all." She grabbed Annalissa's arm with her fingers digging into the flesh.

Just then the door crashed open and Vinny appeared as an avenging angel. Sharon turned in a panic, but Annalissa moved quickly to shove the gun down.

Vinny's pistol appeared but with Annalissa right behind Sharon he did not have a clear shot. "Get down," he ordered. Gordon screamed and dropped immediately to the ground.

Annalissa tried to drop, but Sharon's grasping claws held fast. The two women's arm's flailed for a second before Sharon's rage gave her the strength to shove Annalissa backward. As Annalissa fell over the railing, Sharon's fingers gave away and Vinny took his shot.

He aimed for her gun arm, hitting her in the shoulder. Howling in pain, she dropped to the floor just as Gabe came rushing into the room, his pistol ready as well.

"Annalissa!" Vinny shouted as he jumped over Sharon, then stumbled on his way to the balcony. Looking down, he stared at the broken harp, Annalissa's blood splattered over the splintered wood. Turning, he rushed toward the balcony, peering down into the inky water. Jerking off his tux jacket and kicking off his shoes, he vaulted over the railing after her.

THE COLD WATER jolted Annalissa as she plunged into its depths. She had managed to take a deep breath before hitting, but could not see in the dark water, quickly losing her sense of direction. She felt her body moving slightly upwards and quickly began to kick. The long dress clung to her legs, making her kicks awkward and slowing down her progress.

Her lungs began to burn just as panic set in. *Vinny. Oh God, help me get back to him.* She moved her arms as he had taught, feeling her body begin to rise. Her injured arm screamed in agony, but she refused to give into the pain. With one last push, her head broke the surface. Gulping in great gasps of air, she tried to dog-paddle to keep her head above the water. Her dress was weighing her down like an anchor. *I've got to get it off,* she thought. The rushing current carried her body until she slammed into a concrete pillar supporting the balcony overhang of the Concert Hall. She felt around as she grasped it and discovered there was a wire fence connecting some of the pillars. Clinging to it, she hefted herself out of the water just a bit and tried to look around. The lights of the hall above reflected on the shimmering surface of the river as it rushed by. She clung to the wire with one hand and pushed her matted hair from her face. Looking out at the exapanse of water, she saw nothing. She knew that Vinny would have seen her go over the edge and would come for her. *If Sharon hadn't killed him. Oh, Jesus.* Her panic rose to a fevered pitch and she moved her free arm to the side of her bodice where the hidden side zipper lie.

Her fingers shook with cold as she grasped at the zipper tab and moved it down, inch by inch. She glanced at her progress and saw the large fragment of wood still embedded in her arm, the sight nearly making her give up. She jerked on the zipper a few more times until she could feel the heavy, wet bodice sliding down to her waist.

Just then she heard a cry from far off. A cry that sounded like…her name. Her eyes searched the moving water but were unable to see anything. *He's out there. I know he is. I feel it.* She tried to scream out in response but was unable to do little more than croak. Over and over she tried to call his name, but the cold water she had swallowed when she fell robbed her of her voice.

I've got to get to him. She began frantically trying to kick out of the dress that now hung about her waist. It was stuck on her hips and she took a deep steadying breath before struggling again. She managed to get her hand on the parted material but the zipper was lost in the wet folds of the skirt. *God give me strength,* she cried as she jerked as hard as she could on the offending garment. It must have ripped slightly because the rushing water began to slide the dress completely off her legs, leaving her in her bra and panties. A crazy thought ran through her head, *I wish I had my old, red, flowered, one-piece swimsuit.*

Still clinging to the wire fence, she managed to reach one foot and slide her shoe off. The other one was a struggle because of the injury to her arm, but she managed it kick it off as well.

Feeling her first sense of mobility since she plunged into the murky depths, she realized she was already exhausted. Looking to the left, the direction of river flow, she knew that was the closest way to get to the riverside where Vinny would hopefully be.

She heard his voice cry out her name once more and finally saw a head bobbing in the water. *That's him. I know that's him.* Determination flowed through her veins as she pushed off of the fence and began to swim toward him. She kicked just as though she were clinging to the side of the pool. She moved her arms in the circular motion that she had practiced. She tried to keep her head above the water, but it slowed her down. *I got this. I can do this.*

With a final prayer, she moved her head into the water, turning it back and forth to the side as he had taught her and swam toward the voice from the depths that called her name.

GABE WATCHED HIS BROTHER dive over the railing and he immediately shouted over the radio, "Annalissa in the river. Back side. Two floors up. Vinny's just gone in to get her. Suspect apprehended."

Gabe knelt down next to Sharon, rage filling him at the devastation she had caused. As a medic he checked her, but noted that Vinny had managed to wing her—a flesh wound that caused pain but no serious injury. *Good shot, bro,* he thought. Then, with reflection, he wondered if perhaps Vinny has been aiming for her heart and missed.

Just then, the fire department came in along with the rescue squad and police. He looked up at Shane and nodded. "She's the one. She and this piece of trash here," he said, jerking his gaze down to the still cowering Gordon.

Shane reported that the rescue was already organized for a river search. Matt called out to two patrolmen who were with him to follow her to the hospital and take her into custody. Gabe looked down for a moment seeing what had startled his twin. On the floor, near the door to the balcony, was Easnadh. Broken. Bloody.

VINNY'S PLUNGE INTO the river's current looked like any training he had endured with his years in the Special Forces, but his heart was far more impassioned than with any other mission. When he had seen Annalissa's body fall over the railing with the broken harp covered in her blood lying at his feet…his heart stopped. It may have only been seconds before he had recovered enough to charge into action, but those few seconds would remain embedded in his memory forever.

With powerful kicks and strokes, he moved upward quickly, his head breaking the surface. He looked about wildly for any sign of her. *She was wearing that god-damn dress.* He knew it would weigh her down, possibly dragging her underneath the surface for too long.

He did not see her anywhere on the light reflected water. He treaded water easily as he removed his tuxedo trousers to allow for easier movement. Crying out for her, he swam in a circle for a moment to see if he could make out any sign of her. He knew the current of the river would have taken her south, so he swam in that direction keeping his eyes peeled for any unusual movement.

Not feeling the cold, he only felt fear. Choking fear that crept up his throat threatening to steal his breath. It did not matter how many times he called upon his training, nothing mattered except finding her. He kept stopping and treaded water, shouting her name, hoping she would answer back.

He looked at his watch. It had been almost ten minutes. *How long can she stay alive in this?* He thought about their swimming lessons. *I shoulda spent more time on her lessons and less on trying to fuck her.* Shouting her name again, he felt desperation as he had never felt it before.

A noise to his left captured his attention and he swung his gaze in that direction. Something was moving. Flailing. He shook his head, swinging water droplets from his face as he fought to see more clearly what was thrashing in the water. Suddenly the movement stopped and an object bobbed on the dark, swirling surface. And a voice cried out over the surface. "Vinny, Vinny. I'm here."

Thank God, she found me. If it were possible for a man to literally drop to his knees while in the water, he would have. Instead, his breath caught in his throat making it impossible to call her name again. Jerking in response, he began swimming toward her, close enough now to see her small arms not strong enough to carry her across the current.

Strong, sure, powerful strokes of his arms had him propelling her way. Within a minute, he was upon her. Clasping his arms around her shaking body he pulled her in tightly, his body tense with the need to feel her. Hear her breath. Feel her heartbeat against his own pounding chest.

Her sobs were the only sound he heard, but knowing she was alive made it a sound to live for. "Baby, I've got you. I've got you."

He realized that she was barely clothed, glad she had been able to rid herself of the dress, but also aware that she was suffering from hypothermia.

She clung to him with one arm around his neck, the other dropped at her side.

"Where are you hurt?" he asked, unable to ascertain her injuries in the dark water. She lifted her head from his shoulder and said, "I...I've...got some wood...in...in my arm." Her teeth were chattering so hard, he could barely hear her speak.

"Babe, I've got you. Relax and I'll get you to safety." With that, he pushed off with a powerful kick, holding her with his left arm wrapped securely around her and using his right arm to stroke through the water.

He came. He came for me. The cold was fading away as consciousness began to slip from her. As the water flowed by, her head held up out of the water by his strong grip began to nod.

The park next to the concert hall had a concrete wall that held the river at bay and on a warm summer day was usually filled with laughing children and their parents. Tonight, it was filled with firemen, policemen, and Tony's group. Huge spotlights had just been turned toward the water, allowing the searchers to see the surface of the swirling waters more easily.

Gabe had made it to the wall, ready to jump in when needed. Tony walked up and had just clamped his hand on Gabe's shoulder when Jobe shouted. "Visual. Man in water. Two o'clock."

The group turned to his directions and saw Vinny swimming toward them, carrying Annalissa. He just made it to the wall when Gabe jumped in next to him. With both of them hefting her body out of the water, Jobe and Tony were able to lean down to grab hold of her.

She was barely dressed and her body had a bluish

color. The men felt the ice cold touch of her skin. Jobe immediately wrapped her in a blanket and began rubbing her limbs to aid in circulation. BJ, Terrance, and Doug had appeared beside Tony and they all hoisted Gabe and Vinny out of the river as well. Tony threw blankets at both soaked men, knowing that Vinny would not even notice. He had already rushed over to Annalissa's side where the rescue squad had placed her on the stretcher.

"Let me get to her, I'm a medic," Vinny ordered.

"Sir, you need to stay back. In fact, you need to be checked out as well."

"Fuck that, I'm staying with her," he growled.

The EMT gave up arguing and turned his attention back to Annalissa. They prepared to move her to the ambulance and did not attempt to dissuade Vinny when he got in the back with her. He looked out of the ambulance before it took off, seeing Gabe, Tony, and Jobe standing together. Always together. Friends. Brothers.

CHAPTER 24

ANNALISSA WAS SITTING in the hospital room, anxious to leave. "Vinny, can't we just sneak out?"

"For the last time, no," he said, pretending to be stern. If the truth were told, he would have given her anything her heart desired, but the ER had admitted her for observation overnight.

She had been saved from hypothermia, although her body temperature was low when she was brought in. Most of her cuts from the small shards of wood had been cleaned and would heal quickly. The more concerning injury was the large, four-inch splinter of wood that had pierced her upper arm, slicing through muscle and almost severing a nerve. That injury had required extensive stitching and would take longer to heal.

She had made the doctor save the piece that he removed. He asked her where it came from, but it hurt too much to tell him that her beloved instrument had been shattered. She shook her head and gave a weak smile. "Just from something I cared for," was all she could manage.

Vinny noticed that she did not speak of Easnadh so

he did not bring it up in conversation either. For him, the vision of the broken harp with her blood spilled on it now replaced the other horrific memory of another harp years before.

Gabe and Jennifer came to the door, smiling to see Annalissa sitting up on the bed. Jennifer rushed over, throwing her arms around her. Gabe walked over, kissed the top of her head and then moved to stand next to Vinny.

Vinny held his gaze for a moment, the secret communication between twins at work. Gabe knew that Vinny wanted to know what had happened to Sharon and what the rest of the story was. He also knew by looking at his brother that Vinny did not want anything said that could possibly upset Annalissa now. With a nod of understanding, Gabe moved back over to his wife.

"Tony said to call him as soon as she's discharged. Shane and Matt will meet over at your house. They need her statement but had enough evidence for now," Gabe said.

"Babe, we don't have to do this today," Vinny stated emphatically, watching her carefully for signs of distress.

The nurse entered, interrupting their conversation, carrying the discharge papers. With everything signed, he wheeled her out of the hospital into Gabe's waiting vehicle.

Arriving at his parking garage, Vinny insisted on

carrying her to the elevator and refused to let her walk.

"This is ridiculous," she protested. "My arm is hurt, not my legs."

"Quiet, princess," he whispered. "It makes me feel better if you're in my arms." He wanted to carry her straight to the bedroom, insisting that she needed to rest, but she equally insisted that she was tired of being in bed. They compromised when he set her down on the sofa and covered her with a blanket.

It did not take long for the apartment to fill with friends, bringing food and good wishes. Matt and Shane came over but kept their questions to a minimum. She recited her side of the events and then questioned them, wanting to know what had happened.

"It appears that Sharon's been a drug runner for a well-known cartel based out of California for a couple of years. She's carried drugs in her cosmetic bags and has gotten more creative in where she hides them for transport," Matt reported.

Tony picked up the story. "She met Gordon at an after opening party for one of his small-time actresses and it seems that she kept him supplied with cocaine for the past year. She wasn't his direct dealer, but as a runner she had access. She also then began to blackmail him into getting jobs for her."

"Is that how she became acquainted with Annalissa?" Vinny asked, his arm protectively around her.

"He introduced her to entertainers who needed her

for their various engagements and traveling around the country was perfect for her to have a chance to move the drugs. I guess one look at your harp and its case and she thought she was in heaven."

"But I still don't understand how she managed to get it done," Annalissa wondered aloud.

Shane explained, "We don't know the specifics yet, but what we could piece together last night with her and with Gordon, he would supply her with the dates, airlines, and travel times for you. She was with you in the hotel suites that would be booked and when everyone was asleep, she would carefully hide the drugs in your harp column. Then she made the arrangements with the airport handler in Dulles. The drug cartel used him for lots of jobs…she was just one of them."

"And," Tony added, "On this trip everything went wrong for her. She has spent the past month trying to figure out how to get the harp alone so that she could remove the drugs, assuming that they were still there. The gala provided the perfect opportunity so Gordon decided to arrange for her to be there and he wanted to cover his ass as well."

"What will happen to her?" Annalissa asked.

"Right now, she is sitting in jail and so is Gordon. We've got her on possession, possession with the intent to distribute, extortion, robbery, kidnapping, assault, assault with a deadly weapon and attempted murder. Gordon, right now, is looking at accessory charges, but more may follow."

"Oh, my God." Annalissa, overwhelmed, leaned her head back on Vinny's shoulder. "I don't even know what to think about all of that."

"She'll probably be offered a deal, 'cause she really is small potatoes in the cartel, but that makes her life worth spit about now. I'm sure they want the larger fish to catch."

Sherrie walked back from the kitchen with a glass of water and as she handed it to Annalissa, she also showed her the newspaper. "I know you hate crowds, honey, but you made the front page."

The headlines screamed about the protégé harpist who had been threatened by a crazed woman at the gala for Professor Feinstein.

"I've been fielding phone calls from fans who want to wish you well and your manager who wants to capitalize on your notoriety," Jennifer said ruefully.

Annalissa cut her eyes over to Vinny, seeing the angry tick in his jaw. Before she could try to appease his anger, Matt and Shane walked over and kissed the top of her head as they made their way out of the apartment.

Vinny looked back down at her and said, "You ought to know that your dad came to the hospital that first night when you were out of it."

Her mouth formed an "O", but nothing came out.

"He wanted to check on you and said he'd come by when you were feeling better. I gave him our address here and…well, we'll see."

She nodded slowly, impressed with that fact that her father actually came to check on her. She wanted to say more, but Vinny stood to let the others out. As Sherrie and Jennifer walked out, he faced Gabe and Jobe.

Jobe nodded toward the sofa where Annalissa still sat, and said, "Take care of her, man. She's a good woman."

"You told me to give her what she needed. Someone to help without taking over her life. That's not easy, but it was good advice," Vinny admitted.

Jobe nodded, a smile on his face as he walked out, leaving the twins facing each other at the door. The silent communication that had served them from the crib all the way through Special Forces continued even now. Unspoken words of understanding.

"See you at mom's next weekend?" Gabe asked.

Smiling, Vinny nodded. "Oh yeah. We'll be there."

With that simple exchange, they parted and Vinny closed the door, walking back to the sofa where Annalissa was still snuggled in the blanket.

Before she could protest, he bent and scooped her up in his arms, walking toward the bedroom. Holding her easily with one hand, he tossed the covers back with the other before placing her on the soft sheets. Toeing off his boots, he stepped out of his jeans and slid into bed, pulling her gently into his embrace.

"You got something on your mind, soldier?" she asked, an eyebrow lifted in question.

"Nope. Not until you're healed." Not paying attention to her pout, he focused instead on the dark circles underneath her eyes. "Now's for resting, and I gotta tell you, babe, all I want is to lie here for a hundred years with you in my arms so that I can know you're safe."

As she burrowed deeper into his embrace, a tear slid down her cheeks. "I know I have so much to be grateful for and this is going to sound really dumb…but I hate that I lost Easnadh."

"I know, princess. I know," he whispered, the vision of the broken, bloodied harp once again in his mind.

Fatigue took hold, pulling them both under as they lay entangled in each other.

MUCH TO HER SURPRISE, Annalissa's father came to see her the next day. She stood awkwardly in the living room as Vinny let him in. He did not hesitate. He walked directly over and pulled her into a hug. Her eyes closed, tears falling as she realized she could not remember the last time her father had hugged her.

He held her at arm's length, his own eyes teary, and peered at her wanting to ascertain for himself that she really was alright. His gaze roamed her face before lowering to her shoulder, where the raw stitches stood out in stark contrast to her pale, smooth skin.

Clearing his throat, he asked how she was.

She answered, smiling, "I'm okay, Dad. I'm really okay. Especially now that you've come."

He stayed and visited for a few minutes, but she noticed he never mentioned Easnadh. He took his leave as she began to tire and Vinny walked him to the door.

"Thank you for not saying anything," Vinny said softly so that she could not hear. "She's thankful to be alive, but not having her harp hurts her deeply."

Steward O'Brian nodded thoughtfully as he thanked Vinny for taking care of his daughter.

SEVERAL WEEKS PASSED, each day finding Annalissa growing more restless. She was physically healed and stayed busy with trips out with Jennifer and Sherrie and her nights with Vinny. Long nights filled with worshiping bodies, whispers of love, and promises of forever.

But she had not practiced. She had not picked up an instrument. The music was silent, both in reality and in her heart.

Finally answering a call from Maurice, she went to visit him and Mrs. Baxter. She had not seen him since the night of the gala, although they had checked on her. As usual Mrs. Baxter pulled her into a tight hug, clucking the entire time, inquiring about her health and harrowing adventures. Annalissa could not keep the smile off of her face as she was enveloped in the plump woman's embrace.

"Well, come on through. Mr. Feinstein is in the back, of course, and I'll go fix a pot of tea."

Walking down the familiar hall, she admonished herself. *It's time to get back into practicing. Perhaps a trip to Ross' school again would be just the thing.*

Opening the door to the music room, she was stunned to see her father sitting with Mr. Feinstein, both with smiles on their faces as she walked in.

"Hi," she said hesitantly. "Am I interrupting?"

"Not at all, Malyshka," Maurice enthused. "Stewart and I were just visiting while waiting for you."

"Oh. Um…okay," she said as she moved over to the settee. Bending to kiss her father's cheek, she turned to greet Maurice, when she saw what was sitting on the stand behind him.

Easnadh. Whole. Restored. Beautiful.

Dropping to her knees at the feet of the instrument, a sob tore from her body, as she covered her mouth with her hands. Tears ran unashamedly down her cheeks as she lifted her fingers to strum a few strings, the familiar sound reverberating all around.

She turned to Maurice, throwing herself at him, her arms wrapped around his neck. "Oh, my God," she cried. "You did it. I had no idea you were even trying, much less able to restore her."

The old man patted her back gently, murmuring in her ear as she cried. Finally, as she lifted her face to look up into his, he said, "Your father brought her to me."

At this, Annalissa's gaze flew to her father's face,

seeing the usually stoic man fighting tears himself.

With a shrug he said, "Mr. Malloy brought the instrument to me after that night and I brought it to Maurice to see what he could do." His voice cracked as he continued, "No one should lose something so beautiful. That makes such music."

Nodding, she said softly, "Yes. She is wonderful."

Her father's smile faded as he gazed down at his daughter on her knees at the feet of her beloved teacher and harp. "No, my dear. You misunderstand. I meant you."

She peered deeply into his eyes, not understanding. *Me? He means me?*

He stood and pulled her into his arms, saying, "You are so beautiful and the music you create would have made your mother so proud." Father and daughter stood quietly a moment as the tears flowed. "So for you, I begged Maurice to work his restorative magic, and he did."

Smiling up at him, she turned toward the beautiful harp once more, this time inspecting the repair. It was flawless. Hearing a noise behind her, she glanced over her shoulder to see Vinny leaning against the doorframe, Mrs. Baxter smiling behind him. Pulling in her lips to keep from crying more, she lost the battle and the tears overflowed once again.

Vinny pushed off the wall, stalking over to her and wrapping her in his arms. Those arms that protect her from harm, cradle her when she is hurt, and hold her as his body rocks into hers with love. After a minute of letting her cry once more, he gently pushed her back. Looking down, he said, "You ready to make some music, princess?"

Nodding, she walked over to the chair and settled Easnadh onto her lap as he went to sit next to her father. She closed her eyes for a moment, letting the muse flow back into her soul. And then her fingers matched her soul, allowing the music to pour forth.

Vinny watched, choking back the emotion. The harp. Once broken and bloody, now restored. The woman. Once injured and bruised, now creating the sounds that allow a man to feel. To heal. To love.

CHAPTER 25

SIX MONTHS LATER

F LYING INTO THE RICHLAND AIRPORT, Annalissa held Vinny's hand tightly, her eyes closed as she listened to his warm voice whisper reassurances to lessen her nervousness. He rubbed her hand, fingering her engagement ring. They traveled every other month for a concert and he always accompanied her, moving the crowds away and protecting Easnadh.

At least that was what he told her. The truth was somewhat deeper. A love of seeing her play her harp. Seeing her sitting in front of the orchestra, her princess dress standing out as the audience sat as enraptured as he was. Every single time. Whether she was playing in their apartment or in front of hundreds, it was always the same. The music flowing through him, touching the deepest abyss inside.

Before she knew it, they had landed. Her eyes opened. Gazing at his smile, her heart stumbled with love. She watched, mesmerized, as his lips moved toward hers. The kiss was soft. Full of promise.

"This will be the last trip for Annalissa O'Brian," he

teased.

Gifting him with her glorious smile, she nodded. "I know. I was thinking about that myself. After next month, I'll proudly be Annalissa Malloy."

"Baby, I've got no problem with you keeping O'Brian as your name."

"No way, Vinny. I'm proud to become Mrs. Malloy. And," giving a little shrug, she continued, "I want the world to know. After all, it was you who helped me realize that I can teach, still perform, and sometimes even play at the occasional bar. I've got it all," she laughed.

"Well, you've got me," he said, as they made their way to the baggage claims to pick up Easnadh. Seeing the familiar case always made her heart pound. Vinny deftly opened the case and carefully inspected the instrument. Giving her a nod, he placed it on the cart along with their other luggage and they headed back home.

The next day found them at the Alvarez picnic. The women excitedly talked about the upcoming wedding plans while the men kept an eye on the children.

"Just wait until you have kids," BJ exclaimed, his twin toddlers keeping him on his toes. Shane and Matt's toddlers were moving around quickly enough and Ross was enlisted to help corral them. Gabe and Tony eyed them suspiciously, both of their wives pregnant.

Ross ran over to Vinny and excitedly told him that

Annalissa had agreed to show him how to play the violin. "I saw her friend, Les, play in his band and I never realized how cool that could be," he exclaimed.

Vinny gave him a fist-bump, knowing that Annalissa would love to teach him. "You'll be great, buddy."

Ross smiled and said, "I kinda worried about trying to play baseball and play the violin, but figured if other kids didn't get it then I didn't care."

Vinny laughed as the others nodded. "You got that right. Nothing says you can't have it all." He looked over at his beautiful fiancé and thought, *yeah. I've got it all.*

SIX YEARS LATER

VINNY SAT WITH his parents, Stewart O'Brian, Maurice Feinstein, Gabe and Jennifer in the audience, his nerves getting the best of him. Taking in a huge breath, he let it out slowly. Gabe glanced sideways at his twin and grinned. His mom leaned over and patted his leg, whispering, "It'll be fine."

The lights dimmed and the curtain rose. A visibly pregnant Annalissa walked out to applause and took her seat in the middle of the stage. Attired in one of her beautiful princess dresses, a lacey headband holding her long, dark hair as it fell in waves down her back, she pulled Easnadh onto her lap. She looked to the side of the stage and nodded. Vinny held his breath. He could not remember the last time he had been this nervous. *Hell, I've never been this fuckin' nervous.*

Just then eight little girls and boys walked out onto the stage, their tiny violins tucked under their arms. The children ranged from four to eight years old, all adorable in their formal outfits. The boys in little suits and the girls in frilly dresses, formed a semi-circle around their teacher. The crowd held their breath when Annalissa nodded to the children and as she began to pluck the strings, the children lifted their child-sized violins and played along with her.

One little four-year-old girl held Vinny's gaze. Her long dark hair was pulled back away from her face with a lacey headband that matched her mother's. Her heart-shaped face was a study in musical bliss. With her eyes closed, the little girl swayed gently to the sounds of her violin, playing in perfect unison with the harp. The children played beautifully as the proud parents videoed the performance. Gabe was taking care of that, knowing that Vinny was unable to focus on anything other than the tiny performer and her mother.

The sounds of innocent music in a war zone once touched Vinny before it was ripped away. Now, at the sounds of innocent children creating the music, he knew he had been healed. As the final notes resonated over the rapt audience, he was the first to his feet, giving a standing ovation. His little girl's eyes opened and she turned them to him, her smile infectious. Those green eyes, like her mother's, pierced his heart as he finally let out his nervous breath. Allowing his gaze to slide back to Annalissa, he saw her stand and lead the children in their bows.

After the recital was over, they made their way over to the reception. Her tiny violin put away carefully, Christina ran straight into her father's arms as soon as she saw him. He swept her up easily, planting a kiss on her chubby cheek. With his praises still ringing in her ears, she hurried over to her grandparents, gaining their approval of her performance as well.

"Ah, little Malyshka," Maurice effused. "You and your mother were superb."

Knowing his daughter was safe and basking in her earned glory, he made his way over to his wife, still accepting the thanks of the grateful parents. Wrapping one arm around her shoulders he pulled her in close as his other hand rested on her protruding stomach, feeling his son kick. "Babe, you were amazing, but you're dead on your feet. Let's get you and Christina home as soon as possible."

She nodded, her green eyes smiling up at him. "She was wonderful, wasn't she? They all were. Oh, Vinny, this feels so right to teach the little ones how to make such beautiful music."

"Yeah, she was wonderful. Just like her mother. And seeing you up there with them? Oh, princess, you did make beautiful music together."

Saying their goodbyes, he finally gathered Christina up in one arm, wrapping the other around Annalissa and they made their way out to the car. After fastening his daughter into her car seat and buckling his wife in, Vinny walked around toward the driver's side. The night was cool and the sky filled with stars. He looked up for just a moment, letting the music of the night float back over him.

Closing his eyes for only a second, he thanked God for the music. Music that tames. Music that heals. Music that loves.

THE END

If you enjoyed Vinny, please leave a review!
Next up is Jobe.

Keep up with the latest news and never miss another
release by Maryann Jordan.
Sign up for her newsletter here!
goo.gl/forms/ydMTe0iz8L

Other books by Maryann Jordan

(all standalone books)

All of my books are stand-alone, each with their own HEA!! You can read them in any order!

Saints Protection & Investigation

(an elite group, assigned to the cases no one else wants…or can solve)

Serial Love

Healing Love

Revealing Love

Seeing Love

Alvarez Security Series

(a group of former Special Forces brothers-in-arms now working to provide security in the southern city of Richland)

Gabe

Tony

Jobe

Love's Series

(detectives solving crimes while protecting the women they love)

Love's Taming

Love's Tempting

Love's Trusting

The Fairfield Series

(small town detectives and the women they love)

Carol's Image

Laurie's Time

Emma's Home

Fireworks Over Fairfield

I love to hear from readers, so please email me!

Email

authormaryannjordan@gmail.com

Website

www.maryannjordanauthor.com

Facebook

facebook.com/authormaryannjordan

Twitter

@authorMAJordan

More About Maryann Jordan

As an Amazon Best Selling Author, I have always been an avid reader. I joke that I "cut my romance teeth" on the historical romance books from the 1970's. In 2013 I started a blog to showcase wonderful writers. In 2014, I finally gave in to the characters in my head pleading for their story to be told. Thus, Emma's Home was created.

My first novel, Emma's Home became an Amazon Best Seller in 3 categories within the first month of publishing. Its success was followed by the rest of the Fairfield Series and then led into the Love's Series. From there I have continued with the romantic suspense Alvarez Security Series and now the Saints Protection & Investigation Series, all bestsellers.

My books are filled with sweet romance and hot sex; mystery, suspense, real life characters and situations. My heroes are alphas, take charge men who love the strong, independent women they fall in love with.

I worked as a counselor in a high school and have been involved in education for the past 30 years. I recently retired and now can spend more time devoted to my writing.

I have been married to a wonderfully patient man for 34 years and have 2 adult very supportive daughters and 1 grandson.

When writing, my dog or one of my cats will usually be found in my lap!

Made in the USA
Coppell, TX
16 November 2021

65831526R00210